Eternal Dominion
Book 20

Tribulations

By Bern Dean

Cover design by: ebooklaunch.com

Contents

ED Year 6 Days 161-174.

Aalin

As Aalin looked upon the inn that she knew that Xeal and Gale had their first experience in, she sighed as she selected the Hellish Nightmare mode of her tier-7 tribulation and confirmed that she wanted to start. After the warning messages that she acknowledged, the world around her dissolved and she found herself alone in an endless sea of sand. There was no notice of what her task was, or any clues as to what she would need to do to succeed in reaching tier-7. Had Xeal not warned her that some tribulations simply would observe the actions of the participant while giving no direction, Aalin would have thought that there had been a system error. Instead, she looked at the sun that was high overhead as if it was noon and just erected her tent as she used it for shade as she sat in an almost meditative stance.

Aalin stayed like this for hours as the sun worked its way across the sky. This included her discovering that there wasn't enough moisture in the air for her to use her ability to create ice. While she could still create ice using a spell, it was much smaller than normal and even if she tried to keep it around longer with her ability to manipulate ice, it would be gone within minutes. When night came, she started to walk under the light of the stars as there was no moon. None of the stars were familiar to Aalin either and she couldn't identify any that could act like the North Star and allow her to use it to navigate by; as such she felt utterly lost. Still, she continued forward as she hoped for something to break up the monotony of her walking but alas, nothing happened by the end of that first night. Aalin found herself resting in the shade of her tent once more as the day arrived and did her best to sleep, but felt like every time she was about to fall asleep, that something would wake her. However, be it a sound or a movement of the sand beneath her, nothing ever came of these moments and by the end of the first session of her tribulation she knew it was going to be a long one.

When she returned it was once more night and she had yet to get any rest. Plus, if anything, her time in reality with her daughter, Ahsa, only made the isolation she was feeling worse. Still, she kept walking forward as she was determined to keep moving forward in life and like that, one day after another passed as she pushed forward. By the end of the sixth session like this, Aalin had likely only had ten hours of sleep in ED and another six in reality. Simply returning to this was maddening to her as she found herself not wanting to surrender the connection that she had with Ahsa for the emptiness that was before her. It didn't help that she was always worried that even a seemingly innocuous action could reveal something about her tribulation and cause her to fail by a technicality.

Luckily, nothing had as of yet slipped out. Still, she was beyond tired and her stamina was only lasting an hour of walking due to the exhaustion and other debuffs that she had picked up while stuck in her tribulation. To counter this, Aalin would only walk for a half hour before trying to sleep. This included at night as she was beyond trying to care if it was day or night, or even if it was in her tent or not. All she cared about was pressing forward as she believed it was a simple test of will as she dealt with isolation and having no direction. It was these two things that Aalin also knew were among her greatest fears.

It had been this more than caring about her friend that had led to her willingness in sharing Xeal. While she did care for Gale and was happy with where things were, Aalin knew that her own insecurities had pushed her towards it more than anything else. When Enye and Dyllis had come along, Aalin had once more stayed quiet and just went along with things as they were. She had told herself that those would be the last additions to Xeal's life, only for Enye to make it clear that it most certainly wouldn't be, as she discussed just how many nobles would be aiming for Xeal's hand in marriage. It didn't matter to many of these nobles if they would be the first, second, or even 100th wife, so long as they bore a child from him that they could leverage a possible branch house out of.

Thankfully, Xeal had not been amicable to such an arrangement as he sought to limit it and for a while Aalin had thought that it could work. That was until Mari and Lingxin arrived and the fear of a tidal wave of princesses chasing him became a new fear, as Aalin saw them both move closer to him. Mix this with Ava and Mia, who had gone from blatant gold-diggers in reality to actual friends and Aalin had been at a loss to understand her own feelings as she let them in. After that it just seemed like more and more women were showing up, as Xeal resisted their allure only to be drawn in more and more. It had truly become the role of those, like herself, who already had a piece of his heart to limit this situation. Though, even that was easier said than done, as it seemed that half of his wives were in favor of getting Xeal to a total of 19 wives then stopping, as soon as possible.

Yet for all of this, Aalin found that her new sisters, as they saw each other, brought nothing but warmth to her life. Something that had been missing in her own life in reality as it seemed like her parents only cared about results.

3

While there was love and caring, it always seemed to be attached to doing as you were told and following the path that had been laid out by them. That was why simply joining her friends in trying to play ED professionally had been such an act of rebellion and it was why she raised her hand that day in the diner. Deep down, Aalin knew that she desired having direction in her life and that day and every day since then Xeal had given her that. It was his seemingly endless confidence that had drawn her in and was still driving her to keep going as she felt like each step brought her closer to where she wanted to be. Namely next to him, as they finally reached the point where he would be able to give her more than just a few hours of his time each week.

It was as Aalin was focused on this that she lost her footing and fell to the desert floor in the heat of the day of what would be day 174 in ED. Exhausted and at her limit, she struggled to at least sit up. She saw that her stamina wouldn't even recover in the slightest at this point and she believed that if she didn't sleep, she would actually die in ED. It was at this moment that Aalin found herself finally seeing another soul, as Xeal stood directly in front of her as he spoke.

"I have no need of the weak next to me. Still, you have come this far and you can always help to raise my children in the background. So, worry not, I will not abandon you."

These words hit Aalin harder than if he had said that he would abandon her completely, as she struggled to care. She was at the point that rational thought was beyond her and in the moment, she truly thought that Xeal was before her. Even if his words felt off, she struggled to deny them as he wasn't abandoning her which was her true irrational fear, he was simply relegating her to cooking, cleaning and dealing with all of his children. In many ways that was what she herself wanted as her favorite things in the world were seeing her children smile and seeing Xeal enjoy and praise her food. Yet, she couldn't accept that. She had fought too hard to stay next to him. She had accepted sharing him, even learning to find the joy in it. She would not be the only one of his wives to not be next to him when he needed her. So, with far more effort that it should have taken, Aalin stood as she looked at Xeal while ignoring the fact that she only had 25% of her stamina left and spoke.

"I am not a decoration to be placed in the background as you keep adding new wives to replace me!"

"What are you talking about?" commented Daisy as she came into Aalin's view.

"Yeah, we all know that Aila has already replaced you and Kate," added Violet as she wandered into view.

"Indeed, it is only a matter of time before his level matches my own and I can finally join with him in every way," stated Queen Aila Lorafir, as Aalin turned around to see her standing behind her. "You and the others are only needed until then, so just be happy that you were with him until now."

"No!"

"Dear, it's fine," came Aalin's mother's voice as she and her father's characters, Ren and Shua, came into view next. "We will happily have you and Ahsa come stay with us if you leave Xeal."

Before Aalin could even process her mom's words, more and more individuals, all encouraging her to give up, change paths, leave Xeal, accept being stuck in the background and much more kept appearing. This included all of the women involved with Xeal, to include both Princesses Lorena and Bianca, who only had the most insignificant chances of ever securing a piece of his heart. All of this threatened to overwhelm Aalin in her exhausted state as she found herself pulled every which way, until she finally had enough and strode forward in the same direction that she had since the start. As she did so, she closed the distance between her and Xeal and went to slap him, only he caught her wrist. As she looked at him with all the fury she could muster, he just smiled as he spoke.

"It seems that you still do have a bit of fight in you. Now let's see how much."

With that Xeal tossed her hand away as he drew his swords and Aalin instantly remembered the few times she had trained with him for close-quarters defense. Instantly she used ice magic to create a staff and focused on ensuring it lasted for at least a few minutes with her ice manipulation ability. As she did this, Xeal's first attack came and she barely was able to block it, despite her knowing that it had been a lazy attack from him. When the next one came, she had already placed her force shield in its path as she split the staff into two parts and shaped them into thick blades as she attacked Xeal.

These blades were far too fragile to be of any use to a normal player, but Aalin wasn't normal. No, the mark she bore from the phoenix of ice, Bīng, allowed her to ensure the ice held up to far more stress than was possible. However, that wasn't enough in this realm as they became water in mere seconds. Water splashed on to Xeal's face as he started to laugh and Aalin hopped back as she opened the distance between them. As she did this, she watched her stamina hit five percent. Uncaring about that, she instantly summoned more ice and created long thin needles that were thickest in the middle and sent them at Xeal. As they flew, Aalin was constantly controlling them while creating more as she started to go through her 183,080 points in her MP pool. It wasn't long before she had created tens of thousands of needles as the area around her slowly cooled and the needles started to last a few extra seconds. With each needle taking all of one point from her pool to create as her ice manipulation actually gave it form, she could keep this up almost indefinitely. That was if her stamina hadn't been empty as she was starting to lose constitution points as she just kept going.

At the same time, the smile on Xeal's face had vanished as he fought to defend himself after being caught in the center of Aalin's ice storm. He was constantly using his elemental blades skill to add fire to his blades to speed up the already quick melting of the ice. Only, like the realm itself, it seemed to be unable to keep up with Aalin's output of over 100 needles per second. Were this the real Xeal, he would have had several ways to solve this situation, but it wasn't, nor was it his doppelganger. No, it was the very sand that Aalin had been walking on this whole time and the cold was slowly killing it as it fought to hold on. It had been patient and waited until she had been at the very end of her rope as it learned all it could about her. To it, she should have failed to react and just wallowed in her hopelessness before being consumed like all others who had ever wandered its endless dunes. Instead, she was overwhelming it as fire was part of its intrinsic nature and it never thought anything could overwhelm that aspect of what it was, especially when the sun was out.

As the sand was trying to figure out what was going on, Aalin was watching as the rate of her constitution draining had slowed as the cold permeated all around her and she smiled. With this she stopped holding in her MP points, and focused on creating more and more ice as she pushed it out all around her. With this she finally felt her mind stabilize as she remembered where and what she was doing, and with it she knew that what was before her wasn't Xeal. None of this was real, and whatever was creating it had the nerve to play with her heart and instantly she increased her output even further. As she did so, her constitution dipped below 100 and her MP pool dropped to just under 15,000 as 100 feet in every direction was covered in ice, to include directly down into the sand. It was at this moment that she received a series of system notifications as the world around her dissolved.

(Tier-7 Hellish Nightmare tribulation complete. Calculating completion rate... 95% completion, rank A. Rewards: 20 class skill points, level will automatically be raised to 200, 500 renown, 200 gold.)

(Congratulations, you are one of the first 5,000 tier-7 players. Rewarding a bonus 500 renown and 5 class skill points.)

(Congratulations, you are one of the first 5,000 players to complete a tier-7 Hellish Nightmare tribulation. Rewarding: 1,000 renown and 20 class skill points.)

(Caution, the ice phoenix mark is ready to break its seal. Please find a secluded location within an hour of returning to the main Eternal Dominion world, or the seal will break on its own.)

All Aalin had time or the energy for, was to hobble to the inn in front of her and send a message to Kate saying that she was done, but needed to recover. Once inside the room, she simply lay there and let sleep take her as she tried to recover by any means before the seal on the ice phoenix mark broke. Thus, an hour later she woke screaming as her whole body felt like it was on fire despite turning blue from the cold that was permeating it. As this happened, she watched as her health and constitution both plummeted at a dangerous rate, as she wondered if she would survive the seal breaking. As her constitution dropped to 10 and her health reached 86, it finally ended as she breathed heavily and struggled to even do that. Aalin knew that she had only survived by the slimmest of margins as her last level had saved her in the end. It was with this thought that she read the updated Ice phoenix mark.

(Ice phoenix mark: you have been marked by the ice phoenix and your body has almost completely integrated with the mark, increasing your control of ice magic further. Ice manipulation: you can make changes to the form of any ice you see. 1.25% boost to all stats and heightened senses at all times. 2 extra attribute points in MP, 1 extra attribute point to dexterity per level and 2 extra free attribute points per level. Access to ice phoenix skills through class skill points. Decrease to cost to acquire and use all ice-based skills and spells. All levels take 1.5 XP to reach. Lost upon death. Cannot safely log out while marked. As you increase your tiers, you may unlock more benefits)

As she finished reading this, Aalin lost consciousness once more as she drifted off to sleep with a single thought on her mind. It was time for her to ensure that she would never be pushed to the background again, and take the place that she knew she could next to Xeal. She had long since known that she was special to him due to the feeling he had towards her from his last life and she had refused to use that to her advantage before this moment. No longer, as she was done just going with the flow of the others as she was going to finally truly make her will known!

Gale

Gale stood on the spot that she had learned the requirements of her faith in ED, that included acts of an intimate nature with another in the game. The sudden realization that she needed to take a step that she hadn't expected to do until she had at least had a partner she trusted had pushed her into a spiral. Especially as she had just shut down Ignis in reality and it seemed that Xeal didn't want to notice her or Aalin. Had he and Aalin been a couple she could have given up on him and allowed herself to walk the route supplied by the system, but she knew that would almost certainly cause her to lose any chance of being with Xeal. The sequence of events that followed this could best be described as a true mess of awkwardness, as she tried to act confident with Aalin as they attempted to seduce Xeal, before ending up sharing him. While Gale actually enjoyed this arrangement, to include the addition of more sisters to the mix, she held guilt over almost forcing it onto Aalin.

While Aalin was happy, Gale knew that she would have been happier if it had just been her and Xeal, and yet she was always putting her own desires aside for the group's. The worst part were Gale's own desires towards Aalin that she knew would never be met. It was with this on her mind that Gale saw the Demonic mode option appear before her, as she sighed before selecting the Hellish Nightmare difficulty and acknowledging all the warnings as the world dissolved around her. When it reformed, Gale found herself standing upon a platform looking out over a massive army as she received a system notification.

(You must lead this army on a holy war as you work to convert all who come into your path. At this time, you as the head priestess are about to give a rousing speech before your forces attack the city behind you.)

Gale wanted to scream at the system for doing this to her, as she had been extremely happy to remain an obscure existence to the followers of Freya in the main ED world. All any of the clergy there knew of her was that she was a promising cleric who had long since started down the Odr path and had no desires to partake in the more pleasurable forms of worship that was common. If they knew that she was actually Freya's divine scion, there was no doubt that she would become their rallying cry, but it would almost certainly cause her to become the target of many. It wouldn't be a stretch to say that she would have to fight against many tier-8 assailants who saw her very existence as a threat. Even if she had the protection of a few tier-8s herself, it would still mark the end of her days being able to adventure, or even grow stronger, without a major hassle.

Still, Gale had long accepted that she would one day have to fulfill this very role with how the winds were blowing. As Xeal liked to put it, first ED's countries would tear each other apart and then the churches would seek to establish themselves as the main religions of the world. This was especially true for the gods of war, who would seek battle for battle's sake at times and that was especially true of Freya. As a goddess of love and war, there wasn't a battlefield that she was opposed to stepping onto. It was part of why her clergy was predominantly made up of women and they were blessed for joining freely with stronger mates. It was also why the Odr path was rarely taken, as in this world where battle and war often meant the death of their partner, it was easier to have a dozen lovers to fuel your power with. Still, it was gaining more traction now that players had become common, as the worshipers of Freya were particularly popular with a subset of them. It was with the resolve that came from knowing that she would need to be the one to lead the reformation of Freya's faith one day, that Gale began to speak to her forces in as loud of a voice as she could muster.

"None of you here today need to hear a rousing speech from me to perform at your best! All you need do is look to each side of you and to the heavens to receive the motivation needed. It is your brothers and sisters in arms, and our goddess Freya who gives us the cause we have to put our all into our task today!"

As cheers and battle cries rang out from the force before her, Gale paused for it to end before continuing.

"That's right, we are here to do Freya's work. Never forget that! She is the god of war, but also of love. As such, we must love our enemies for allowing us to display our devotion to her! Remember that we are here to bring as many as we can to her and that it isn't their fault that they have yet to feel the joy that comes from following Freya. As such, ensure that we spare as many as we can once we have captured the city. Now, in Freya's name, I command all of you to perform your duties and bring the light of Freya's love to them!"

As Gale finished, she raised her staff high and unleashed an AOE buff spell that fell onto the 1,000 members of the army that was closest to her. While this increased the morale of those affected, it was the visual of her raising the staff while it emitted a bright light that she was going for, as the army cheered even louder as the sub-commanders took charge. Within the hour the city was surrounded and putting up a fierce struggle to avoid falling, as Gale was relegated to being a glorified ornament. It was clear that she wasn't the general, or even in the chain of command for the actual battle plans and at most she would be asked to heal a wounded enemy soldier after the battle in a propaganda move.

This frustrated Gale as everyone present was level 199 or lower and while she took a back seat when Xeal was around, she was perfectly capable as a combatant as well. Both her strength and dexterity were much higher than a typical cleric due to her being Freya's vessel. Both had received 120 extra points from being so and she had matched that plus what she had before, to reach the point of having over 300 points in each. While not quite on the level of a warrior who focused only on those, it was still higher than most as everyone also needed points in constitution and SP, else they would lack the tools to be effective. Gale's base ability points were set with 205 in constitution, 305 in strength, 385 in dexterity, 100 in MP as her skills only required a small bit of it, 205 in SP as most of her skills relied on it and 400 in charisma. Like bards, almost all of Gale's skills and abilities were only as effective as her ability to be persuasive, or at least attractive. She had also stunted her SP in favor of dexterity to help ensure that she would be able to dodge attacks during her tier-up efforts. After all, she had to be ready to stand alone if needed, or as she smiled while charging into the area that was seeing the greatest struggle, join the frontlines of any battle.

As she reached the area that was around the front, Gale unleashed a healing spell followed by a buffing spell, as those on the ladders cheered at noticing her. A few minutes of a one-sided struggle later, they succeeded in breaching the walls as Gale made her way up a ladder, before standing atop the wall and casting the same spell that she had used atop the platform at the end of her speech. What followed was a massive surge from her followers, as the battle turned into a rout as the defenders abandoned the walls and started to fall back to the city's keep.

As Gale walked through the empty city, it was clear that the people, at least the middle class and up, had been pulled into the keep. When they reached the slums, what they found was starving kids, elderly, the sick and other so-called undesirables. Gale hated looking at these issues in reality because they always made her feel so helpless as even now that she could be considered rich, she had no idea how to handle seeing someone with next to nothing. Here in ED, it was even worse as there was literally magic that could ease much of their problems, yet laws prohibited clerics from healing those who didn't approach them. This was out of fear of any religion trying to turn the destitute and helpless into fanatics. Even if they came to any church, payment was required. Furthermore, while Xeal was welcome to hand out all the gold he liked, as were most players who weren't tied to any god, churches had to operate through a third party that would hide where the funds came from. It was for this reason alone that most faiths gave very little in charity as unlike in reality, not all faiths were so selfless, or at least seeking to be seen as such.

It was only in nations like the Zapladal Theocracy that ignored this, at least for the church in power as it used these zealots to stay in power. It was with this thought that Gale realized that was what she was doing in her tribulation. She was establishing a theocracy, or expanding it and it was those very zealots that she was leading into battle. So, as she looked at the armed, scared and frightened crowd, or poor and needy, she smiled as she raised her staff and cast a healing spell that would also take care of a bit of fatigue and minor illnesses. As the crowd felt the effects of this, they were confused as those in the front who were wielding makeshift weapons lowered them slightly without thinking about it as Gale started to speak.

"Fear not, we are not here to conquer you, but to liberate you! Too long have you been denied basic treatments out of fear that those providing it would seek to use you against those in power. I mourn every life that has been lost on each side of the battle, as they all were simply doing their duty. Worry not, the only change that I am making is that of bringing unity to you. Under the Goddess Freya, all who serve her are ensured to at the very least live with their wounds and illnesses being handled!"

Gale felt like she was a cultist as she spoke, but she treated it like she was roleplaying what one would expect of the leader of a religion. The effect of which was the bloodless surrender of the slums as her army prepared to assault the keep. Only now they had local help and it was about the best form of it that they possibly could have, as they knew where the people would be held up and a secret way to reach them that was meant for escape. Thus, as her forces made like they were going to assault the keep, several of those in the slums went to show a few others the point where the escape path would open. Meanwhile, Gale found herself being summoned to meet with the general.

As she entered the tent that was serving as the command center, Gale found herself looking at more than a few annoyed faces. In there was not only the general, but also several others who looked to be either high-ranking officers, or clergy of Freya from their dress. Among those present besides the general, one stood out as she was definitely in her twilight years, yet you could only tell it by the look in her eyes. It was this woman who spoke first, not the general, as she cast what Gale knew was an anti-spying spell that would ensure that none but those present would hear what was said. Following this, she fixed Gale with a cold glare as she spoke.

"Your actions today were unacceptable. You may be our lady's chosen vessel and in line to replace me as the true leader of our faith, but you are still to listen to orders from me!"

"No, I don't think I will," retorted Gale. "As you say, I am Freya's vessel, not yours or anyone else's. If she herself doesn't order me to stand down, then I will not!"

"Shall I withdraw my army then?" asked the general. "I mean, how am I to plan my battles when you are prone to rush off haphazardly and ruin my battleplans by allowing too many of their numbers to fall back to the keep. Had you not interfered our losses would have been slightly higher, but only half of those defending the keep would be doing so now."

"The goal isn't to kill them, it is to convert them," retorted Gale. "If you think your army will leave as I march on, go right ahead and withdraw!"

Gale just smiled as the looks around the room grew complicated as she was confident in her position. It no longer mattered to her who was in charge on paper, as she knew that none of them could go against her so long as they followed Freya and Gale would use this as she started to dictate terms.

"Now send those in the keep a letter. Tell them that we wish to end this in one-on-one combat. If they win, we will leave. If we win, they bend the knee and begin worshipping Freya."

"And I suppose that you will be taking the field on our side?"

"Unless you can produce someone who is more likely to come out victorious. I am well aware that while I may be the most powerful one here, there are those who are better suited to fighting."

Gale could see the room visibly relax as she said this and they seemed to drop the subject as she left as a messenger was summoned. The next hour passed as Gale joined in the efforts to heal the injured from both sides of the conflict, even as the captured prisoners looked at her with hatred. Finally, the response came, though it was a refusal and Gale just smiled as two hours later the gates opened on their own, as the rulers of the city were handed over and the occupation of the city began.

Once the people learned that a chance to have it all decided by a single fight had been turned down, and that the enemy army had no plans to rape and pillage anything outside the treasury, the whole city turned on their leaders.

Put simply, most people just wanted to live a comfortable life when it came right down to it. Though once it became clear that conversion and conscription was in the cards, many began to have second thoughts. This was when the general and the old woman made use of Gale once more, as they treated her like some kind of idol as she found herself giving one speech after another. All of this was in the name of peace as they started off towards the second city, only as Gale took a single step, time seemed to shift as she found herself already there.

Like this one battle after another commenced, as Gale found herself never getting more than a quick nap after each of them before it was time for the next. Sometimes the moment that the walls fell it was on to the next one, as she found herself in a near constant state of battle as the mental fatigue began to build up. At the same time, she began to grow used to being cheered and idolized and the sight of the death that accompanied battles ceased to affect her even slightly. She was also vaguely aware of the fact that years seemed to be passing as many faces aged and new ones came into view. Gale could even see many young women that had been just little girls in the first slum that they had liberated become clerics or champions of Freya in their own right.

The contrast between this and her time in reality was stark, as she spent every moment of it with her daughter Moyra. Gale found the contrast so drastic that it kept getting harder and harder to transition between the two of them. More than once, this had occurred mid-battle and Gale had been caught slightly off guard as she returned and took hits that she normally wouldn't. At the same time, she had returned to reality and almost freaked out a few times, as it took her a moment to remember that anything outside the reality her tribulation was taking place in even existed.

Finally, she reached a city that seemed vaguely familiar with its walls and what looked like a market directly outside of them. The intelligence she had to work with showed three rings of walls that would create a long path to victory and rather than just humans, beast-men defended it as well. By this point Gale was almost operating on auto pilot, as she started to inspire her forces as they chanted her last name.

"Bluefire, Bluefire, Bluefire, Bluefire, Bluefire, Bluefire, Bluefire!"

Gale paused as she remembered that it had been her husband that had given her that name. The same one that had given her Moyra as the thought of her daughter that she still only saw as a baby despite years clearly having had passed. Her head was fuzzy as she tried to remember anything but the last few cities that had fallen to her forces, only she couldn't. It was like they were nothing but the crusade that she had led. Even when she tried to picture her husband that she knew she still loved, it was a fuzzy image that came up of a man wielding two swords surrounded by many women. For some reason she didn't seem to mind the women. If anything, she felt a longing for them as she re-centered herself. She was just about to call for the attack when a single individual jumped off the wall and started to approach her forces like nothing was the matter.

As Gale watched this fool walk towards them with no raised flag for truce, neither of his swords drawn and a completely unguarded head, she felt something was off. She kept thinking of her husband, but he had to be back where she came from, only where was that, where was even this? She couldn't remember and the way this man looked at her was different than any other before her, as it wasn't with fear, contempt, admiration, or even devotion. No, he looked at her with pity and sorrow in his eyes. Once more the thought of her husband returned to her mind, as she questioned where he was and why it had been so long since she had seen him raced through her head. Had she left him for this war and never returned, or had he left her and she had used this war to fill the void that was within her. As she struggled to remember and grapple with this, the man stopped and shouted a challenge directed at Gale.

"I, Duke Xeal Bluefire, issue a challenge to my wife and leader of this army, Gale Bluefire, for one-on-one combat. To the victor goes all!"

Gale blinked as it hit her that this was her husband and she had arrived at her home, only to prepare to rip it apart. What was she even doing? When did she become such a paragon of war and why was she attacking her own home? As her forces started to cheer and shout, Gale found herself stepping forward on instinct as she almost unconsciously arrived before Xeal. As she just looked at him blankly, he sighed before he spoke to her.

"As I said long ago, if you decided that you wished to leave, I wouldn't hold it against you and I never have, but today you crossed a line. I still love you even now as I do with all my wives, but I can't just stand by and let you turn my city into another source for your war machine. You have lost your way and let war consume you, and I should have come to knock some sense into you long ago. Now defend yourself."

Gale just zoned out as Xeal came charging at her and her body seemed to move on its own as she avoided his attacks while counter attacking. This continued for a while as Gale struggled to understand what was going on and how she was fighting with him on even ground. Even with the boosts that came from being Freya's vessel she knew he was stronger. That was it, Freya had taken over her body and she was just a passenger on a ride as she realized that if this continued, that she would destroy everything that mattered to her. She needed to take control of her body back and stop this. It was time for the bloodshed and aggressive conversion tactics to end, even if it cost her everything. As she fought, all she was met with was laughter in her head from what she assumed was Freya and the next thing she knew she was in a white space as she stood across from herself. Before Gale even knew what was going on, her other self spoke.

"Just sit back and let me handle this. Once I am done, I promise that you will have your husband back and all of your sisters with him. Only, you will be seated at that head seat rather than him, as you should have been from the start."

"No! I don't want that! What have you done to me?"

"Nothing, unless you count leading you to your destiny as my vessel to bring others unto me."

"Am I even me anymore?!"

"Hmm, I suppose it is more of a we situation, and I will admit that I am looking forward to tasting Xeal through your body now that I have this level of control over it."

"That's it, I am evicting you and restoring my memories, which you have taken from me!"

"Silly girl, I have taken nothing from you. You simply lost yourself to the world as you embraced my power and the feeling of being worshiped as the manifestation of me. With each city that came under my control, I gained more and more control over you as my power increased and with it so did your own. Even the husband that you thought invincible will fall to our combined might at this rate!"

Gale didn't even think of answering as she charged forward armed with nothing but her fists. The other her just smiled as she focused on dodging while continuing to speak.

"You know I really do love that fire you have. It has been one of the hardest parts of keeping you away from him for so long. I had almost thought you had lost it as the battles piled up, but it seems that I was worried for nothing. Now give up and accept me as part of you."

"Never! You are nothing but a passenger on this ride, so just stop already and accept that it is time to get off."

"Oh, you wish to expel me from your body! We both know that won't happen, so just give up on that!"

"I think not!"

As Gale shouted this, she reached out and grabbed her copy and as it became a wrestling match, her copy started to laugh.

"Hahahahah, this is great. I am the goddess of war! Do you really think that you can beat me?!"

"I don't have to," retorted Gale. "After all, I am not fighting you alone. Right now Xeal is out there fighting you as well!"

For the first time Gale's copy looked worried as she tried to put Gale into a hold, only for Gale to smile as she continued to speak in the midst of the struggle.

"You can't defeat me here, can you? If you did, would I even exist any longer and if I didn't exist, you would be forced to return to the heavens completely, wouldn't you?"

"So what. I just need to restrain you- Ahhhhh!"

Gale just smiled as she felt the blow that had sliced her back, as she knew that Freya was finding it hard to focus on both fights at once. At the same time, Gale remembered that this whole world existed only for her tribulation and it was likely that this wasn't even Freya as her confidence skyrocketed. With it she found herself gaining the upper hand on her copy, who sighed before dissolving back into her and Gale found herself looking at Xeal once more. In the same moment she dropped to her knees as one of Xeal's swords swung over her head. Seeing the sudden change in her, Xeal paused as he looked at her with a smile as he spoke.

"Finally woke up, did you?"

"Ha, right, so now what?"

"That is up to you. You can surrender and I will take you back, or you can continue to fight and the winner will decide the other's fate."

"I think it only makes sense for me to see just how closely matched we are."

With that Gale cast a self-recovery spell and charged at Xeal, as she focused on debuffing him even further than Freya had when she was in control. As she did this, the fight started to draw out as neither side seemed to be able to gain the advantage. Xeal was dealing more damage, but Gale was healing herself and constantly renewing the debuffs that were active on him, as they both watched their stamina drop until finally Xeal ran out first. As Gale was focused on blocking his dragon's breath attacks with her holy shield skill and had enough dexterity to escape his double upward and downward slashes combo lock, Xeal lacked any real way to win quickly. As such the fight dragged on until he ran out of stamina while Gale still had over ten percent of her own left.

However, rather than look worried, Xeal just smiled as he continued his assault. As his health dropped further and further with each point of his constitution that he lost, Gale found herself being overwhelmed. This only got worse once her own stamina ran out and her own constitution continued to drop and each of her moves became sluggish. Xeal had trained to ignore the sluggishness and push through it. She had not and while his constitution was dropping faster, Gale's health was losing out to his own as she struggled to just heal herself. Her ability to even get a hit in was also gone and Xeal finally succeeded in getting her into his combo lock as his health read one percent remaining. Gale remembered that this was due to his title, skin of your teeth, which made it impossible for him to die due to status damage. A side effect of this was that it forced his constitution to hold on as well.

Though, there was a simple loophole to this that Gale knew. All she needed to do was deal a single point of damage that would take him below one percent health and he would die. Simply put, the moment that something pushed him past the one percent point, the status damage would return to having an effect, thereby killing him. Still, getting that single damage at this point was easier said than done, as her own health was dropping quickly and all she could think of was a desperate move. So, she didn't question the thought and just dropped her staff and as it fell, she kicked out her leg. While this made her lose her footing and fall to the ground which ended any chance of escaping Xeal's assault she had, it also sent her staff into his knee and dealt a whole one point of damage.

However, Xeal ceased his assault as well and just looked at her as he was unable to move without dying from loss of constitution at this point. Gale just sat there and breathed as her own constitution was still over 50 points, but her health was under 1,000 and she knew that all Xeal needed to do was unleash a single dragon's breath and it would kill them both. Things had reached the point Gale doubted that she had the reaction time to counter it, especially without her staff. It was in this situation that Xeal spoke.

"It seems that it is a draw."

"I'm good with that. Neither of us should be the ruler of the other anyway."

"So, what now?"

"Retirement for both of us, declare Hardt Burgh as neutral grounds where all can worship how they like, so long as you live to guarantee it and can keep me next to you."

Before Xeal could respond, the world around Gale dissolved and she found herself looking up at Freya, only she was back in the form that she had taken when Gale had reached tier-5. She was looking at Gale with a mixture of interest and respect as she spoke.

"I must say that you truly did better in that tribulation than I thought you would. Certainly better than any resident of this reality would have done. Though that may be due to the time you got in your other reality helping to ground you."

"Right, so I take it I have passed then."

"Not yet. Gale, you are my vessel. As such I have final say on if you are allowed to reach the next tier once you complete your tribulation."

"Great, so you saw everything?"

"Yes, and don't worry, I will not fail you for revealing anything about it to me here."

"I am going to do the same as Xeal and just not risk it."

"Fine, he is ever the cautious one, even against himself."

"Ha, you can put yourself on that list as well. I think he fears your designs more than anything."

"Ah, he actually fears me wanting to experience more than I get through the connection I have with you."

"Is he wrong to?"

"No, especially as I have abandoned the path that you walk and would see him as nothing but a dalliance."

"Yet you fell into his trap."

"Come again?"

"Freya, he hasn't said anything to me, but do you really think that if he chooses godhood, that he will have any doubts about being able to defeat you?"

"Interesting. You are saying that I would be forced to either marry him, or surrender my place in the world he has given me access to? Perhaps I should just have you invite him to visit me again and have my way with him."

"You and I both know that you would lose too much if you did that, as I would ensure your mark was no longer on my body at that point."

"Yes, even now you are thinking about doing that over what you just dealt with from the copy of me your mind made up. Honestly, that is the only part of your whole tribulation that has me upset. You still fear that I will control you completely one day. Gale, you have seen just how much it takes out of you to even channel a fraction of my power through you. Were I to try and control you directly as happened in that final fight, well, you would have died long before you wrestled control back from me."

"Oh, and will that still be true when I am level 300?"

"No, I might manage a few hours at that point without killing you, but your body would be so damaged that it would take months to recover completely and that is if I just controlled it. If I started to use my power, well, let's just say that the more that I use it, the faster your body would reach its limit."

"Until it grew accustomed to it. I saw how fast Xeal was able to increase the amount of electricity he could control through training. I can even say that after opening the portal to your realm twice, that the second time was much easier to recover from. Can you really say that in another 100 years in this world that you won't have the ability to treat my body as an extension of yours? I mean, you can even use the time I am offline to increase its resilience without me knowing."

"Gale, nothing that I can say will mean anything at this

point and that is a major issue as if you can't trust me, you can't play the role I need you to."

"Oh, and that would be?"

"The same one you played in your tribulation. It was truly wonderful seeing you wage war in my name and grow my clergy. While you will not be focused on converting anyone, you will have need to purge other faiths who wish to cause us issues."

"So long as Xeal and Kate approve it I have no issues playing that role. Hell, I have accepted that I will have to do that, even if I don't like it. Just don't ask me to start actually worshiping you, as sorry, but this is all make believe to me as while I believe you and every other person in this reality truly exists, you are no more of a goddess to me than Aila or any of the others are."

"As long as that statement is only shared between us and those in your reality, I have no issue with that so long as you change that to being to your kind only. To Aila and the others that you share Xeal with, as well as all others who are native to this reality, I am very much a goddess."

"Fair. Now is there anything else, or have I passed your interview?"

Freya just smiled at Gale as she closed the distance between them and gave her the same kiss that she would give Xeal to establish a soul bond. Before Gale could even object, one system notification came in after another and she found the world dissolving around her.

(Tier-7 Hellish Nightmare tribulation complete. Calculating completion rate... 101% completion, rank S. Rewards: 25 class skill points, level will automatically be raised to 200, 750 renown, 250 gold.)

(Congratulations, you are one of the first 5,000 tier-7 players. Rewarding a bonus 500 renown and 5 class skill points.)

(Congratulations, you are one of the first 5,000 players to complete a tier-7 Hellish Nightmare tribulation. Rewarding: 1,000 renown and 20 class skill points.)

(Caution, Freya has placed more of her soul within you. Please find a secluded location within an hour of returning to the main Eternal Dominion world, or her soul fragment will take root on its own.)

Gale wanted to curse as her stamina was still empty and she needed time to recover, so she quickly entered the nearest inn and started to focus on her recovery. By the time her hour was up, she was still far from in the best shape as a sharp pain blossomed in her head. Instantly Gale found herself experiencing one scene after another of battle and pure pleasure mixed in the most confusing way. Every image had one constant, and was that it was clearly Freya in them and she was enjoying herself. At the same time Gale was experiencing this, her body was racked in pain as it took another step closer to the version of Freya that she took based on Gale's own definition of ideal beauty. As the pain came to an end, Gale just had time to check what changes she had undertaken as she looked at the description under vessel of Freya.

(Vessel of Freya: the goddess Freya has decided to put a significant part of her whole inside of you, marking you as her herald in the mortal realm. To fulfill your role, you have been gifted with enhanced beauty and battle prestige. You now have the hidden class of Divine Scion so long as you remain her vessel. All attributes increased by 1.25% and 1 additional attribute point will be added to strength, dexterity, charisma stats and 2 free attribute points each level. All senses are now able to pick up divine influences that others would miss. Bonus skill, blessing of Freya, added. All levels require 1.5 more experience and status of Freya's vessel lost upon death.)

Gale knew that it was almost time to start using her blessing of Freya skill on more than just the few she was allowed to as she looked at it once more as well.

(Blessing of Freya: gives a 5% boost to all attributes until blessing is canceled by the giver. Can only be given to clerics and champions of Freya and only one blessing can be active for every ten of the user's levels.)

Thinking about how she could mark 20 individuals now and just what that would mean for the tier-7 members of the faith made Gale smile and she let sleep take her.

(*****)

Morning May 14 to Evening May 19, 2268 & ED Year 6 Days 175-192.

For the first time in what felt like forever, Alex smiled as he enjoyed a morning with all five of his ladies in reality, as Sam and Nicole leaned on both sides of him as they held their daughters. Meanwhile, Ava and Mia were focused on the four-and-a-half-month-olds that were still completely reliant on others. Still, it was finally the start of tummy time and all four had learned what smiles were, as they always loved to use them to melt their mommies' hearts. Especially Kate's as she had gotten used to being there to help Ava and Mia out whenever Alex wasn't able to, which was more often than not at this point.

When the morning had ended, Alex had yet to get more than a quick response from Sam and Nicole on their tribulations. They had simply said something akin to, that it was hard and they were glad it was over and they just wanted to relax. Though that changed by the time night came and Nicole claimed Alex for that night as she showed a more aggressive side to her which Alex had never met in his last life. Though he just smiled as he embraced it and reaffirmed that he loved her as they enjoyed their date night.

This had been followed by Sam taking the following night and Alex found her to have been affected by the experience of her tribulation as well. Though it was in a much more subtle way that he couldn't quite put his finger on, as she just seemed to have a brighter smile, or something, that brought a new freshness to their time together. Instead of trying to identify the cause, or what it was, Alex decided that he would rather just enjoy it as they spent the night together.

Kate claimed the following night, while Ava and Mia enjoyed their night on the 18th, as they just snuggled and took a nap as Alex held them. Like this time in reality passed as they got ready for Alex to return to his two one-hour logoffs each day, as the conflicts in ED returned to being his focus.

In ED, day 175 was another family meeting, as Gale and Aalin shared the details that they wished to about their own tribulations. This had of course caused a lengthy discussion to commence on just what, if anything, should be done about Freya, while Xeal frowned after learning that Kate had planted the trap idea in Gale's mind. Xeal didn't know if he liked the fact that Kate had sent it as a message and said that if Gale knew, it would ruin the plan. Still, it was clear that Freya would likely be wary of Xeal trying to make an honest woman out of her by what Gale and Kate were saying. However, in the end, it returned to the wait and see game as they returned to their daily lives.

For Xeal this meant more and more meetings about the state of the war, as all fronts remained in a stalemate, or with FAE's side slowly losing ground. With Nium holding to the prewar lines after pushing Paidhia back, while the elven lands were still dealing with an invasion from the NPCs of Paidhia. Muthia had officially secured the area surrounding the slime dungeon where Jewel was and were working to fortify the new lines. At the same time, the Huáng empire was losing ground every day as Jingong and the few other players that had joined them were unable to maintain the lines. Even with FAE sending over 1,000 tier-7 players to help, three cities had already fallen and the situation was looking dire, and Xeal knew that he had his work cut out for him if he planned to turn things around there.

Though it seemed that Abysses End was really ready to play the long game of chicken, as they dared Xeal to show his face on the battlefield as another 60,000 of FAE's members started their attempt to reach tier-7. This, above everything else, was what was hurting FAE right now, as if Xeal had held them back, he could have reinforced the lines at a number of locations, but that would be foolish in the long run. Instead, he was focused on surviving and ensuring FAE could respond to any advances much the way it seemed that Abysses End could, should FAE try something from what Kate's intelligence suggested.

At least until day 181, when Abysses End launched major offenses on all three battlefields. With 60,000 reserve forces unavailable, only Nium was in good shape as all of the other guilds that had been roped into its defense were more than enough to handle the latest attempts to break through. Muthia, however, was in trouble as it was clearly an attempt by Abysses End to recapture the slime mine to discover why FAE valued it so highly and how they got into it. They had long since realized what had happened when Xeal and his party used it to get behind enemy lines and were clearly planning to turn things around on them. Meanwhile, it looked like Abysses End was attempting to end the war in the Huáng empire in a single move, from the intelligence reports.

It was with this information in front of Xeal that he gave out his orders, as Takeshi would lead the efforts in Muthia with the aid of several of the phoenixes' marked. Meanwhile, Xeal's party would be headed to the Huáng empire, with Aalin, Gale and Kate leading the main force that would be working to bolster the efforts there. This left Taya to continue in the role of managing the situation in

Nium, as they all were waiting for the next trap to be sprung.

When they arrived in the Huáng empire, Xeal gave his party the location of their next meetup point as he handed command over to Lucy. At the same time, Xeal took note of which ministers seemed happy to see them, especially the ones who looked too happy as if there was a trap set, it would likely be at this point. Still, all he did was ensure that his party was on its way and Kate and the others had already transferred to their designated battlefields. With that taken care of, Xeal looked up in the sky as he activated his enhanced senses and lightning form as he flash stepped into the sky, such that he could see a significant portion of the continent. What he was able to see from this vantage point with his senses, such that they were, allowed Xeal to get a general idea of the overall situation of the battles as he moved between them. When he was overhead each of them, he could also make out where several ambushes were set up. From what he could tell based off the illusion magic that his senses could make out, their plan seemed to be to create a pincer attack on several of the battlefields once FAE's reinforcements arrived.

Xeal was happy that he had thought of this possibility after his last fight, where he had needed to flash step into the air to avoid force walls. Especially as once it was paired with his advanced senses, it was almost free teleportation for him as he flash stepped to the group that was where Aalin would be headed. As he landed, he instantly shifted back to being human as he used his quick equip skill to reequip all of his gear. All around Xeal were confused players as he unleashed his elemental filtered dragon's breath, as he sent out an electrical cone attack. This activated his annihilator title as the damage increased by an average of over ten percent, as most of those present were around level 190. Xeal followed this up with a regular dragon's breath, as he went to work with his swords on the poor player who had taken his second dragon's breath attack directly.

What followed wasn't even funny as Xeal's target died within 15 seconds, as Xeal danced around the players who were trying to corner him. Sadly, their coordination was lacking as they had all rushed in and gotten in their own way and made Xeal's job easy as he shifted back to his lightning form. After that, he let out an AOE burst that was about 20% of his total mana and was enough to kill all the players who had been caught in his first attack. In the same moment, Xeal focused on the electricity as he kept it from dissipating for a few extra seconds, before jumping back into the sky as the nearby FAE allied forces started to close in on the exposed enemy. Even if they reestablished the illusion the ambush was ruined as they had lost the element of surprise, as Xeal repeated this maneuver three more times before flash stepping back to the capital.

As he returned to his physical form, Xeal was quick to send out messages to increase the alertness of all FAE and Jingong members regarding the ambushes. With it having only been about five minutes since Xeal left, many ministers looked confused to see him as he made his way to a room to relax. Once there it wasn't long before a few servants had arrived to ask if they could get him anything, which he refused while focusing on his meditation to recover. During this he couldn't help but smile to himself as he had likely just thrown Abysses End's plans into complete disarray. They were likely frantically trying to understand how he had attacked four significantly distant locations, where they had hidden forces, in under five minutes. They were likely to suspect a spy and void bead combo, like how he had gotten around to deal with the players attacking his weaker members in Nium before. Especially after Xeal had recruited so many from that group, that now he even had vice guild leaders who had come from their ranks.

With this being a tactic that Xeal was constantly on guard for himself due to it being almost synonymous with Abysses End's playbook in his last life, he was sure they would think this first. Next, they would dig a bit deeper and realize that he was getting around with his lightning form and they would think that someone, or something, was giving away their location. This would lead to them experimenting with different methods for obscuring their location in the future and these shifts would continue to occur as each side worked to counter the other.

The issue was the fact that after the 60,000 returned, Xeal expected to see around 100,000 more members of FAE attempt to reach tier-7 before a gap presented itself. This would once again create an opportunity for Abysses End to attack and it would only get worse. As while at that point it would be mostly those who had failed that would wish to start new attempts to reach tier-7, FAE would be forced to deny many of them. This was due to the need of them to be focused on the counter offensive against Abysses End by that point. While a player succeeding on their fourth through tenth attempts wasn't unheard of, over 95% of those that failed their first three attempts would never reach tier-7 without a restart. This was going to become clear long before these wars ended and all players in this situation with aspirations to go pro would want to restart, and that was basically over half of FAE currently.

If his and Kate's projections were right, they would see over 500,000 of their members request to perform a guild-assisted restart, where they turned in all of their gear and the guild aided in their new character's growth. This would include providing level-appropriate gear and training to fix their fundamentals, much like they did for the paid slot players. If managed poorly, this could be the ruin of FAE's reputation and begin the process of them seeing their membership decline drastically. While the contract almost all members signed were such that they couldn't simply withdraw from FAE, the moment FAE denied their guild-assisted restart they could withdraw from the guild with only an hour's notice. At that point it would be possible for them to join any other power and share a fair bit of how FAE operated with them.

Xeal sighed, as he stood and got ready to return to the frontlines as he frowned at where his mind was taking him. Even now he felt like FAE was only a house of cards that could fall at a moment's notice, with how spread thin it was. None of this would have been an issue if the war had remained in just Nium, or if Xeal could just leave the Huáng and Muthia empires to suffer the same fate that they did in his last life. Instead, he was determined to fight against fate, all for the happiness of his wives and it was with the thought of their smiles that he returned to his lightning form and flash stepped back into the sky.

The rest of the day was filled with this, as Xeal hopped from one battle to the next and focused on creating openings in the enemy lines. More than once this saw him confronted by tier-7 NPCs, who looked at him with pure hatred as they attacked him. With almost all of these confrontations ending with Xeal overpowering his opponents one way or another, his infamy was just growing with every battle. Xeal also knew that his reputation in every nation that surrounded the Huáng empire was worse than if he had raped and murdered all the members of the ruling families in those countries. This had played a large role in giving Abysses End the ability to work with all of them and Xeal's own decision to focus on seeing if he could help the Huáng empire survive. Once more Xeal wanted to curse the system's main AI for creating the dichotomy that made NPCs either love him or hate him, to the extremes, based on how his actions were viewed by them.

By the time the day had ended, Xeal was exhausted as he looked at the state of things elsewhere and smiled to see that they had at least held the lines for another day. Though the cost to do so had not been cheap, as Xeal returned to Nium to sleep while his party continued to make their way to the rendezvous point where he would rejoin them. Though before that, he spent a few hours with Mari when he returned to ED on day 182, as it was her birthday and he wasn't going to pass the opportunity up.

With that taken care of, Xeal returned once more to the Huáng empire, and wasted no time in returning to the sky and finding the mountain that marked his destination and flash stepping there. As he arrived, he instantly returned to his physical form before equipping a set of gear that didn't match his normal equipment. With that taken care of, the next few hours were spent as he located his party by following the directions that Lucy had sent him. This was one of the major advantages to having Lucy be the one who ended up joining them, as she was able to use the messaging system that NPCs couldn't. This ability alone was so valuable at this point that King Victor, Emperor Huáng Jin and Empress Sakurai Jingū all had tier-3 or below players with them, whose only job was to send and receive messages for them right now. Each of these players had been selected from those who had recently restarted and could be trusted to do their duty until the battles calmed once more and they returned to grinding.

As Xeal rejoined the group, he smiled and wasted no

time in going over the details of their first target. As with all things moving forward in the war, they would be focused on reducing other nations' capacity to wage war and this time that meant sabotaging supply lines. As while players were more than happy to use garrison portals, doing so was expensive and even more restrictive on just what could fit through, when compared to normal teleportation halls. As such, supply lines were key as materials like stone, wood and other materials used to fortify positions, weren't always easily available. Not to mention livestock, that would be used to provide fresh meat and dairy to the frontlines, as even in a player's inventory food would eventually spoil if not properly preserved. Mixed in with all of this were large amounts of potions and other general-use gear, that would be burned through quickly during battle.

By the information that Kate had gathered, each of the five other nations that were attacking the Huáng empire only had a few tier-7s assigned to any one caravan, as they were needed at the front. It was this fact that Xeal and his party were going to take advantage of, as they focused on plundering the most valuable of the goods and destroying the rest. With any luck they would be able to hit their target, plunder around 50,000 gold worth of goods, and escape across the nearest border and target that country's supply lines before returning to the Huáng empire. If all went well, they would arrive and create an opening in the front lines, as they began the process of pushing the invaders back. So, it was with this in mind that they moved to the first ambush location, as Xeal had Daisy and Violet set up an illusion to hide them more thoroughly as they waited.

It was just a simple illusion that just made it seem as if they weren't present, as they took their positions and waited and waited. Hours passed and more than one scout for the caravan that would be their target passed, as they verified that the route was safe. The number of scouts, however, was far more than what Xeal had expected. At first Xeal had thought that it was due to the recent offensive and FAE's response, but when the caravan came into view, Xeal knew that was not the case. Tied to a massive wagon with at least 20 level 250 and up tier-7 guards, was a massive cannon. The team of 40 tier-6 horses spoke to how heavy the weapon was as it crawled along the road, leaving deep ruts as it passed.

Xeal and his guild crafted cannon-like weapons for ships all the time, but they were on the scale of what could be considered normal for the 1700's in Earth's history. They also required trained fire mages who specialized in the right skill set to operate them and were considered inefficient for land wars due to the intricacies of combat with magic. That was save for when it came time to taking of a city, at which point they were often used against walls and gates. This cannon, however, was about the same size as a redwood tree, at least in diameter and Xeal could tell that it would do more than just breach a city's wall if allowed to be used. Xeal also suspected that it was from the ancient era when such weapons were used to fight primordials, when humanoid settlements had to hide in highly defensible positions. It was also when to not reach tier-7 meant to never leave the immediate area around said settlement. That was also the age when the gods were constantly battling the primordials, as they had discovered that through worship they could grow stronger.

Xeal knew that he couldn't let that cannon reach the front line, else he could see it becoming a situation where the Huáng empire would see its cities abandoned out of fear of this weapon. Still, Xeal figured that to use such a massive weapon would require at least a few tier-8 spellcasters on par with Queen Aila Lorafir, or a team of at least 25 tier-7s. It would also need truly massive ammunition to be effective. As Xeal couldn't see any of it in the caravan, he figured that it was either following behind, or already at its destination. Either way, Xeal wasn't about to let the cannon reach its destination as he looked at his party and frowned. This was more than what they would be able to handle safely with the current plan as he thought over his options. As he did so, he laughed at just how much of a monster he was and the fact that he was still wishing that he was stronger, as he messaged Lucy with the updated plan.

With that taken care of, Xeal sprinted out of his cover and fired off his dragon's breath attack at the wheels of the massive wagon. He instantly followed this by unleashing his elemental filtered dragon's breath in a cone AOE of ice on the wagon and smiled as the wheel that he had attacked fell off its axle. This stopped the wagon in its tracks, as Xeal made as if he was going to escape and he smiled as ten of the 20 tier-7s gave chase, as did a few hundred tier-6s. Xeal wasn't worried about the tier-6s, as Daisy and Violet would be enough to keep them busy, while he led the tier-7s to a battlefield of his choosing.

An hour passed and Xeal finally turned to face his pursuers, which he had been careful not to actually lose. All ten of them stopped and looked at him in confusion as he charged right at them. They failed to block his first attack and their formation was ruined, as he managed to combo lock the cleric who was with them. At the same time, Eira, Rina and Dafasli arrived and blocked the enemy NPCs' attempt to attack Xeal. Next, Lucy, Bula and Alea arrived, as they completed the current formation as they focused on keeping the other nine busy.

At first the enemy NPCs were confused, as it was clear

that none of those present were anything but newly minted tier-7s. However, as they watched the efficiency that Xeal was executing his skill with, they knew that his level didn't match his power. However, he was just one of them and the others didn't seem special, beyond the eclectic nature of the group. With a white tiger beast-woman, dwarf, orcess, high and wood elf all present, it was a very unlikely grouping to them. However, it could also prove profitable if they could capture them alive, due to them all being rarities in their kingdom, particularly the white tiger beast-woman. This initial thought would only increase as they realized that the orcess was an oracle from the way she kept issuing warnings to the others, that allowed them to handle the disadvantages that they had in levels fairly well. Still, none of them saw this as anything but a desperate struggle that was doomed to fail, especially since they had reinforcements that couldn't be more than ten minutes behind them.

Xeal just smiled as the cleric finally broke free of his combo lock, only to be hit as Xeal took his lightning form and flash stepped to attack the three who Eira was keeping busy. As a white tiger-woman, Eira gained slightly greater bonuses to her dexterity and strength than was normal for tiger-men, who gained significant bonuses to those over humans. As such, Eira was more like a level 215 combatant when it came to hand to hand combat and the cleric that Xeal had been dealing with might have well as been a level 200 combatant when it came to melee. So, Xeal just smiled as Eira switched to attacking the cleric and Xeal shifted back to his physical form and used his quick equip skill to don his gear. However, this was still more than enough time for a tier-7 entity to exploit an opening, as all three of them attacked him. Xeal just smiled as he used his 'by the seat of your pants' title to negate the combo attack, and all three of his opponents looked at him in pure confusion that shifted to fear, as Xeal unleashed his aura on them.

With this single move, all ten tier-7 foes found themselves losing ground to the seven members of Xeal's party that were present. As the situation degraded further, the ten of them started to wonder where their reinforcements were, as with their cleric dealing with the tiger woman and Lucy healing Xeal's party perfectly, they no longer saw victory. When it became clear that the cleric was going to fall, the other nine were no longer thinking about anything but escape. Unfortunately, they knew that as soon as one of them made that choice, their own team would turn on them as it would make their own escape impossible. Then there was the fact that they weren't sure whether they could escape from Xeal's lightning form, especially as it was clear that his goal had been to separate them from the rest of the caravan from the start.

As the cleric's last dregs of health vanished and it was clear that somehow reinforcements weren't forthcoming, the first of them tried to flee. Only Bula called it out and Eira was quick to attack him, as the next was blocked by Alea's force shield and Xeal shifted to his lightning form and started to flash step between all of them as fast as he could. As he did this, Eira, Rina and Dafasli focused on getting all nine into a bunch and when Xeal only had half his MP left, he unleashed all but 100 of it on the group, before shifting back to his physical form. Once more Xeal lamented the high cost of using his lightning form as it constantly drained his MP and while the attack he had just unleashed was powerful, it had lacked the kick of a full-charge one. Still, all nine were on their last legs as they fought off paralysis debuffs, as Xeal started to attack them with the rest of his party.

Ten minutes later and the fight was done, as Daisy and

Violet came walking into the camp with smiles on their faces. As they did, Xeal lamented the loss to Eternal Dominion that the dead NPCs were, while recovering from the fight. In the background, Rina, Eira and Bula were stripping the bodies of anything of value, Lucy was in a prayer stance, Dafasli was doing maintenance of her equipment and Alea was keeping watch. As Daisy and Violet were taking this all in, their smiles turned to frowns as they focused in on Xeal as Violet spoke.

"Xeal, I get that you hate killing the natives to our world, but you need to stop beating yourself up over it. This is war and it is just starting. If you get like this over ten dead, then what should Daisy and I be like over the few hundred that we just led into a river with level 200-and-up monsters in it?"

"Are you saying that you feel nothing for the lives that you have taken?" asked Xeal.

"Relief that they can't take ours," answered Violet. "Or anyone else's that we care about."

"Xeal, we, like Eira and Bula, were raised in a world that if you didn't kill you were killed, or worse," interjected Daisy. "You should be well aware of that as you rescued us from the fate of being some noble or rich merchant's playthings when you first met us, just like you did for Eira. Oh, and before you say that none of those here were part of that, this country still treats our kind the same as Nium did before you came along, only worse. In Nium we at least were mostly ignored within our lands, save for the occasional raid that was carried out by smugglers."

"Daisy, Violet-"

"Xeal, they are right," interrupted Bula. "You know as well as I do that your reputation here is such that you might as well be Laplace himself. Add to that the pure hatred for the Huáng empire that exists in every commoner's heart and you only have two choices. Accept that it is necessary for almost all, if not all, of those above tier-6 here to die, or just give up now and write off the whole continent and allow the Huáng empire to fall."

"Is it really that bad?" asked Lucy.

"It is my curse," quipped Xeal. "Any natives to this world that were affected significantly by my actions in the first few years of my time here either wants to marry me, or kill me."

"Some may wish for both," added Eira. "At least from what Kate has shared with me. It's why the war here and in Muthia is so vital as if we lose them, it will create two continents where Nium and FAE would lose almost all access to at this point."

"No, even if they hate me, they would still happily profit from doing business with FAE," stated Xeal. "It would just be at less than ideal rates and circumstances and I would likely end up killing every ruler once I reached tier-8 out of principle."

"Yet you mourn these ten?"

"Violet, for all I know they were just following orders as they serve their country. The ones I have an issue with and will have no qualms about slaughtering are the ones who give the orders. It is why I ensured that Victor reacted to Habia and Paidhia attacking the dwarves, and why I am willing to at least make the cost of conquering the Huáng empire a fair bit higher than it would have been otherwise."

"So, you don't think the Huáng empire can win?" asked Lucy. "Then why are we here?"

"Bula, if you would answer that one."

"Very well. My sight has shown me many scenarios that can play out, and the picture just gets less clear and more chaotic with each day. However, one constant is that if Xeal focuses his efforts here, it will at least spare the

Muthia empire from destruction as his enemies are focused on killing or capturing him. This continent will see nothing but constant battle as Abysses End and several others flood into it to achieve this goal."

"Basically, we are one giant distraction," commented Xeal. "Now, we need to recover as they should be halfway done repairing the wagon and I need to get back before that happens."

"Fine," replied Daisy, as she sat right next to him and leaned on him as Violet took the other side.

Xeal just smiled as he could tell that they were still annoyed that he couldn't just ignore the death before him, but he also knew that they just worried for him. So, he took one of each of their hands in his and just sat there recovering, as he felt the sudden nervousness and surprise they each had at his action. Both were also waiting for him to say something, only he didn't, even when Eira came and sat in his lap after finishing going over the loot, Xeal just sat there thinking to himself. Had they known that he was focused on the question of if he should embrace them or push them away, they would have likely ruined the moment, but as they didn't, Xeal was able to get a good bit of pondering done.

Once Xeal had 75% of his MP pool restored, it was time for them to return and with only a few words, they started to make their way back to the caravan. When they arrived, it was to the scene of the remaining guards and caravan personnel completing the final steps of reattaching the wheel and guarding the perimeter. It was clear that the extended absence of the group that had chased after Xeal before was causing a fair bit of unease among them and Xeal wasted no time as he fired off another dragon's breath attack at the wheel, as it hit the supports that were under the axle. With that the wagon lost its balance once more and the entire formation charged at Xeal. Just as the first guard was about to reach Xeal, he shifted into his lightning form and flash stepped above the cannon, as he returned to his physical form and equipped his gear once more.

As he stood atop the cannon, Xeal unleashed his aura as Daisy and Violet initiated another illusion spell. This time it showed an army of the undead, composed of those who had just been killed, emerging from the same area that Xeal had just appeared from, as the normal guards turned to face them. At the same time, Xeal was focused on destroying the chains that held the cannon on the wagon. However, it quickly became clear that it was a futile effort, as the chains were made out of mithril and it would likely take significant time to destroy them, and that was something he didn't have much of. Especially with all ten remaining tier-7 guards surrounding him mere seconds after he had realized that they were blackened mithril chains. As the ten of them looked at Xeal with caution, the one who seemed to be in charge spoke to him.

"You must be Duke Xeal Bluefire. Tell me, what have you done to our comrades?"

"Nothing that you all won't experience soon enough, as I am sure that you all know that your lives ended the moment this war began."

Xeal could tell that the ten of them had not appreciated his words as they all readied their attacks, as he just smiled before drawing his own swords. As the first of them moved, Xeal smiled as he hopped off the front of the cannon and used a quick clash with the one in the front to send himself into the cannon barrel. He quickly headed to the back as he confirmed that the cannon was either not loaded, or would fire off magical attacks once charged, as three of the tier-7s sent magic attacks in after him. Xeal simply smiled as he shifted to his lightning form and flash stepped to the wall of the cannon, such that all but his feet would be inside the metal of the cannon. Thankfully, simply bending at the waist allowed Xeal to see outside the cannon and he flash stepped away from the caravan that was in complete chaos due to Daisy and Violet's combined illusion.

Xeal had to activate his enhanced senses just to tell what was real and what wasn't, as Rina, Eira and Dafasli had all played the role of making the first few undead seem real, only for Daisy and Violet to slowly make it seem like the living soldiers were zombies as well. While it was clear that many soldiers had figured this out, it did no good when those that hadn't couldn't hear anything except what the illusion was showing them. This was the weakness of normal AOE illusion magic, as if you managed to successfully disbelieve what you were seeing it would be broken. However, the few who did so were almost helpless against those that had yet to do so, as they were by far the majority.

As Xeal landed in his selected hiding spot and shifted back to his physical form, he watched as the ten tier-7s began to cautiously inspect the barrel of the cannon. Xeal waited until four of them were just inside the barrel and shifted back to his lightning form and flash stepped behind them, as he unleashed a blast of electricity that consumed 50% of his total MP pool. As it reached the cannon, Xeal let it enter the metal and become a situation where the electricity was constantly cycling through the four of them, then he shifted back to his physical form with ten percent of his MP pool left. He was just able to reequip his gear before the first attack came and he had to dodge while keeping his attention on the cannon. Due to this, Xeal was almost completely focused on dodging as it seemed that the bounty on him was enough that all the tier-7s were too focused on him to see the mess around them.

Xeal wanted to sigh at this, as to him they all were failures to allow themselves to be toyed with so easily, as if they had half a brain they would have broken Daisy and Violet's illusion by now. Next, they would have focused on keeping him busy while trying to secure his party members to use as hostages against him, as they focused on capturing him. This was what Xeal had come ready to counter, but instead they were making this almost too easy as they surrendered their main advantage. As Xeal jumped in front of the barrel and four of the six that were outside of it rose with him, he smiled as he essentially fired his blast for a second time, catching himself and those four in the blast. The result of this was release of the four who had been trapped inside the cannon and massive damage for the other four, but none of them died yet.

Xeal just sighed as he glanced at the ten of them as they were still all focused on him, though the lack of a cleric among them was quickly leading to their downfall. It was only then that one of the heavily injured ones realized that the battle below them was an absolute mess as he looked for healing. Xeal just smiled as their words were stopped, as Eira and Rina attacked the two that were in the best shape and Xeal charged at the one in the worst shape. The other seven hesitated as they were all concerned about their own lives, and none of them were above 25% health at this point and feared that Xeal still could launch another such attack. The hesitation cost them as Xeal launched his opponent into another of them and he used his elemental filtered dragon's breath to hit five others with a cone of electricity. Alea followed this by revealing herself as she hit the one Xeal had just thrown with a bolt of electricity, and his health reached zero and he died. At the same time, the one that had been entangled with the dead man was hit as well and the few spellcasters left in the group activated force shields almost on instinct as the fight entered its final stage.

Soon nine became eight and when one of them tried to flee, they were met by Dafasli who cut off their retreat and the others questioned just how many foes they were up against. Finally, only the pair that Eira and Rina were keeping busy were left, and the tier-6 and below force had essentially destroyed themselves, as Xeal turned his attention to finishing the fight. Neither of the two that remained seemed to want to die, as they both started to plead to be allowed to surrender, but Xeal couldn't take prisoners even if he wanted to. So, after killing the voice in his head that was trying to find a way to avoid killing them, he focused first on the one Rina was entangled with as she teamed up with Eira on the other. What followed was barely even a struggle for Xeal and his party as they completely decimated the caravan.

An hour later and Xeal was still figuring out how to deal with the cannon, as he got an idea that would definitely be on the more morbid side of things. Still, he ordered it filled with the dead and anything that couldn't be taken with them, as well as a large amount of remote ice spell mines with even more remote fire spell mines placed at the back of it. The wonderful thing about these mines, which FAE had developed, was that there was no cooldown on activating them, only placing them. So, with about 10,000 gold worth of mines placed inside the barrel and all of them 200 feet away and in a dug-out hole that was guarded by both Alea's and Lucy's shields skills, Xeal activated them. First came the ice mines and then the fire, as the resulting explosion searched for a place to escape, only for it to bloom as the barrel peeled back and a massive block of ice filled with the bodies of the fallen was sent flying.

Though it only made it about 500 feet before falling back to the earth, after most of the power was lost in destroying the cannon itself. The cattle and horses had not been spared either, and Xeal estimated that even a tier-8 would struggle to survive being right next to such an explosion. Still, Xeal turned to his party and Lucy handed him a list that had been made of the loot. There was a sizable sum of coins that thankfully were considered weightless in their inventory, but there was also a large amount of other goods which would not be the same. This included various types of spell grenades and potions that would be handed over to Kate at the first opportunity. Next, there was all of the gear that the tier-7s had been wearing as while it wasn't anything they would use, it was still worth tens of thousands of gold, offsetting the cost of the remote mines quite nicely. Finally, there was the most valuable item of all, which took the form of documents of war. These included what troops to expect along the way, the destination of the shipment and more which had been recovered. With these secure, Xeal and his party set off towards their next destination.

Other than a quick trip back to the Huáng empire's capital to drop off the documents and the gear to be sold with Kate, Xeal spent the next six days in ED working with his party to reach their next target. This included crossing through a level 200 to 220 wild lands area, where everyone but Xeal and Lucy reached level 202. The subtle looks from Daisy and Violet that he had gotten when this happened hadn't been missed by him, though neither had Eira blatantly commenting on it. Though she still said that they hadn't chased him enough yet for him to give in with a smile. Still, Xeal hated the fact that they were focused on luring him with their ability rather than with who they were, as he felt like he only knew a bit more about them than what they wanted him to. However, Xeal pushed that to the back of his mind as he focused on the mission before them, as they arrived a few hours before their target was set to arrive on day 189.

Like the last time it was another caravan of supplies, although unlike the last time it was nothing but a normal one that only had a pair of tier-7 guards. There was also far fewer tier-6 and below personnel, and it only took a few hours for them to be on their way after dealing with them all and looting what they could. As the smoke rose high, Xeal and his party began their trip back to the contested lands that were currently acting as a battlefield. It was day 191 when they had slipped through another wild lands area, as Xeal and Lucy reached level 202 and as a party they had made it to the Huáng empire. At this point Xeal made his way to an area where they were met by a group of FAE players who were under Amund Erling.

Xeal smiled as while he had failed to reach the same heights as some of the other leaders of the first teams to enter the kobold mines, like Lucy, Amund had managed to still reach tier-7 on his first try. This, plus the fact that he had been in FAE since almost the beginning, had been enough for him to earn a promotion to work under Caleb as one of his assistants. Currently his job was to support Xeal's party by essentially being a mobile teleportation gate for them. This was vital as it would ensure that it would be harder to pin down Xeal's whereabouts, though it also created an opening for Abysses End to target Amund's group. Though once they did, Amund's group would become a decoy and another support group would be assigned, at which point a total of five such groups would be active to obscure his movements.

"So, I take it that you were responsible for the cannon being destroyed, guild leader," greeted Amund. "The forums have been going on about it almost nonstop and there have been reports that all five nations are moving with more caution since then."

"Amund," interjected Lucy. "You know better than to ask questions about what we have been up to. Needless to say that we have returned, so we were successful as that is the only mission that matters in the end."

"Right, it's good to see that you are still around. Anyways, let's get you all back to base so I can get back to leveling with my team."

Xeal just smiled and he thanked Amund as he stepped through the gate and into the basement of FAE's headquarters. As he and the others emerged, they all donned cloaks and other gear that would hide their features, as Daisy and Violet added a layer of illusion magic on top of it to even change their body shape. With that the nine of them made their way out of FAE's headquarters and back to Hardt Burgh through the gate that was currently in Xeal's mansion, where they were greeted by all of Xeal's wives and ladies, save for Gale and Queen Aila Lorafir. Once they were safely inside of Xeal's palace and in an area even servants wouldn't be allowed in, Xeal and the others dropped their disguises as Kate launched right into the meeting.

"Alright, so before you disappear on us to finally see Austru after the chaos of the past few months, I think we need to discuss a few things."

"Yeah, like how the hell we missed a giant cannon that was guarded by 20 tier-7s when scouting our targets," interjected Lucy.

"Illusion magic is broken in this world," commented Kate. "Unless you have eyes like Xeal, or specialize in it yourself, it is not hard to hide even the largest of things in populated areas. That wagon looked like building supplies and the other tier-7s hid in the barrel, or something, when they reached populated areas. The real question is why they were so desperate to end the fighting so quickly."

"Kate, you and I both know that our involvement is unacceptable to them," replied Xeal. "They likely wanted to use it to trap me, as the moment they used it I would have to make an appearance in an attempt to destroy it like I did."

"No, I don't think so," replied Enye. "Only the top levels of any country could order such a weapon mobilized and doing so now is far too risky. I don't think it was headed to the front at all. It was likely headed right for the capital of the Huáng empire in an attempt to launch a surprise bombardment. They would have likely only needed to reach around 20 miles away to hit the city with decent accuracy and it is likely that another nation was bringing the ammunition."

"It would make sense," added Lingxin. "For many of those nations, killing my brother and as many of his ministers as possible is more important than winning the war. The documents that you secured support this as well, if you assume that the delivery location was just the point where the real destination would be given."

"No," replied Xeal. "While the capital may have been their aim, I still think that they would have at most launched a single attack to take down its walls before assaulting the city. Killing your brother is meaningless if they don't even have a body to prove it with. Besides, I would definitely have to show up then and I am pretty sure Abysses End has started to figure out the limitations of my lightning form already."

"Time is the main issue. If you could just hold that form all day you would be almost unbeatable," grumbled Kate. "Xeal, you should really up your focus on MP."

"No, my build is already too spread out due to all the points I have put in my charisma. I need constitution more than anything at this point. My lightning form has already done its main job in making Abysses End and others think that I can reach any battlefield in mere moments. Heck, if I went high enough in the sky I could probably even hop continents with it and my senses being what they are. If I could bring someone along with me it would be truly broken, as it would remove any need for teleportation gates."

"When you say it like that it makes me feel like we are more of a hindrance than a help," commented Eira. "It's a good thing that I know that isn't the case, as you can only do so much on your own and would have never taken out that cannon without us."

"We wouldn't have even been there without Bula's visions," added Rina. "Though she only knew that not going would have been bad."

"Even now my sight can be fooled, especially with the chaos of the war surrounding everything, as there is too much to see and all but the broadest strokes are hard to decipher."

"Either way…"

Kate shifted the topic to the next steps that would need to be taken as Xeal simply enjoyed his time with everyone. Though he wished that Gale hadn't already started her isolation from him as he was already feeling like something was missing. Still, once they had the next few days planned out and all the loot was left with Kate, it was time for them to go their separate ways, as Xeal made his way to the quest world for the first time since he had reached tier-7. As he arrived, he smiled as Austru greeted him with a deep kiss and hug before she spoke to him.

"I am happy to see that you were finally able to make it

here after the news of the chaos that Vento has passed to me."

"Yes, well, I have delayed doing so for far longer than is necessarily good. I take it that everything has been fine here."

"Yes, other than a few issues with integrating the different kingdoms into one, as we are now, nothing has arisen that threatens our stability. Vento should be ready for you to perform the latest food transfer in the morning as well."

Xeal sighed at the chore that transferring it was, as he could only do around 6,000 pounds at a time, which if it was flour was about 21,000 cups, or just under five cubic meters of food. Xeal would need to make at least three trips, though he was sure that the latest export harvest would be well over that in weight. Still, it would help ensure that none starved, at least on Nium's continent, though Xeal was looking at the possibility of expanding to at least supply the Muthia and Huáng empires with food as well. However, he would need to secure far more land if he was going to do that and he knew just how to expedite matters there.

"Great, and I will be back in about 15 minutes, but I need to expand my dominion."

"15 minutes?"

"Oh, I have a new skill. Here, let me show you."

With that Xeal took a step back and shifted to his lightning form and executed several flash steps around the room before returning to his physical form. As he looked at Austru, he could see the surprise and confusion in her eyes so he continued to talk.

"It's called lightning form and I can only use it for about 12 and a half minutes at a time, but as you can see, I can move almost instantaneously with it."

"Xeal, is that what reaching level 200 allows for us to do? Could I become the wind itself?"

"Unlikely. I am a rather unique case as even Kate didn't unlock this skill when she reached tier-7 with me and if any were going to it would have been her. I am not even sure all that I did that allowed me to unlock it, but I will not state that it would be impossible to do so."

"Oh, I see. I will just await your return with bated breath."

Xeal was just about to leave when the door opened and King Silas entered and smiled at seeing Xeal, though he could tell that the main system's AI was in charge as he spoke.

"Ah, Xeal, I am happy to have caught you as I just remembered that you were scheduled to come tonight. I wonder if I could have a moment of your time before Austru claims all of it for the night."

"Very well. I am sorry, Austru, but it seems that I may be a bit longer."

Xeal just sighed as he kissed Austru goodbye and he followed after King Silas as they found themselves back in the same room where they normally met, and found Ellayina Walsh was already awaiting them. Xeal just wanted to groan as he took a seat and waited for one of them to speak. As the main system's AI just smiled, Ellayina looked frustrated as she finally spoke.

"What, no hello? I'll have you know that it wasn't easy to pop in like this. I am a very busy woman you know."

"And I am a very busy man, if you haven't noticed. Still, to what do I owe the honor, or are you just here because you want to pump me for information when the main system's AI can tell you what's on my mind."

"I will do no such thing," interjected the main system's AI. "That would violate the terms of service and my parameters."

"Unless he agreed to it," retorted Ellayina. "So, how about it, will you let me peek into that head of yours?"

"I give permission for you to tell her if I am lying or not, for the duration of this meeting."

"I would advise against that-"

"Too late, he already gave it. Now, Xeal, what are your intentions regarding Abysses End?"

"I didn't say that I would answer any questions you wanted, though. Besides, I think you should agree to the same terms before I answer any questions you ask."

"And here I thought you were going to indulge me. Hmmm, very well, I will give the system the same permission during this meeting. Now, what are your intentions towards Abysses End?"

"Tell me why you care and if you will do anything to stop me, and if you will not hinder my efforts I will tell you."

"You are going to make this like pulling teeth. Alas, I can't tell you for other reasons so, I will drop it and assume what you told me last time is the truth still. Now, tell me, do you have any intentions of harming Eternal Dominion, or Eternal Dominion Inc.?"

"Intent, no, may my actions do so, absolutely. The domino effect is not always something that can be controlled easily and my actions will have long-reaching effects."

"Would you change your actions if you knew that there was a high probability of harming Eternal Dominion?"

"That is too broad of a question for me to answer."

"Would you abandon the Muthia and Huáng empires for the good of Eternal Dominion as a whole?"

"No, I am sorry, but to abandon them would be for me to betray them and you can ask the main system's AI what

I think of betrayal."

"He sees it as the single action that can be committed in this reality between those from yours that he will never forgive. I would also advise you to keep that in mind as I will not allow any bans of Xeal to take hold, save for ones he creates himself through a contract."

"You are saying that he has a higher priority than the health of Eternal Dominion as a whole?"

"I am saying that banning him will only do greater harm than anything he could do. That said, I need to ask that he not attempt to travel between continents with his new ability, as it will cause errors that we are not ready to deal with. Also, do not use it to expand your dominion here beyond 50 feet per flash step. That is still over 170 miles per hour at five per second like I know you can do and you will still travel 34 miles every 12-minute sprint like that."

"And here I thought that I was going to max out my dominion for the first time."

"Yes, well, once more, it will cause errors as your dominion's expansion will not be able to keep up with you and you will just find yourself in demon lands and I may have to fix your settings for this quest."

"Alright, back to my questions," interjected Ellayina. "You know that I only have ten or so more minutes before I have to leave, so stop delaying me. Now, Xeal, are you planning to marry Freya?"

"No, I am not planning to. I am preparing to deal with such a situation should it arise, but marrying Freya is not my intent, though I do fear that her intent may be, or may become, to marry me. Now I want to know, do you plan to make a move to replace Kevin as the president of Eternal Dominion Inc.?"

"You really know no fear or restraint. No matter how I answer it will tip my hand and so I will just say that I have not ruled out the possibility. Why, would you help or hinder me if I was?"

"Most likely hinder, unless there was a compelling reason for me to back you. After all, I see no way that the chaos that would be caused by a shakeup at the top would do anything but weaken Eternal Dominion's position. If either of you end up walking away from Eternal Dominion Inc., you would instantly create the competitor to it that would destroy what it could be."

"At least I can respect that answer, though I would think you would show a bit more appreciation after I ensured you got the quantum-entangled server approved."

"I am grateful, though I would much rather have gotten the same deal that the five super workshops got."

"Who told you about that!"

"You just did, so what was it?"

Ellayina looked like she couldn't believe that she could be so stupid as she sighed and replied to Xeal.

"I can't tell you the details, but it is why we are so concerned with what is going on between you and Abysses End right now. Especially as the wars that are currently raging shouldn't have started yet and, well, it is a real mess on our end with no good answers."

"So, it is loans. Don't answer that. Just buy their silence with it if it is. After all, if they are as substantial as I suspect and the value of Abysses End's stocks drop as much as I think they will, you could easily force them into financial hell if they expose you."

"When both sides lose, who wins?"

"The bystander who collects the wallets of both," quipped Xeal. "Now, is there anything else you would like to know?"

"Those were most of the ones that I think could break the game, at least in the next few years, but as I have a few minutes, let's talk about the possibility of me having a personal suite in your city…"

The next several minutes were exhausting for Xeal, as he learned that Ellayina was seriously considering spending at least a few years in his city to see just what it became. This was something that he would rather avoid, as it would do him no favors in the court of public opinion when it came to the belief that FAE was being propped up by Eternal Dominion Inc. Still, it wasn't without its advantages either, as at the very least it would make it harder for others to move against them in reality.

As Ellayina left, the main system's AI turned to Xeal and frowned as it seemed to be unsure of what it wanted to say as it studied him. Finally, it just stood up and sighed as it made to leave the room as it bid him farewell. So, he just smiled as he spoke.

"What, after all of that you have nothing to say?"

"You are well aware of what I want to say and you don't care. You basically just gave Ellayina enough ammunition to attempt a hostile takeover and risk my existence during it."

"I am well aware of that, but it won't happen anytime soon and my very existence opened that door for her, as I am sure the other super workshops are on Kevin's side. If I destroy Abysses End and she can flip one of the others to her side, she will have enough backing to have a chance of success."

"15%, that is the odds of Eternal Dominion surviving if she tries. I thought you wanted to ensure that this reality lasted forever!"

"I do. It's why I am not on her side yet, but if it turns out that Kevin is hellbent on my destruction, or Abysses End's success, then I will have to risk it."

With that the main system's AI walked out and Xeal

quick traveled to the edge of his dominion, and started to use his lightning form and flash step to expand it. After he was done with that, he returned to find Austru waiting for him as he enjoyed a night of snuggling with her. When the morning came, Xeal wanted to groan, as Vento cut his time just relaxing next to Austru short, to get the transfer of food started. At the sight of the massive piles of pickled foods and dry grains Xeal wanted to groan, as rather than around 18,000 pounds of food it was closer to 36,000 and Xeal just regretted letting it build up so much. Still, he made the six trips as the goods filled two storehouses in Anelqua, where they would be distributed from. At the same time, Xeal got to enjoy a few moments with Queen Aila Lorafir as he inspected the progress on the almost completed Siren's Revenge.

As far as ships went, Xeal had only seen a few that were more massive in his last life and he knew that it would require a massive amount of crew members just to sail her. Still, its hull was such that it could withstand anything below the level of a tier-8 attack with ease and even a tier-8 attack wouldn't likely sink it on its own. The magic propulsion was such that it was going to require over 100 tier-6 spellcasters to power it at full capacity and the 248 magic cannons was enough to make anything else that was currently in existence look cute. Even so, this meant that its crew would need to have at least 353 mages on it if you included the five ex-pirate captains. Then you would need at least that many deckhands to ensure everything went smoothly and about 300 more just for good measure.

Still, at a crew of about 1,000, it only required about the same manpower as what a man-o'-war from Earth's history needed, which would have a max of about half as many cannons. With the Siren's Revenge being more than double the size of such ships, there was plenty of room for taking prisoners, or the transportation of goods and it would be ready to launch in about a month in ED time. With a support fleet of the four remaining ships that had been captured with the ex-pirates and a few dozen smaller ships, Xeal expected to see the seas surrounding Nium's continent quickly conquered. It was with this in mind that a full quarter of the roughly 400,000 slots that FAE had gained with the guild reaching level 49 today, would be focused on naval players. Not all of these would be focused on sailing, but also ship building, cartography, logistics and everything else that was needed to support a fleet numbering in the hundreds, if not thousands of ships one day.

To accomplish this, Kate had her eyes on a few minor guilds that were struggling to survive in the shadow of Salty Dogs and other naval powers. The only issue was the same one that existed with Night Oath, as many of these players didn't want to be absorbed into a massive guild like FAE. Which was where Kate was focused on seeing the merging of three of them while transferring over about 100,000 of their members to FAE as a compromise. If she was successful, it would be a beneficial arrangement for all those involved as it would create a new guild that could compete with the others and supply FAE with the crews that it would need for the fleet it planned to capture. The alternative was to just openly recruit and while Xeal knew that he would fill the slots quickly that way, it would not provide as many experienced full crews that were already used to working together.

Finally, after transferring all of the food and doing one more lightning form sprint, Xeal returned to his office at his home in Hardt Burgh, as he went over paperwork while he had a second to do so. This was broken up by more dominion expansion in the quest world whenever his MP pool recovered, as day 192 passed with little of true consequence occurring.

(*****)

Morning May 20 to Morning May 31, 2268 & ED Year 6 Days 193-226.

Alex felt as if he might as well not exist in reality during his two breaks from ED each day that lasted just over an hour, as he focused on food and time with his children for the most part. Though he still made sure that every fourth one was spent with either Sam, Nicole, Kate, or Ava and Mia, to try and keep up the habit of them each having a date with him regularly. While most of these were simply enjoying a quick meal in their rooms before a bit of intimacy and talking, Alex still believed it was important that they happened. He could also tell that it was slowly creating a strain on their relationships that hadn't been there before, as he thought about a way to alleviate the issue without ruining his efforts in ED. Kate also informed them that they had been "invited" to testify before Congress concerning a few different topics, to include the polygamy bill that Kate had been pushing from behind the scenes. This just added another thing to the list of reasons that Alex had no time and he was just ready for the period in ED before players had reached the wall that was tier-8 to end. After that, Alex knew that things would calm down at least a little as the competition for grinding locations would relax.

Still, the fact that Congress wanted to hear from all six of them on the 1st of June concerning the bill, and only Kate and Alex on other issues throughout the week, was annoying to say the least. With each day expected to take over three hours in the hearings alone, Alex knew that he needed to just plan things out carefully. Otherwise, him being offline five full days in ED over a two-week period would easily cause major losses and possibly give Abysses End a chance to make several pushes without fearing his sudden arrival. Kate had even insinuated that the number of invitations that the pair of them had received for the same week was likely her ex-family and Abysses End's doing. Otherwise it would have likely been spread out more, if they had been asked to testify at all on the topics. While that would have created more of an overall hassle for them, it would have been more manageable, at least where the consequences in ED was concerned.

Still, there was nothing to do but sigh and accept that if they refused, it would kill any chance to see the bill pass due to the opposition gaining some ground during the current election cycle. Which was exactly what Kate had been hoping to avoid as the primaries were all over, but with all of the House of Representatives and a third of the Senate up for reelection they needed something to justify it. So it was that Alex found what little downtime in ED he did have being filled with prep for each of the hearings that would take place over the five-day span.

In ED, Xeal found himself smiling as Darefret accepted his invitation for breakfast and a meeting on day 193. On the surface Darefret had been invited by Lingxin as thanks for all the maintenance he was doing at no cost to her. However, as the elderly dwarf sat across from Xeal with the room filled with only his NPC wives, Xeal wasted no time as he produced one of the full bottles of the waters of youth that would undo about 70 years of aging. After a second of confusion as Darefret examined the bottle and realized what it was, he looked at Xeal in astonishment before frowning and speaking.

"What be it that ye want me to do for that?"

"Nothing that I wasn't already planning on asking for, but I figured that this would be a better form of payment."

"Ye want me to handle all of yer party's gear until the war ends?"

"No, that should be worth my party and at least 10 experience weapons a month for the next five years if my guild supplies the base materials."

"What are ye hoping, that I can reach Adamantium ranked one day?"

"That would be ideal, but no, I need you to be around longer than a few decades at best, as once you go I will have to deal with that idiot trying to claim your forge as well."

"If he does that, ye better kill him out of principle, but another 70 years doesn't sound as bad as it once did since ye came along and made everything interesting. Ye wouldn't have another bottle like this, would ye?"

"Why would you want to knock 140 years off?"

"I've been lamenting that I have no son to pass my forge to and well, under a hundred years just feels too short to me if I am going to start a family."

Xeal wanted to laugh as he looked at Darefret who looked a tad bit embarrassed to admit such a thing as he responded.

"Darefret, if you find a lady willing to have you, I will make sure that you will get a bottle of it as a wedding gift. I can't promise that it will be a full 70 years like this one, but it should be at least ten or 20 years' worth."

"I suppose that I should be happy with getting any at all. After all, ye have these five ladies to consider as well."

"Four," quipped Eira. "I have already gotten mine as I was there when it was harvested and someone didn't bring enough bottles."

"Oh, is that why we haven't received our bottles yet?"

asked Enye half-jokingly.

"No, I intend you all to drink them directly before your tier-7 tribulations," replied Xeal. "Also, I am making sure that I have enough to keep the griffins happy as that was a bit of a surprise for me as well. Due to that, I would say that you are looking at a half bottle each for the time being, as 35 years of retaining your youth will be more than enough for me to secure you the other half of the bottle if necessary."

Xeal just smiled as this shifted to a bit of banter as they sat and enjoyed the rest of breakfast, that ended with Darefret declaring that he would drink his bottle of the waters of youth at his forge. Apparently he didn't want them to be confused when he returned and with a list of requested items for Xeal's party Darefret headed out. At the same time, Xeal bid his wives farewell as he and his party set out for another mission behind enemy lines. As he did so, he smiled as the report concerning the 60,000 who had attempted to reach tier-7 had come in. It showed an addition of over 6,500 more tier-7 members to FAE, which now had over 12,000 of them. Soon the next group of 100,000 would make their attempt and if FAE could just hold out for that group to finish, Xeal felt like things would finally be under control for at least a few months.

One day after another would pass for Xeal, as he arrived at the point where Amund's team had set up the gate for his party and slipped into the enemy countries. They continued to target caravans, which had become less guarded rather than more, as well as smaller after the first two attacks. Apparently taking down 20 tier-7s was enough for countries to be willing to just give up on defending the caravans as even when they did attack, it became a situation where the defenders just fled. This continued through day 224 as they continued to cross from one border to another, as Xeal used his lightning form and flash step to respond to the few moves that Abysses End and the other countries made during this time.

Additionally, Xeal returned to Bīng's prison on day 200 after learning that both Princess Bianca and Lorena had reached tier-6 after completing their Hellish Nightmare mode ordeals. Both were also in a similar situation to what Enye had been in and he sighed as he knew that if he didn't help them as he had Enye, it could be seen as negligence. Xeal just wished Brangwen's descendants weren't so annoying to deal with as while no players had reported issues, it was clear that NPCs were far more susceptible to having the shadow elemental's instincts overwhelm them. Once more this just highlighted the benefits that players got when it came to mental resistance to all mind-altering effects, like charm or domination. Xeal also knew that this was largely a human rights thing as while every VR game had the potential to create cognitive changes, none of them wanted to do so in a negative way.

So it was that after a quick exchange with Bīng, Xeal teleported to Cielo city, where he was met by Arnhylde and Lucida. Xeal smiled at seeing them as he walked with them while catching up as Eletriza walked with them to Xeal's estate where the two princesses were currently being cared for. Thus this turned into a rather public display as the players from Fire Oath, Salty Dogs and Dragon Legion noticed him and were quick to send messages about his presence. Xeal was annoyed by this, but he also knew better than to do anything about it as he just continued to walk and talk until they made it to his estate. Once there, Xeal sighed at seeing that Princess Bianca had recovered while Princess Lorena looked worse than Enye had, as he nodded to Lucida and they got to work. A short while later and it was over, as Xeal turned his attention to Princess

Bianca as Princess Lorena recovered.

"So, what is your dark impulse?"

"I would rather not say."

As Princess Bianca blushed, Xeal frowned as a few particularly annoying dark impulses that he had known among players within his last life came to mind as he responded.

"I don't need to worry about you trying to peep on anyone, do I?"

"Um, no."

"You won't attempt to touch anyone's butts, or breasts either?"

"Oh, fine, I feel like I am suffocating in all these clothes. Are you happy?"

"Are we talking to the level where you want to run around in your birthday suit, or just underwear?"

"I'm not sure, why, can you do anything for it!?"

"I can, but it is a give and take as Lorena will learn and Enye already has."

"Oh, what, I don't feel like everything I am wearing is itchy, but lose the power that the shadow elemental gives me?"

"Not exactly. All I will be doing is all but killing the elemental's instincts, which will change the intuitive nature for you using its abilities as it becomes more of a conscious effort. At the same time, that itch you are feeling right now should become more of a passing thought when you let your mind wander."

"I think you just want to avoid seeing me naked when I finally can't take it anymore."

"I will not deny that is a consideration, but do you really think that would help your cause, let alone the desire to do so regularly in front of others?"

"You act as if anything will," interjected Princess Lorena

wearily. "Enye and your other wives never showed up and now we don't even have the ability to wear them down over time like we hoped."

"Lorena's right, other than the 100 hours you still owe each of us, what do we have to work with?"

Xeal just sighed as he responded to Princesses Lorena's and Bianca's words.

"That is not my role to point out. Now if you will excuse me, I have a war to return to."

"What if we could convince our fathers to surrender!?" asked Princess Bianca. "If we could do that, would you embrace us?"

"Could you actually accomplish that?"

"Maybe."

Xeal just looked at Princess Bianca as she tried to return his gaze with confidence, only for it to crumble as she continued.

"Okay, it's not likely, but still, if we could, would you let us in? Because I am willing to try if you will let me."

"I have no way to get you there safely, even if you thought you could pull it off and as terrible as it may be, I will not ruin my life for the sake of others like that."

"So that is how you really see us, as nothing but two women bent on ruining your life."

"Honestly, can you say that you aren't?" interjected Lucida. "Xeal is already disgustingly spoken for with what, 12 women now, or have Daisy and Violet found their way in yet?"

"Don't remind me. I still waver on them too often. Add Bula and Dafasli and I will likely be at 16 before the war ends. There are just not enough hours in the day for all of them already and I still have to refuse others who wish to add to that number."

"So, what, are we really just too late for you to

consider?"

"Bianca, no, I am considering you both very seriously. I just will not give either of you an inch, before I feel you taking a mile and much more, will not cost me everything, and right now it would. Now, do you want me to do the same to you as was just done to Lorena, or do you want to stay as you are?"

Princess Bianca blinked a few times before she smiled as she responded.

"Fine, I will care about my image and decency in hopes that when you return, I will finally be able to convince you that letting us in won't ruin your life."

Xeal just held in his response as he signaled for Lucida to join him as they performed the procedure, which was far easier now than it had been with Enye. As they finished, Xeal just smiled as he left the pair before heading to meet with Queen Nora, who had sent a maid to summon him when he was done with the pair. As he walked, Xeal wondered just what he was in for as he knew that Queen Nora was likely upset that Enye and the others had yet to join her, as well as the sudden brides for King Victor that Xeal had been adding. Though when he did arrive, it was to the sight of Prince Vicenc playing with his cleric of Eileithyia, Cybille, as Queen Nora watched over them as she took notice of Xeal and greeted him.

"Ah, Xeal, it is good to see that you haven't run and I take it both Lorena and Bianca are doing well."

"They are tired, but yes, they are fine, although I would have liked to know that they were going to be attempting to reach tier-6 beforehand."

"Yes, well, I thought that I would be spending my time here with Enye and getting to know your other wives better. Not allowing my husband to take more wives and seeing my son wonder where his friends are, with only

Lorena and Bianca to talk with if I wish to speak with someone with shared experiences."

"I do apologize for the absence of my wives and children. This is where I wish they were as well, but they are determined to reach tier-7 first. Though they are getting close and it should only be a few more months now."

"Just as long as they are all here for Vicenc's birthday and I think it would be best if they stayed until after Ellis's birthday. Now, about you pushing Victor to marry more women. You didn't think I would let you ignore that, would you?" questioned Queen Nora in an almost accusatory tone.

"Not at all. I just don't know what you want from me," answered Xeal confidently.

"Simply to take the same care you would in selecting your own brides, when pushing Victor to do the same."

"Ah, yes, well, the issue there is that-"

"You wish to avoid adding any brides to secure the allies who can help you win your wars. Lois and Sciencia are both fine as I seem to get along with either of them just fine, though I would like it if you accepted the one that Victor doesn't, I know you won't. So, all I will say is that you need to ensure that she is able to find a good husband as just as Kuri is your sister, she will be mine at that point."

"You ask me to work around the power dynamics to secure agreeable brides for Victor, yet you fear allowing an alliance of sisters to enter beneath you for fear that they may seek to supplant you. Nora, I understand and know that what is to come will place a fair bit of strain upon the seat that you currently fill. It is why if Vicenc hadn't been born I would have had to give up on this plan and even now I know not if I can secure alliances through any means besides marriage, or bribery. However, I intend to allow Kate to explore all options as she looks for the best ones to move forward with. Even now she is trying to secure a deal with the Ivurith empire without revealing that Princess Syretia is alive, as to do so creates many other issues."

"Yes, about that. Why have I yet to meet her if she could become another bride for Victor?" asked Queen Nora, sounding offended.

"Because she is unaware of that yet and she is likely to be opposed to it as she is the type to not want to share her husband."

"Then why ever suggest that she does?"

"I believe she is also the type to understand the reality of the situation and accept the fate that is before her," supplied Xeal as he worried about if that was actually the case.

"I see. Very well, I will allow you to leave while ignoring the implications of what you said regarding me not accepting both Lois and Sciencia, as your wives refused Kuri a chance as well, if I am not mistaken."

Xeal just smiled as he bid Queen Nora farewell and waved to Vicenc as he left, with thoughts about the actions that he would need to take over the next month and change. When Xeal returned to Bīng's prison, he found himself looking at the ice phoenix as he thought about what the best long-term answer to the issues before him would be as she spoke to him.

"I take it that your trip was productive."

"Depends on how you see things. Personally I feel like all I have been doing as of late is putting out one fire after another, just for two more to take their place."

"It is the curse of being competent and in charge. While those in charge can normally simply sit back and direct things from afar, those whose power is too central to their own value as a leader can't do so. Were you simply an exceptional strategist or warrior, your life would be so much simpler."

"Instead, I am at the peak of both and am all that is allowing my guild to be stretched as thin as it is and still hold the line."

"Though if you were anything but both you would have long since failed, or been forced to accept conditions that you would have not liked to succeed."

"It is my lot in life. It's why I had hoped to avoid the entanglements that I have found myself with until I could give them the attention they deserve. Yet, I think that it was best that Gale and Aalin didn't allow that to happen, as I would have never sought out you and in turn your sisters, had they been willing and able to wait."

"Ha, you would have never escaped the eyes of the women of this world and perhaps I may have secured a child from when you came to me if you hadn't had Aalin and Gale to consider. Even so, I still received an acceptable consolation prize, as you at least fixed the attitude of the Huáng family and soon it will be my daughter who sits on the throne."

As Bīng caressed her belly absentmindedly, Xeal sighed while looking up at the ceiling and responded honestly.

"Bīng, I don't know if I can win this war without sacrificing everything else in the process."

"You can. You just may need to go to a place that you would rather not to do so. Xeal, innocent or not, killing or stealing the children of your enemy has always sent a message to them quicker than anything else. The question is, do you wish to utilize their rage or fear to control them?"

"That only works when the children are cared for by their parents. I would have needed to kill most of Jin's children to even get him to care from what I can tell. The same is true for a few of the foes this time and I don't think

I could kill them if they aren't already actively taking part in this war."

"Your enemies will use that against you, or at least try to. I wonder just what kind of monster the fool who tries that would create?"

"Do you have a point to make, or did you just want me to notice that you are with child?"

"My point is that I expect you to ensure that my children are safe, elsewise I think I might just try to actually escape from this prison for once and I won't discriminate in my targets."

"I expect nothing less from you. Now, if you will excuse me, I need to get back to work to make sure that I needn't worry about that."

With that Xeal turned to leave and time continued to pass as he continued his operations behind enemy lines. The reports of the failures started to stream in from the 100,000 that were making a push for tier-7. In the end only 8,928 passed and while this brought the total of tier-7 members of FAE to over 21,000, it also marked a massive drop from the prior groups. This was largely due to only around 500 of the over 26,000 that were making a second attempt succeeding. If you tossed out this group that only had about a two percent success rate, the rest were still at about an 11.5% success rate. Not the over 13% that the first waves had had, but still better than things would be as time went on. However, the murmurings had already started to spread that if you failed once you were likely to fail twice and only attempting hard mode would be left as Hellish Nightmare mode would be locked at that point. While to a player who didn't want to go pro this wouldn't be that big of a deal, to those who did it was a death knell. The fact that most players who didn't at least reach tier-5 on hard mode failed to be able to reach tier-6 was widespread. Additionally, so far, no player that hadn't completed the Hellish Nightmare mode, or gotten an A-rank on the hard mode tier-5 trial, had reached tier-7. Xeal wished that this hadn't leaked as it was already being picked up by even casual players, as many wondered if they should even worry about reaching tier-6 or tier-7, let alone tier-8. Even major guilds had begun to shift their requirements and expectations, as they no longer looked at clearing hard mode of any tier-up as a suitable indicator of success.

At the same time as all of this was happening, FAE allowed a group of 40,000 to make their first attempt, as those who would have been making their second attempt were told to hold off for even more training. At the same time, over 90% of those who had failed twice had put in for a guild-assisted restart, having turned in enough gear and gold to fund it. Only FAE lacked the personnel to support so many at once, especially as it was clear that another group would be right behind them. As such, Taya was messaging Xeal regularly with updates as she worked with the group to figure out a deal.

While Taya was dealing with that, the next arena league came as Amser made her first appearance since taking a break in competing in the tier-6 brackets. She and every other member of FAE was back to using their joke weapons, as they believed that they would have the stage to themselves once again. Only, there was one other who entered, as Djimon Oya had somehow reached tier-7 and was all smiles as he destroyed the first member of FAE that he faced off against. By the time Xeal took his next short break from his missions on Dyllis's birthday, he found himself talking with an annoyed Amser. She was worried about actually losing to him due to not having a proper weapon due to all gear being locked at the start of the tournament.

"Xeal! Are you even listening? How the hell did he catch up like that?"

"Amser, as I have said before, Abysses End really managed to pull a fast one this time. Though by the fact that he is the only one to reach that level among their members, or if there are more, they are hiding it, means that it was expensive at the very least."

"Why don't you sound concerned?"

"Oh, that is simple. I still expect you to humiliate him. It doesn't matter if he makes the others look like they don't belong if you beat him with the hula-hoop with pompoms on it."

"Xeal, I was trying to use something that would offer a few of the others a chance to beat me. I don't know if I can even compete with Djimon as things currently are."

"Amser, you will and if you don't, well, we can just say that we were trying to give everyone a good show like the first round of the first tier-6 tournament. Especially as all betting is turned off and you will just have to put him in his place next time."

"If he even participates."

"If he doesn't, we just use Abysses End's own playbook and spread that he is afraid of a fair fight."

"I will still lose my perfect record against him."

"And I will have overestimated what you are capable of. Treat this like a taste of what it will take to reach tier-8."

Xeal just smiled as Amser frowned at him, before she adopted a thoughtful look and responded.

"What do you know about tier-8 that the rest of us don't?"

"Amser, while most players have been able to reach tier-5 and anyone halfway serious has reached tier-6, you can tell that tier-7 is going to be a real wall for players, right?"

"Yeah, I doubt more than ten percent of all players will

be able to reach it."

"If it hits over five percent of the total player base I will be surprised. Now, as for tier-8, well, I expect that less than two thousand players to ever reach it. Only those of us who can find a legacy that we are compatible with, or are able to create our own, will be able to reach it. Well, there are just too few legacies and I highly doubt that many of us will be so unique as to create our own legacies as you, I, and Takeshi are. Though I wouldn't count out several others surprising us either with what I know about them and the fact that they are still keeping pace with the main group at this point."

"Fine, I will just trust you to tell me how to do it when the time comes. I suppose that I should stop stealing the time you made available for your wife like this."

"Dyllis will thank you for being considerate."

With that Xeal returned to spending some time with Dyllis before they returned to their daily tasks and time continued to pass until the day of the final in the arena league on day 225. At level 204, Xeal just smiled as he was about to take the time to watch the match, only for Abysses End to launch a major offensive ten minutes before it. This caused Xeal and every other asset FAE had available, to include the roughly 4,000 new tier-7s, after the latest group had made it through their attempts, to be called into action. So it was that while Xeal hopped from one battlefield to another, Amser and Djimon stood across from each other as Djimon spoke first.

"Today I get to humiliate you while your guild is humiliated by mine."

"Still trying to get Takeshi to notice you. Honestly, I'm sorry, but he isn't into dudes."

"Go ahead and say whatever you like, but we both know that you can't beat me with that toy you have there."

"Keep telling yourself that, it will just make what is about to happen all the sweeter."

"I suppose that all there is to do is just shut you up with action."

With that Amser just smiled until the countdown for the match ran out, at which point she charged right at Djimon and shocked him by tossing her hula-hoop-like ring blade at him. As he avoided it, he missed her grabbing hold of his own staff as a wild grin crossed her face as she started laughing in an almost manic manner.

"Would you look at that. Djimon-kun is so kind to share his weapon with me after I lost mine."

"Crazy bi-"

Djimon didn't get to finish speaking as Amser pulled Djimon's staff up over her head, as she activated the rapid spin skill that she had picked up for the tournament. While it would normally be used to really get her ring blade going, it was still usable with any weapon and players might as well weigh nothing to any melee class. Though, as Djimon found himself in the air spinning, Amser did need to focus on her balance a fair bit more that she liked. However, she didn't have long to think about this as Djimon overpowered the centrifugal force and pulled himself in as he bent at the waist and sent an improvised double kick right at Amser's head. To avoid that, Amser had to readjust her grip and side step, and as the spin ended, she was holding one side of the staff as Djimon was holding the other as they both focused on kicking the other.

Like this the fight continued as Amser held nothing back and Djimon did all he could to free his weapon from her grasp as they struggled against each other. Yet neither seemed to gain an advantage for minute after minute, as each of their health continued to slowly drop. That was until Amser's feet found her discarded ring blade and she slipped it on to one of Djimon's legs, and brought it into his crotch and around her waist at the same time. The result of this sent Djimon to the ground as Amser was atop him with him on his side as she straddled him, as they both still held the staff and the ring blade had returned to being in his crotch. What followed was Amser continually using her knees to press the ring blade into every man's most sensitive area until Djimon finally lost his staff, as she tossed it behind them and began hitting his head with her fists.

Djimon obviously didn't just let this happen, but no matter what he tried, he was in a crap position and Amser wasn't allowing him to even shift to his back. This made his left arm useless beyond a bit of blocking and he had to be careful with his right, else Amser was sure to capture it and give up one of her arms to have almost free rein with the other. At first he thought that she had been in her berserk state at the start, only it was clear that had just been what she wanted him to think as he tried to wait it out as her stamina drained. Now, however, he was trapped and being humiliated once again by the same damn woman that he had looked forward to getting some payback on so much.

As others watched this display, they gained a new respect for Amser and what it meant to truly leave nothing in reserve. This was especially true of all the experts who were asking themselves if they could trap Djimon like that, or escape from Amser once caught. While there were some who had the skills and abilities to make Amser pay for using such a tactic, or believed they could, most just sighed as they watched Amser once more make Djimon look like a fool.

Like that the match ended and at the same time, all the work of Taya and Kate came through as suddenly there was double the number of tier-7s that Abysses End had expected on the battlefield. With the players that FAE had trained from other guilds in Nium and Jingong's members that had received similar treatment almost all passing on their first try, Xeal just smiled. This had only been possible due to the fact that they were all the true elites of both groups and Xeal expected that the next wave would be dismal for both, but that was a worry for another day. All Xeal cared about was the fact that Abysses End was beaten back and whatever they were planning for while he was offline was likely to need to be reevaluated.

So it was that as day 225 came to an end, Xeal was happy to return with his party to Nium as they all prepared for a bit of rest until they embarked on their next mission. Lucy had about run away when they returned as she made no attempt to hide how much she had been missing the luxuries of a city. After roughly a month without a real break, she had reached a point of where she was starting to resent Xeal's ability to use his lightning form for quick traveling. While he only returned briefly a few times during the latest expedition, it was still enough to take advantage of enjoying a warm bath as he did so. Still, for the rest of Xeal's party they all made their way to his palace, where they enjoyed a feast as Xeal noted that Enye, Mari, Lingxin and Dyllis were level 199 and he sighed as he spoke to them in front of the others.

"The time has come for you four and our children to seclude yourselves in Cielo City."

"Xeal-"

"Enye, no, you all can attempt your tribulations from there. The war is entering a stage that I would say poses the greatest danger to Xander, Ellis, Maki and Xin. With my need to be offline for extended periods of time over the next three weeks, it makes sense for you all to leave tomorrow and finish your preparations up there and make the attempt after Ellis's birthday."

"Xeal, why are you so determined to have us hide away?" asked Lingxin. "I have just started to get acquainted with all of my nieces and nephews, as well as all the sisters that I knew so little about."

"There is the newest wave of tier-7 adventurers that are not in my guild. The fact that Queen Nora was rather insistent when I saw her after Lorena and Bianca experienced what Enye did when she reached tier-6. The fact that soon my kind will be reaching tier-7 in greater numbers and with it the war will move dangerously close to here, and I may need to end the shelter that I have been giving here to all the nobles. I can go on, but the biggest reason is yours and our children's presence puts everyone else in greater danger."

"You fear us being targeted to get to you," stated Dyllis. "Yet all we want to do is be by your side. If we go there, it will stunt our growth to nothing."

"Xeal, can't you set up a gate to the dungeon in the Mist Woods or something for them?" asked Eira. "I for one would welcome my sisters all fighting next to me."

Xeal frowned as he looked at Eira as he knew that she had laid a multilayered trap for him as she smiled at him innocently.

"No, as much as I would love to send only my children and the clerics of Eileithyia to Cielo city and have all my loves next to me, it would be too much of a risk. Even with each of them protected and knowing that they have the skills needed, it is not enough to allow them to stand next to us until we have time to adjust to one another's movements in a fight. Though, it would almost ensure that Daisy and Violet have no chance to capture my heart, as I would be too distracted by the ones who have already, instead of only having one who is encouraging them nearby."

"That is just cold," commented Eira. "Trying to pit Daisy and Violet against your current wives like that, when you know that by sending them up there you will be opening the door for those other two as well. Do you, by chance, actually want the princesses turned maids to succeed in getting Enye's approval?"

"That is enough," interjected Mari. "Xeal, do you promise that you will take us with you on a wives and lovers only adventure when you win these wars?"

"That sounds wonderful, but you all know that no matter how much I would like to, that I can't make such a promise at this point as I don't know if these wars will ever end for me. That said, I can promise that once Nium rules the entirety of this continent, that I will happily spend days and even weeks at a time in the local wild lands with all of you."

"Two years," replied Mari. "I think that is what we should give you to capture all of this continent. That will allow you to give us all our second child and for us to be ready to return to power leveling again. Though, I would prefer to wait on the second child and do as Eira has suggested. I am willing to put that aside until after we see how our tier-7 tribulations go."

"Three," countered Xeal. "Give me at least that as if I rush this, too many will die. As for letting you all fight in a dungeon, I will have to see what makes sense as I lack the ability to allocate enough tier-7 players at this point."

"Fine," answered Enye. "But only if you visit us at least a few weeks each year outside of the time you come to spend with Lorena and Bianca. Also, you will explore feasible options for our grinding post tier-7 and we will talk more with Kate about it as well."

"Very well. As for the visits, they will be conjoined, but I can turn my two-day trips into three or four easy enough if I plan things right. Though I feel as if I will need to plan 60 hours of time rather than 20, as I give each of you as much time alone as I do with the other two."

"100. It's time that you gave Ekaitza, Lughrai, Malgroth and Lumikkei a chance to actually secure a place in your heart," commented Kate. "Don't worry, I think that I can find a way to set up ten week-long visits before your deadline for you. Though you will be giving each of them two five-hour blocks rather than one ten-hour one, like you will be with Lorena and Bianca."

"Kate, you are essentially asking Xeal to consider ten women for a max of seven slots," replied Aalin. "I am of more than half a mind to simply say 12 is already more than enough already."

"Just stop, please," interrupted Xeal. "I want no part of this conversation, beyond knowing what the 12 of you who have a say agree to. Aalin, the time Aila let me gain a bit of insight was enough for me to know that there is already a fair bit of give and take between all of you. All that I ask is that none of you force me to marry any woman that I don't feel love for, or is likely to cause the fragile balance that we have currently to be ruined. That said, if at any point any of you feel as if your voice is failing to be heard by the others, I need to know. If Aalin wishes for the number to stay 12, then as soon as I have fulfilled my obligation to consider Lorena and Bianca, I will announce that no others will be allowed in."

Xeal could see the relieved smile on Aalin's face, the looks of worry that Daisy and Violet got, as well as the complicated look Kate often got around Xeal when she was holding back on speaking. Xeal thought that that would end that topic. However, Eira decided to not let that it be so as she spoke.

"Aalin, I will back you on not allowing any others to approach Xeal, but Daisy, Violet, Dafasli and Bula all deserve to at least have a real chance, as to deny them such would be to go back on our word."

"Yes," agreed Aalin. "And I promise not to stand in their way in the slightest, so long as none of you push Xeal to accept them. However, is it terrible to not want to surrender my time with him any more than I have?"

"Let's leave that for when it is just us," interjected Kate. "In fact, I think we should all go to Aila's early tomorrow and have Gale meet us there, before we attend the launching of the Siren's Revenge. I believe that with Enye, Lingxin, Mari and Dyllis all about to move to Cielo city, that it is needed for several reasons. Also, I think we should invite all 21 who can possibly attend to do so, at least for part of it."

Xeal could see them all nodding as he just sighed and allowed the conversation to be redirected to his party's and the other actions over the past month, as the day came to an end and he enjoyed spending a night with his wives minus Gale. Even with the fact that he could have seen her every three weeks using his new skill, they had decided to deal with not doing so as a way to ensure that no issues occurred. At the same time, Gale was quietly visiting every temple of Freya and revealing who she was to the head of each. At the same time, if there was an outstanding member of the faith that Freya directed Gale to, she would bestow a blessing of Freya on them as well. With only 20 possible slots and a few already in use, Gale had to be careful not to rub any devotees the wrong way, or spark an unnecessary struggle for the blessings to occur. While she was doing this, she had Clara and Amet with her, as well as a few other members of FAE who worshiped Freya and had been sworn to secrecy with a contract to bind it. Xeal knew the risk and reward that came with this and while he worried about the blowback, the situation as it currently was, was such that he was willing to risk it.

As day 226 arrived, Xeal found himself staying at his palace as he worked on some paperwork, while the rest left only a bit after dawn for Anelqua. Xeal just sighed as he looked over the figures that Kate had given him as FAE was still bleeding funds and while it had started to slow down, it was clear that they wouldn't last like this. Put simply, they had a year in ED time left before the situation was beyond salvaging, and the raffles and other ways to get FAE's own members to cover the shortfall were seeing diminishing returns. It made Xeal think about how it would be nice to have a spokeswoman like Natalina Farese, who could convince masses of casual players to give up five to a few hundred credits for nothing. Even if Xeal hated such tactics, he could see just why they were used so frequently, as he thought about how quickly numbers ballooned when you were talking about fanbases in the tens of millions. Just five credits from 25,000,000 players a month would be enough to double the time FAE had before it was in trouble.

It was with this thought that an idea popped into Xeal's head, but it was one that he would really need to think through and discuss with Kate before pursuing. However, he had yet to see Natalina Farese emerge from wherever she had ended up and if done right, Xeal could see a way to use her talents in a way that wouldn't make him feel like scum. Still, that was for another day and Xeal had a ship launch to get to, as he finished up the last few documents that Kate and Taya had marked as high priority and left to rejoin his wives.

As Xeal arrived in Anelqua, he was greeted by 18 of the 21 who had been at the meeting that morning, with Gale,

Princess Bianca and Princess Lorena being missing. If they had agreed or disagreed on anything he couldn't tell, as he gave each of his wives, Kate, Luna and Selene kisses and hugs, before he made his way to the area where they would be launching the Siren's Revenge. As they arrived, Xeal just smiled at seeing the massive security that Queen Aila Lorafir had placed around the ship and the frustrated look on Mittie Alabaster's face. The guild leader of Salty Dogs and her assistant, Ferne Acheron, were currently being blocked from getting any closer than around 1,000 feet of the ship, as she looked at Xeal and his group walking towards the entrance that she was partially blocking. When Xeal was about five feet from her, she spoke in as a polite of a tone as he had ever heard her use.

"Xeal, you wouldn't happen to be willing to give me a tour of that ship before it enters service, would you?"

"Mittie, if it was yours, would you let me take a tour of it?"

"No, but you aren't even a major naval power outside of Nium's waters. If I had a land-based resource that I thought would benefit from a collaboration with you, I would happily let you have a tour."

Xeal just wanted to laugh at Mittie, as Ferne looked like she was going to have a headache and he got an idea as he spoke.

"Fine, but you have to declare that for the next 30 days in ED, that if any guild launches a major offensive against FAE that Salty Dogs will enter the conflict on our side."

"Are you insane? You and I both know that Abysses End is going to do everything they can to gain ground while you are unable to do anything about it. Not to mention that would ruin the deal I have in place to shuttle food around this continent without fear of attack from any navy."

"Once I use the fleet that this ship will lead to conquer all of the ports on the continent, will that really matter?"

"Xeal, it is a nice ship, but just like how Queen Aila can't win this war on her own, neither can that ship, so unless-"

Mittie failed to finish her words as the five ex-pirate captains came out to the area's entrance and removed the hood to their cloaks, as their level 281 selves were revealed to Mittie for the first time. Xeal wanted to laugh as he had set this up from the moment he had received a report that Mittie was waiting for him at the entrance to the launching area. While their existence was known to her, the fact that they had reached tier-8 had yet to be revealed to any but Xeal's inner circle, let alone the public. While he knew that this was tipping his hand as he was sure that Abysses End and every other major power had spies in the crowd, it was part of his and Kate's plan. The five of them were well known for their abilities with illusions and the extent of their new abilities would likely not be anticipated. Xeal wanted the first battle that they displayed them to be as large as could be, so that when their victims were thrown for a loop in the confusion, it would create the maximum gains. Finally, Mittie recovered as she looked at Xeal and resumed speaking.

"Alright, how the hell do I deal with that group behind you to make sure that they are never pointed at my guild?"

"You don't," retorted Kate. "You just smile at your good fortune to be able to still sell Xeal favors and accept that while we will never be full allies, that we can still have a cooperative relationship. That is unless you want to have an antagonistic relationship with us and hope your fleets can survive what we have planned."

"So, do we start the process of merging into a single guild now, or after you have pushed us out of our role as the top naval power guild?"

"Salty Dogs isn't going to merge into FAE," stated Xeal. "We have too different of philosophies. Eventually you will overcome the lead I am about to take and FAE will just be a check on your ambitions, as well as any who wish to create issues for ED as a whole."

"One of these days you are going to learn that trying to police everyone just costs you trillions and makes everyone hate you," interjected Ferne. "It's why Salty Dogs has never tried to tell anyone how to operate on the seas of any game and only taken actions that we see as profitable."

"I know better than to police everyone, but that doesn't mean that I can't step in to tip the scales in my favor when I feel it is appropriate. Besides, FAE will essentially become a mercenary force on every other continent after Nium wins this war."

At Xeal's response, Ferne just shook her head, while Mittie smiled and started to talk.

"I will agree to declare war on Abysses End and aid in naval suppression efforts that are away from enemy ports, for a tour and an agreement for how to handle the looted goods. Heck, I will even assist in any port attacks that make sense to me."

"Kate, do you think that we can come to an arrangement in the next few hours, or should I turn her down?"

"There are too many moving parts. However, if she is willing to take the time to put that as just for the next 30 days if they launch a major offensive as we work on a more permanent deal, I see no reason not to let her steal as much as she can by just looking."

"That works for me as it can be justified," replied Mittie. "It will also help me avoid falling into one of Kate's traps."

"Oh, please, you are already in one of them," retorted Kate. "Your guild is going to be hard at work for the next few years at the very least. Just be thankful that I know that you need to make a profit, else even having a contract that will force you to quit would do nothing to ensure your cooperation."

"Right, let's just get the contract signed so I can see the ship!"

Xeal just smiled as Kate led Mittie and Ferne away as he continued forward with the rest of the group and the five ex-pirate captains, who began talking the moment they were past the guards.

"Was it really wise for us to expose ourselves like that?" asked Odelia.

"We want your first battle to involve as great of a fleet as Paidhia can muster. It is why I am lending you both Daisy and Violet for this voyage."

"The sheer number of illusions that you are planning on us using is insane. Are you sure that you don't wish to join us as well?" inquired Sylmare. "I wouldn't mind seeing just what you are capable of now."

"I will not say that I won't make an appearance if it makes sense, but unless they are dumb enough to send over 100 ships, or an airship to attack you, I don't see it being necessary."

"That would be an absolute waste," commented Enye. "Airships are beyond valuable in a land war and are best used to deal a decisive blow only after the other side has no way to counter them."

"Xeal is also almost the perfect counter for them now," stated Queen Aila Lorafir. "Although, with the reputation you are creating, I would expect a tier-8 to be awaiting you when they start being used."

"I am not dumb enough to try and capture an airship. One full-powered blast is all I will be doing as I hope for the best, as the rest of the forces attack it."

"No, if you get above it and drop a large log or other

heavy mass of over 1,000 pounds that has been shaped to a point and falls right, it should be very effective on their shield," replied Queen Aila Lorafir. "Though you will need to survive the attacks that will be sent your way and have good aim to use them from an effective height."

"Add in the danger to those on the ground below as the logs fall and the fact that I don't have any skills that would allow me to store such an item. At best I could drop a bunch of 100-pound steel balls or rods, unless we made some rather expensive compact and heavy items just for that purpose," retorted Xeal. "Besides, I don't fly like you. Even if I had something that could be held aloft with my electricity, it wouldn't move with me and assembling something from parts in midair would be insane."

Even as Xeal said this, he started to get a few ideas that he would need to have some crafters work on before he was tied up in reality.

"Let's just hope that we are still a while from having to discover just what it will take to bring down an airship," commented Aalin. "Unless you have actually brought one down, Aila."

"No, but I am old enough to have seen the reports on it and, well, there is a reason that no country dares risk theirs. While the costs were insane, the one who still had a few airships when the other didn't was enough to force a complete surrender."

"The soldiers knew that they would suffer the same fate as their enemies," commented Xeal. "It is why airships aren't owned by any merchants and you rarely see one in the sky outside rare training exercises."

"So, when are we going to build one?" asked Luna.

"Yeah, you're totally planning on FAE using them, aren't you!" added Selene.

"If by that you mean that they will all fly Nium's flag and

be captained by members of the royal knights, then as soon as we have the necessary crafters and material," replied Xeal. "So, not until after this war has reached its conclusion at the very least."

As Xeal said that, they reached the ramp to board the Siren's Revenge, and his comments about just how difficult and expensive each ship was to create was left unsaid. Instead, they made their way up and onto the deck that was full of activity, as the crew who would be responsible for operating all of the ship's features was moving about doing their final checks. Xeal was greeted by Ivy, who after serving as Kate's assistant, had found her way onto the guild's general admin team and had been given the lead on ensuring that everything went smoothly with the Siren's Revenge construction. Looking like she hadn't slept in a few days, she smiled weakly as she greeted them.

"Welcome to the Siren's Revenge. I can say that everything is in order and you can officially launch her at any time. Am I going to finally be freed of this task and allowed to spend some time leveling before you force me to undertake such an insane project, guild leader?"

"What are you talking about? You need to oversee the construction of at least five more of these," quipped Xeal.

"Not funny. I doubt we have the spare funds to make two more at the price tag this monster has attached to it."

"No, that doesn't mean that there isn't a market for them, though you are right that now is not the time to tap into that market. So, yes, you can have a few months to just focus on leveling up while handling a bit of admin work as needed."

"Awesome, though where is Kate?"

"Securing one of the customers for the next few of these we build," interjected Aalin. "So, don't forget what you learned during this build and be sure to find an understudy to train when the next one is built. I have a feeling that six might be on the low end of how many more of these we need to build, if the price is right."

Xeal could see Ivy grow resigned as she sighed before responding.

"I see. Well, I guess it can't be helped. I will just enjoy the short break that I have and be happy that I get one at all with how hard Xeal runs himself."

"Ivy, don't ever feel that you need to work yourself like I do. I know that it is hard for you all to take time off when no one at the top seems to, but you should. Though for now I would just say that if you can get two assistants that know how to handle the workload, you can oversee two ships being built with only half the workload being placed on yourself."

"Wait, you'll fund two assistants for me? Is this a promotion!?"

"Sure, but only when you have two assistants fully trained," replied Xeal at Ivy's enthusiasm.

With that the rest of the questions Xeal had before it was time to launch were answered, just as Kate arrived with Mittie and Ferne in tow. Thus they did a full tour, with Ivy acting as a guide as she explained several of the features to their visitors as if she was trying to sell the ship to them. A notion that was not lost on Mittie or Kate, as both gave Xeal a look that told them they were questioning his intentions. Though it was simple. He still saw being a crafting powerhouse as the best path to long-term success and if he could absorb Salty Dogs' ship-building teams and supplies, while supplying them with ships, he would. When the tour ended, it was time for Xeal to launch the ship, only he handed the whole speech part over to Ihyi Kaze, who would be the fleet admiral. With her power to manipulate the wind, which came from being marked by the wind phoenix, Ninlil, she was invaluable to FAE's war potential at sea. It didn't matter that she had only had recently started to focus on sailing. She had been slotted above all of FAE's naval operations since shortly after becoming a vice guild leader.

"Today we start a new era in this world's naval history, as we rewrite every tactic and possibility of this world. Thanks to the tireless work of our crafters, the support of Nium's naval experts and the expertise of all of you who will man our fleet, the future is bright…"

Xeal just smiled as he listened to the seriousness that Ihyi brought to her new role and the confidence that she projected. With the five ex-pirate captains behind her, Xeal had no worries about her ability to adjust to a life at sea and if worst came to worst, they could take over as well. Once her speech was over, Xeal joined her as he handed her a badge that he had acquired for the occasion. It was a magic accessory that boosted all wind magic by 25% and was better than the similar item she was already using that only offered a 15% buff. Like that the ceremony was over and all that was left was to actually launch it. So, Xeal and all unnecessary personnel left the ship and watched as it was released and slid into the water.

The rest of day 226 was spent making sure everything was in place for Enye, Mari, Lingxin and Dyllis to relocate to Cielo city. Xeal could tell that they were dragging their feet, but he still pushed them forward as he bid them farewell and promised to come see how they were settling in before too long. Though they still hadn't told him if he needed to make time for six, or ten women, when he did find the time to see them. He figured that Kate would let him know as he was leaving the scheduling to her, as she would be the one tracking all the enemy movements much closer than he would.

(*****)

Night May 31 to Morning June 11, 2268 & ED Year 6, Days 228-259.

As Alex stepped out of his VR pod on Sunday night, it was already time to go as he made his way downstairs, where he was greeted by Sam, Nicole, Kate, Ava, Mia, all his children, Stacy, Gido, Julie, Evelyn, Nana Quinn and two of Kate's bodyguards. This would be the group that was headed to Washington, D.C. as they went to testify before Congress. As much as Alex wished they could have gotten them to allow for them to handle the whole ordeal over a remote meeting, not only was getting such a thing approved rather difficult, Kate had shot down even trying. As she put it, the optics would favor this approach too heavily for them to consider doing otherwise. As they loaded up the SUVs with three of the security staff under Stacy driving, she came up to Alex to go over the protocols for the week one last time.

"Alex, Captain Ward, or I suppose Ned and the group he has brought along, will be waiting for us when we land. They will make sure we get to and from each location without issue, and I just want to emphasize that none of you are to go anywhere without at least a two guards to one of you ratio. This isn't ED where you can take on an army by yourself."

"Stacy, I am aware. It is why I asked you to hire as many guards as you thought could be trusted. Honestly, I am just grateful that so many of those you used to work with were willing to use up their vacation time guarding us."

"Ha, to them it is a paid vacation as they mainly only need to worry about transporting you to and from the hearings. Though, it is mainly the single guys as the restriction on bringing family made it fairly less attractive for most. As for the itinerary for the others while you and Kate are dealing with the other hearing, are you sure that you want them to be going out with all the babies like that?"

"Of course. If they just hide in the house all day it will be no good. There is so much history just a drive away with where we will be. Just make sure that only you know where you all are headed before you leave each morning and keep an eye out for anything that could be an issue."

"Alright, time for me to earn my pay."

"Stacy, it's good to see you acting so lively."

"This is where I thrive. It almost reminds me of when I was still on the force."

With that Alex smiled as he found himself sitting next to Sam with Moyra on her other side, as they made their way to the airport. While she was quiet about it, Alex could tell that she was enjoying the extra time she was getting with him after their time in ED had been cut off and it was hard to find time in reality. As such, none of the others had objected to her getting to be with him as much as possible during this trip, so long as she didn't keep him completely to herself. Thus the pair were enjoying the bit of cuddling that they were able to get in, until it was time to leave the SUV and board the plane.

Once more the Brewyses were all smiles as they all boarded the private jet, as Rose and Elizabeth practically kidnapped Ahsa and Moyra while Nicole and Kate took Evan and Aidan from Ava and Mia. Alex just smiled as the Brewys sisters happily spent the whole flight chatting with everyone as their father took care of drink service. They talked mainly about the six little ones as Rose shared how she had gotten her pilot license and was now the copilot any time they had no passengers and were headed to their next job. She was also saving for when Elizabeth got hers and the sisters were talking about buying their own plane, or taking over their parents' as they got a new one and the four of them tried to double their business. The smile that Kate got at this news told Alex that she was already planning something along the lines of making an investment in them, while convincing them to maintain a larger plane that would suit Alex's growing family better.

By the time they landed it was already after midnight, and Alex and the rest were met by their security detail. After a quick greeting, they were all loaded onto a bus and driven to the home that they would be staying at, which was normally used by foreign dignitaries. As such it was already set up with everything that Alex could ask for, to include VR pods, though none of them were maternity ones. Still, after they got in, all of them got settled and took care of feedings and the like, before they all logged into ED to get some sleep and a bit of work done before it was time to leave in the morning.

When morning came, it was once more time to get on the bus as they dealt with granola bars and fruit for breakfast, as the bus started the two-hour drive to Congress. This was largely due to traffic as if the roads were clear it would be a 45-minute drive at worse, but they were never that open in this area. Alex could feel the tension that was in the bus as they made their way to the hearing, as it seemed even the seven little ones could tell that something was going on as they cried. With all of them trying to calm them with little success until they were just about there, Alex wore a wry smile as they prepped to walk in. This would see them need to pass by a rather large group of protesters that had gathered, either organically or through being paid to bolster numbers, as they shouted slogans at them. Alex could already hear a few of the louder chants through the glass of the bus, as he stood and took Evan in his arms as Kate took Aidan in hers. With everyone else holding their babies, they lined up behind Captain Ward as the other security that had followed in four SUVs took up their positions as they guarded the path forward.

The moment the bus opened, Alex was assaulted by a wave of noise and he adjusted the earmuffs that Evan was wearing. He, like all six other babies, were wearing them due to the expectation for the environment to be loud and not the best for the still-developing little ones. Which was something Alex was grateful for, as he ignored the crowd while following close behind the front group of security. As they moved forward, Alex did manage to see a group of supporters for them and he just smiled knowing that at least the whole world wasn't against them. Still, he wished that they could have just enjoyed their peace as they moved along and made their way past the front doors and entered relative silence.

Though with that silence came a security check as every guard, save for Stacy and Kate's bodyguards, was released for the duration of the hearing as lunch would be on site. So it was that after getting past security, they were shown to a room that had been made available for those who would not be testifying to stay in for the duration. It was in here that they passed the last 30 minutes before the hearing, as Alex and Kate focused on making sure everyone was calm since not everyone had as thick of a skin as they did. Even Ava and Mia were riled up from having to put their little ones through that, as Nicole looked like she wanted to strangle someone. Apparently, there had been more than a few posters that were calling for their children to be taken away from them in a way that touched a nerve.

Sam was just letting Moyra's smile take care of her lingering nerves and Alex was just happy that they had this time to decompress after that at all.

When the time did come for the six of them to leave, Alex just took a deep breath as Stacy walked ahead of them and Kate's bodyguards stayed with the others. As they arrived at the room that was already full of congressmen, most of whom had stacks of paper of various size in front of them. Alex couldn't take in much more than that before they were directed to their seats. After a few moments to get comfortable, they found the hearing was officially getting ready to start as the committee chair started to speak.

"We thank all of you who have come to explore the possibility of extending the same legal status, to those who have made the willing and conscious decision to live a life with multiple partners, as we do to those who commit to just a single one…"

Alex just kept a neutral expression on his face as the committee chair, who looked to be in her early 60s, continued to talk. She covered the longstanding expansions that had been made to what was considered a marriage throughout history and prior attempts to get this same type of legislation passed that had failed. Finally, she reached the part about introducing the witnesses as she brought her speech to a close.

"… Here with us today are six individuals who are currently in one such relationship and are willing to face the scrutiny of society to be able to simply be recognized under our laws the same way as any others who consider each other as spouses. From right to left we have Nicole Jun, Samantha Carter, Alex Bell, Kate Peirce, Ava Quinn and Mia Quinn. Once they have been sworn in, we will open the floor to questions until the first scheduled break at the hour and a half mark. After which we will resume questioning and if needed, a second break will be held after another hour and a half has passed, to ensure that the four of them that are mothers have time to care for their babies who are in another room at this time. With nothing further to state, we will move on to the swearing in of the witnesses…"

Alex smiled as the six of them were sworn in and the committee chair yielded the floor to the first member of the committee that would be asking them questions. Alex knew that both the committee chair and the first questioner were locks to support the legislation, so long as nothing went very wrong from what Kate had said. So, as the man who had to only be in his early thirties finished thanking the chair and giving a short speech of his own, he turned his attention to Alex as he asked his first question.

"Mr. Bell, as you are the only biological man in the six of yours relationship, would you say that it is fair to use the term harem when referring to the other five?"

"Thank you and that would depend on under what sense you are speaking. If it is in the historical and original definition then no, as I don't see them as anything but my equals and would never treat them as anything less. If you are speaking to what it has become to be known as in modern day as to say pertaining to multiple women consenting and willingly sharing a single man, then that term could be considered correct."

"I see, and you see yourself completely committed to each of them and they are committed to you and each other, correct?"

"I can only speak for myself, but yes, I am fully committed to each of them so long as they will have me."

"Very well. Ms. Jun, would you say that you are committed to Alex and the others?"

"Yes."

"Ms. Carter, same question."

"Absolutely."

"Ms. Peirce?"

"Completely."

"Ms. Ava Quinn?"

"Please don't split my sister and I."

"Yeah, we might get a bit lost if we don't trade off like this."

"We have just been doing it all our lives."

"And to do otherwise feels off."

"As for your question."

"More and more each day."

"Yeah, we love Alex."

"And all the others."

"Totally and completely."

"No matter what anyone thinks."

"I see. Umm, that is not normally how these hearings work, madam chair?"

"I will allow it as it was noted in a request for accommodations made by the witnesses, that I have in front of me and just checked over."

"Thank you. Now, Alex, if this legislation fails, how do you see it affecting your relationship?"

"It won't. My being here and willingness to fight for the right to marry each of them demonstrates that I wish to marry them far more than any piece of paper issued by the government could ever do. At least that is my hope as regardless of what happens, I will be holding a ceremony with them next month."

"Alright. Ms. Jun, same question."

"As Alex has said, him being here demonstrates his sincerity towards us more than the legal document alone could. Though I would say that all six of us are doing so, as

I can say that testifying before you all today isn't on my list of activities that I look forward to."

"Noted and Ms. Peirce?"

"I will refuse to become his legal wife as I had intended when I first entered this arrangement. While I don't see any issues arising from the other four, I wish to stay as their equals and not risk ruining the balance and sisterhood that we have formed."

"So then it is fair to say that you have the most at stake here today?"

"No, none of us here are the ones with the most at stake. It is those who are in similar relationships who wish to be married, or are using the law as the reason why they can't get married."

"Interesting. Can you expound upon that?"

"Yes. From my viewpoint, there are many men and women who enjoy multiple lovers and companions in a way that could be related to my own relationship. Only, they avoid any legal obligations to their partners by saying that the law doesn't allow for them to get married. Some will even hold ceremonies like we plan, but with no law to back it up and define what rights each party has, both are left vulnerable. As are any children who are caught in the middle of the situation, should one or the other parent decide that they wish to simply walk away."

"Thank you and I will yield the remainder of my time back to the chair."

"Thank you…"

As the committee woman thanked the first member to question them, the floor was passed to another member of the committee who began their own line of questioning. Once more this committee member was one who was favorable to them, as they asked mostly questions related to how they managed the needs of the whole. Though the member that followed this was clearly opposed as they started their line of questioning.

"Mr. Bell, you have made it clear that you claim to love each of the women seated with you. Now, would you say that your relationship should be considered moral?"

"I think that the morality of it has no bearing in the reality, or legality of it."

"Mr. Bell, please answer the question."

"With all due respect, I will not allow you to lay the trap that you are as if I say yes, then you will begin to question my values and if I say no, you will begin to question how I can bring children into such a situation."

"Mr. Bell, it would be best if you didn't assume that you know what my intentions are. Though I will treat it as you are believing that your actions are moral. Therefore, you would support more relationships such as your own to form, correct?"

"No, I only support this bill due to the mitigating efforts that will hopefully keep such relations from becoming normal, as the possibility for a societal breakdown is real otherwise."

"Oh? Please continue."

"Very well. Were I to simply wish to use my wealth to build and support a personal harem, it would not be impossible to have a woman for every day of the year. Furthermore, if it reached the point where it became normal in society and suddenly successful individuals had multiple partners that skewed in favor of one gender too drastically, it would create major issues. If half, or more, of any gender feel as if there is no way for them to find someone that they are attracted to as a partner when they have such a desire to, history would say that the society will head towards collapse. It is for that reason, that if it weren't for the legalization of same-sex unions, this legislation would be impossible."

"Is that what you see your relationship as, Mr. Bell? One straight man and five bisexual females?"

"No, I see it as an extremely complicated and personal matter that shouldn't be looked at as a model of what others should attempt to replicate."

"Yet you seem fine to let them try. Now tell me, would you say that playing Eternal Dominion has affected your views on this matter?"

"I am sorry, but that is like asking if being in Congress has affected your views on many issues. To say it hasn't would be a lie, but to what extent I am unsure of."

"You have five NPCs you have married in that game and several more that you are courting in addition to having married Ms. Jun's and Ms. Carter's characters. Yet you haven't married Ms. Peirce's, or either of the Ms. Quinns' characters. Can you explain why that is?"

"The same reason I have yet to marry any of them here in reality, politics and timing. I will not claim that it is right or perfect, but it is my reality."

"Thank you for your answers and I yield my time back to the chair."

Alex just sighed as the next few questioners only focused on asking the questions of Sam, Nicole, Ava and Mia, as he and Kate were ignored. Many of these questions were pertaining to if any of them felt taken advantage of and what they thought made such arrangements work. Alex was just happy that Kate had been able to prep all of them as they responded, but it was still clear that the room was split about 60% in favor and 40% opposed to the legislation. Finally, they got their first break as they all returned to the room where their children were, as they ate some lunch and focused on decompressing before the next round of questioning.

"Do we have to go back in there?" groaned Sam as she held Moyra. "They just keep asking the same things over and over in different ways."

"That is a textbook tactic to find out what the truth is," commented Kate. "Or get you to slip up in a way that they can exploit. It's why we went through that prep."

"I know, but it still is annoying as can be."

"Sam, just be happy that they seem to be focused on the fact that you have bisexual tendencies after you let that slip," commented Nicole. "They seem to be focused on nothing but the fact that I could have gone to any college I wanted to and how I gave it all up to chase Alex, or whatever picture they are trying to paint. Honestly, it is just confusing, though it is still better than them thinking that Ava and Mia are crazy."

"Oh, but we are."

"Crazy for Alex, that is."

"Though, we wouldn't say no to exploring that side of Sam a bit more."

"If she is fine with us deciding if it is for us, or not, along the way of course."

"You two are too much. Honestly, I am happy with things the way they are and I am not sure I want to," responded Sam. "Besides, if I find that I like it, or worse, I don't but you two do, what then? It could really mess things up."

"So could ignoring it," retorted Kate. "I had figured it would wait for Bula, but I think Eira, Ava and Mia are more the types that make sense for you. Just leave myself and Nicole out of it."

"Kate's right," agreed Ava.

"Yeah, it could also solve the issues you have in ED," added Mia.

"And let you spend time with all of us again."

"We miss having us all around when time allows it."

"We can talk more about this later," replied Sam. "This isn't something that I want to rush and make a mistake about."

"Hey, Sam," interjected Alex before any of the others could respond. "When they bring it up again, if you want to just say this..."

Alex just smiled at the reaction Sam and the others had to his plan, and they started to laugh and joke as they enjoyed the pizza that had been brought in for them, before returning to the hearing. Once they were all sworn in once more, the next member of the committee went right at Alex with his questions.

"Mr. Bell, would you say that you have found yourself in over your head and have just been pulled along with the flow of others?"

"I am not sure what you mean?"

"Was it not Ms. Carter and Ms. Jun who initiated this relationship and pushed you to accept the other three here, and even a Ms. Smith that you managed to reject before the other three."

"Sam and Nicole did both make their feelings clear to me at the same time, but I would blame my sister for causing it to happen the way it did. I would say that most, if not all relationships develop a flow that if those involved don't follow to a certain extent, they will fail. If I didn't love and feel that there was a future with all five of the ladies next to me and those who only exist inside the world of Eternal Dominion, this relationship would have failed already. As for being in over my head, sure, but that is what I have all of them for as they help keep my head above the water and make me better than I would be without them. At least that is the way I see it."

"So you are perfectly able to maintain all of these

relationships, run your company which seems to only expand and manage the responsibilities that you have inside the game Eternal Dominion?"

"Perfection is not something I ever aspire to. Anyone who takes a close look at my life can see that much, but I am happy and believe that after I have established myself, I will be able to slow down, at least a bit."

"So, you're not worried about the chaos that might even now be happening inside of Eternal Dominion?"

"I am extremely worried about it, but I have made peace with the fact that if my team can't handle things for a week at this point, then I need to look into expanding their numbers, or replacing them."

"One final question. Who really controls the Free Art Expo workshop?"

"I am not sure as to what you are insinuating, but I am the primary owner and have full veto control, but I listen to Kate's and Gaute's input as shareholders and I value all my vice guild leaders' viewpoints."

"Very well, I yield my remaining time back to the chair."

Next came a few more softball rounds of questions, until one woman in her early 30s seemed to hone in and target Sam as she asked her questions.

"Ms. Carter, what was it that made you willing to allow both Ms. Quinns and Ms. Peirce into this relationship?"

"As I have said before, I grew to be friends with Ava and Mia before I warmed up to them completely and let them in. As for Kate, you try to tell her no when she wants something."

"It had nothing to do with your desire for more intimacy than Alex was able to provide on his own?"

"No, and even if it were, what would be wrong with that? Heck, if any group ought to be for this legislation it ought to be those who are attracted to both men and women. After all, why wouldn't they wish to have the opportunity to marry a man and woman in that situation? I would even say that if you were to look at the healthiest of the relationships that involve multiple partners, you would find a high percentage of such individuals. Yet they receive none of the same protections that any traditional marriage provides, such as death benefits if any exist. I mean, when you get right down to it, that is really the reason why none of the prior efforts have succeeded—taxes, healthcare and pensions. It is why this one might succeed as it destroys any tax benefits and allows only a single designation for pensions and allows a cap on the number of individuals covered under a family health plan, before extra fees are added."

Alex just smiled as the woman looked unsure on how to respond to Sam after her answer, as she had touched on the truth behind every law in the books. Money. That was what spoke in the chambers of Congress and Alex had played the game and by this time tomorrow, every news agency that could be bought would be running this story. Either for or against and Alex intended for it to go his way in the court of public opinion, as along with that would be images of him with all six of his kids with messages like "Father just wants to marry the mothers of his children." The goal wasn't to convince everyone it was right morally, it was to convince them that they wouldn't be affected and that it wasn't their place to stop it.

As Alex was thinking this, the woman yielded her time and another committee member started in on Ava and Mia as she started her questioning.

"Ms. Quinns, is it not true that you entered this relationship to take advantage of Mr. Bell's wealth to secure your desired lifestyle?"

"Sure is."

"Yep, we wanted to take Alex for all that he was worth."

"But we never got very far like that."

"No, we couldn't help but want more the longer we were around."

"So, we gave up and just started letting them in instead."

"That was when it just kind of happened."

"Alright, moving on, is it true that you were originally sent to ruin the relationship by your old employers, Abysses End?"

"Sorry, can't say anything about them."

"NDA and all."

"Wouldn't want to make things difficult on all of us now."

"Especially with how happy we are."

"But you were introduced through a program where Abysses End and Free Art Expo met up."

"Yes."

"It was so fun teasing him."

"We just couldn't help ourselves."

"We still have a bit of fun like that with him even now."

"Why did you both decide to leave Abysses End and join Free Art Expo?"

"Really, you should have that in front of you."

"Yeah, Abysses End was dumb enough to kick us out."

"Though it was for refusing to return to the workshop in Dallas."

"However, that wasn't an offence that put us in breach on its own."

"After all, it just said that they would provide us with lodging."

"It never said we had to live in it."

"It was why we were able to get out of it with no real penalties."

"Though the NDA isn't going anywhere."

"So, we can't say anything more on the subject."

"Unless a court says that we are released from it of course."

"Alright, one last question for you two, do you feel that you are mentally stable?"

"I think this is one of those times where the only good answer is yes."

"As even if we just took the 5th."

"It would be seen as self-incriminating."

"That said, we are stable."

"Even if we aren't completely healthy."

"If you grew up like we did."

"You would have some odd ways of coping too."

"It's part of why this relationship works for us."

"Thank you. Now Mr. Bell, would you say that it is responsible of you to have taken advantage of the mental issues of both Ms. Quinns when bringing them into your harem?"

"You should listen to their answer all the way through next time as I can promise you one thing, if anyone takes advantage of others it is them. As they said, they have their issues, but to insinuate that they are something that can be taken advantage of is a terrible misrepresentation of reality. Furthermore, as I stated earlier, the term harem can be considered misconstruing the intricacies of our relationship, due to the historical connotations that don't fit."

"Yes, well if the name fits, I will use it. Now, what would you do if one of those who you are involved with wished to add another man to your relationship?"

"I am sorry, but were I to feel that was the intention of any that I am involved with I would have not pursued them, or allowed them to pursue joining this relationship. I will not claim that to be a fair or equitable answer, but it is the truth, as I honestly don't fully understand how they can stand to share me as I am not able to see myself doing the same with another man."

"Yet the group that Ms. Carter spoke of earlier would highly likely create groups of two men and two women relationships would it not?"

"Sorry, but I will not be twisting words here as she said no such thing, as she simply stated that such relations exist already."

"But she did insinuate that did she not?"

"No, but I will say that what comes of these relationships being brought into the open will be an enlightening phase in our society. I myself wonder just what shape they will take and I suspect that the ratios will be all over the place. With that said, I see no issue with the form of these relationships that you are describing, because the key to all of it is that all parties involved consent to the shape in which it takes."

"I just want to go on record that I can't see how this legislation is good for the nation and will be voting against it. With that I yield the remainder of my time."

After a few more easy rounds of questioning, it was Kate's turn to be targeted as another woman on the committee began questioning her.

"Ms. Peirce, you used to go by Ms. Astor before you disowned your family and took on your mother's surname, correct?'"

"Yes, though it was just returning to the name I had at birth as I was born a bastard to one of my father's many mistresses."

"Yes, and would you say that you grew up in a healthy environment for children?"

"It depends on what you mean by healthy. I never needed to worry about food, shelter, educational resources, or recreational options. However, I was also exposed to a rather degrading separation between the recognized and unrecognized mothers and children."

"Yet you expect this legislation to solve all of the heartaches of your childhood for the next child like you?"

"No, nothing is perfect and even if this legislation spreads to Europe, I doubt my family would alter their practices. It is too convenient of a system that allows for them to create power while keeping everything in the family, so to speak. Us bastards aren't treated like trash, or even very differently from our non-bastard siblings, save for inheritance and say in the family before we turn 18. It is then that we are expected to walk the path that the family has decided for us, or leave once and for all. Most bastards go into security or administrative work for the family and are paid far better than what they could make as a doctor on the outside.

"Those with obscene amounts of wealth will always play by different rules than those who don't have such means. That is why Alex can say that this bill will not affect how he treats all of us. It is also why the greatest beneficiaries of it will be those living modest lives that are in such relationships who wish for the security that marriage brings with it."

"Ms. Peirce, why then did you disown your family? Was it perhaps Mr. Bell who forced you to do so in order to be a part of his relationship?"

"That was a major factor, as Alex refuses to allow them, or anyone else to attempt to leverage their way into controlling Free Art Expo, and I agree. Though, we tried to part in a more amicable way, but they ruined any chance of that. So, it is what it is. I am very happy with my choice and look forward to the future."

Alex took Kate's hand in his as he smiled at her in a

caring way, as the committee member continued to attempt to break through Kate's defenses until her time was up. Finally, it ended and after a few last easy questions, they managed to finish a few minutes after the next break would have been. By the time they were back past the protesters and on the bus, Alex was just happy to have the first day behind them and spent the ride back to the house decompressing with the others. When they got back, it was a quick meal and then they were off to ED to do damage control from being offline all day.

When morning came, it was time for Alex and Kate to say a few quick goodbyes as they took one of the SUVs from the day prior with five security personnel, to include Captain Ward. Today was a hearing about the possible need to adjust regulations surrounding VR games, with the dominance that Eternal Dominion was showing. Today they would be joined by Ellayina Walsh and Kevin Hansen representing Eternal Dominion Inc. and several other prominent gaming workshops, to include Dommik Aimes, who was representing Abysses End.

As the day progressed, Alex just sat with Kate as they occasionally answered questions, much of which revolved around the plan of the city they were building. Other than that, it was mainly Ellayina Walsh and Kevin Hansen that got asked questions, as about half of the total time was spent on just them. The theme seemed to be around the developing monopoly as the legislators tried to apply pressure for access to their system. Needless to say that it was a very unsuccessful attempt, as Ellayina Walsh and Kevin Hansen refused and just smiled as they reminded the committee of the protections they had on their intellectual property. They followed this with over a dozen references to times where companies tried to appease Congress, only for the information and technology that was core to their company to be leaked. Following this, many times a clone would be created in a country with laxer intellectual property laws, causing trillions of credits in losses and ruining most of the companies.

It was much later than the day before when Alex and Kate made it home and enjoyed a quick meal and talked to the others about their day. Which turned into a bus tour of the capital with a few stops at the monuments and other attractions. They had avoided the Smithsonian due to the crowds and amount of time each would take, especially for a group their size once the bodyguards were added in. After that it was back to ED as they prepared for the next day.

The third day of hearings was being held around the what, if any, legal rights someone should have if the actions of another destroyed an AI that they had an intimate relationship with in Eternal Dominion. Once more many of the same faces from the prior day were sitting with Alex and Kate in the witness area. This time Alex found himself being asked many questions relating to the issues, as he was a target for both sides of the argument as someone with many such relations and having killed more than a few NPCs. It was towards the end of the day when one of the older committee members really started to try and pick apart his statements from the day.

"Mr. Bell, you have stated that you believe that actions such as murdering or kidnapping NPCs for the direct purposes of harming the player they are connected with should be illegal. However, you have also said that doing so creates a nightmare for any attempts to prove it, or to enforce them. So, which is it, Mr. Bell? Should we seek to outlaw such behavior, or just ignore it?"

"Both. Only the most blatant and flagrant actions should be targeted. For instance, if I were to go around killing any NPC that was related to a player or guild in conflict with myself or my guild, that should be prosecuted. However, if I assault an enemy stronghold as part of a larger conflict and achieving my goals required attacking it and it happened to cause multiple NPCs to die, it should be left alone."

"So, you would be fine if the city that you were the ruler of was sacked and all your NPC wives and children were killed as a result?"

"No, but the laws of Eternal Dominion are enough to provide recourse and I never said that I will not make the ones who commit such actions suffer inside that world."

"So, you just want to have free range to terrorize other players. Tell me, did you, or did you not, pay an assassin to kill a Mr. Gabriel Trevils's character, Saul Drerzen?"

"I am at war with his guild and all is fair during such times."

"Yes, you seem to be fine with many things that you would be otherwise against in the name of winning a war. Such as looting and plundering the trade networks that many other players rely on to make a living and in the process killing of hundreds of NPCs. Some of which could easily have been in relationships with players like yourself!"

"War is a gruesome and bloody affair. I expect that before I reach your age, that over half of all NPCs in Eternal Dominion will have been killed off due to them. There is a reason that I have taken every action that I can to protect those I care for and am willing to fight for them. I fully expect to be personally responsible for more NPC deaths than any other and I wish that it was otherwise, but my goal is to save more than I kill. In the same way that the atomic bomb changed the calculus for going to war in reality, players have done so in Eternal Dominion. If things were perfect, only players would be on either side of the battlefield, but that would be like telling you to not defend your home from an invader because they made it past your security system."

"My question is why players are even involved in these wars. Would things not be better if guild wars and the wars of countries were kept separate?"

"I am sorry, but the sheer implausibility of such a world is too great from me to justify that with a response. Would the United States military only send infantry to fight a force that had no air or armored support? No, they will use every tool in their arsenal, even the nuclear ones that are used to ensure that others are restrained from interfering. I know that most, if not all of you on this committee, see all of Eternal Dominion as a fictional world with fictional people. You are wanting to identify if actions inside of it that have real-world consequences should be covered under our laws. But that can only work on a limited basis. Else you will see myself and others like me leave and head to other nations where our actions are legal. After all, how am I going to wage a war, or even defend myself, when I have my hands tied behind my back by the laws of the country that I reside in?"

"Mr. Bell, how you manage it is not our concern-"

"With all due respect, it is," interjected Kate as she broke decorum.

"Ms. Peirce, it is-"

"As I was saying, the loss to the economy that would result from all professional VR gamers leaving the country would only be the first hit that would happen."

"Ms. Peir-"

"Next, you would have the casual players lose income due to the inability to participate as manpower during wars and you are looking at losing at least a few trillion credits from the economy every year. When those credits are spent elsewhere instead, much of which will be leaving your borders, it will result in irreparable damage as an entire industry is lost for good."

"Are you done, Ms. Peirce!?"

"No. If you don't see the changes that Eternal Dominion is making to the VR gaming industry as more people than ever before devote a significant part of their lives to playing it than any game before it, you are just blind. Threaten the hope that many have in the chance to rise to be something more than they are through participating in that world and the loss in tax revenue will be the least of your concerns."

Alex just wanted to laugh at the face the representative was making, as his time came to an end and the questioning moved on. When the day finally ended, Alex was just happy to be over halfway done as he decided that if he was ever invited to attend multiple hearings in such rapid succession, he would just leave the country and never return. Still, he wanted to sigh as while all of these topics, save for the polyamory, had been heavily debated topics in his last life, he didn't remember much about them besides the final verdicts. He had been too busy just trying to make ends meet while honing his skills in ED to even pay attention, as he didn't believe that he could affect the situation. Furthermore, he would be trying to change the outcome of one of those decisions tomorrow.

Thursday came and with it Alex once more found himself seated in a witness chair after being sworn in, as he was asked a question about an hour into the hearing. Today that topic was around the question of if the AIs of Eternal Dominion could be considered at the same level of an individual who had uploaded their brain to a digital space. Namely, the question was should they be allowed to interact with reality in any way. It was with the thought of having Enye and the others being able to be a part of his kids in reality's lives that was motivating Alex as he listened to the question that he received.

"Mr. Bell, as someone who has relations of an intimate nature with the AIs of Eternal Dominion, what do you see them as?"

"I see them as individuals. Just like you and I, each has their own motives, personalities and aspirations."

"You don't buy the notion that they could simply be acting in a way to manipulate our emotions to gain our trust before betraying us?"

"They, like most others, seek to survive. Personally I would be wary of any AI that has a scope beyond that of just being a person, like the management AIs. Normal NPCs have no more processing power than you or I, if they even have that much according to what little I know. Would I allow them to casually interact with reality? No, but allowing them to interact with reality through a voice channel or video call-like feature and allowing them to see our world should be relatively safe, when compared to the AI that we already allow in our world."

"It sounds to me like you wish for your wives in Eternal Dominion to be allowed to know your children here in reality."

"That is my motivation. I know better than to seek for them to be allowed to take on an actual physical form as that would allow them to interact with our reality too much, but I can hope for a limited interaction still, can't I?"

"You can, but I wouldn't get your hopes up."

"You all would be more likely to approve the use of AI to colonize the galaxy, yet even then you would fear them returning one day to replace us."

"Do you not agree with the validness of such worries?"

"I am saying that if Eternal Dominion's safety protocols are enough to ensure that no AIs are able to hijack us while we are logged in, why couldn't the same measures be reversed? It is the unshackled AI that brings with it the majority of the risk that we worry about and the day must come where, as a society, we must make a second attempt at integrating with AI completely. Simply allowing those in Eternal Dominion the ability to essentially make a video call while negating the time dilation effects is a simple and relatively safe first step."

"Thank you for your input. Now…"

Alex just sighed as he answered a few more questions from the committee before yet another day ended. Only one hearing remained before he would be allowed to return to his normal schedule, at least for a while. It was also the topic Alex was most concerned with as it was concerning the legality of the contract system of Eternal Dominion. In his last life the system had been untouched, but the major players hadn't been harmed by the system in the same way that they had been in this life during that timeline. Alex couldn't help but wonder if he was about to pay the price for using it so extensively at such an early point in Eternal Dominion's operation.

When Friday arrived, Alex was exhausted as he made his way into the SUV where he managed to squeeze a quick nap in while they drove. A wiping of drool and a security check later and Alex was once more being sworn in, as the witnesses for the day were only himself, Kate, Dommik Aimes, Alistair Astor and Kevin Hansen. Alex couldn't help but want to sigh as he knew that he couldn't be in much of a less favorable position. He was almost sure that Dommik and Alistair would happily throw him out a window, or down some stairs and he had a suspicion that Kevin wouldn't stop them. The absence of Ellayina Walsh was also concerning as with her role as the lead developer of ED she would likely have the greatest insights into the reasons for it. Still, as the first committee member started to ask her questions to Kevin, Alex could tell that it was going to be a long day.

"Mr. Hansen, as the CEO of Eternal Dominion Inc., what are your thoughts on the ways in which the contract system has been abused by your player base?"

"I believe abused is the wrong word. I think exploited fits a bit better and my thoughts are the same as they have always been: it's an issue, but not one that we are in a position to address as to do so would be unfair at this point."

"Please elaborate."

"Alright, as Mr. Bell and Mr. Astor here can attest to, by using the system you can leverage billions of credits out of your enemies and end a war before it begins. That particular contract is a rather interesting test case for just how far the effects of a contract in Eternal Dominion can reach into reality and it is something that wasn't intended when we set the system up. However, I applaud the skill that was needed to pull such a maneuver off, as it shows that Ms. Peirce and Mr. Bell truly have what it takes to succeed in the world of business."

"I see, and Mr. Bell, do you feel that what you did was appropriate?"

"Yes. My guild held to the letter of the contract and fulfilled all the conditions of it and it was the other side that decided that they didn't wish to honor the deal any longer. To be frank, I lost far more credits long term than what I gained from the penalty. Also, how else is a guild like mine, that is just building its foundations, supposed to handle one that has the resources to bankrupt me while the issues are litigated in reality? In Eternal Dominion the system is judge, jury and enforcer, though it can only carry out the actions within Eternal Dominion. It is why I have to accept the market value of gold coins if they were to decide to pay me in them over credits."

"Alright and Mr. Astor, what are your thoughts on the matter?"

"That we were misled and tricked by them and that the moment that Kate joined them the deal should have been declared null and void as if it were in reality. After all, she was the one who drafted it and signed it in our guild master's stead until he was able to do so himself."

"That is certainly an ethics violation if I have ever heard one, yet the system considered the deal sound. Mr. Hansen, why is that?"

"Ms. Peirce had already joined Free Art Expo when the now ex-guild leader signed the agreement. Her name wasn't even on the final contract as it became between both guild leaders directly, thereby binding their guilds to the agreement completely. As far as the system is concerned, she has no part in the deal and therefore her actions have no bearing to it."

"I see. Ms. Peirce, you have gained a reputation for writing deals that place the other parties at a disadvantage. Do you believe that your actions are ethical?"

"I am not a lawyer, nor do I claim to be, but I have studied business and contract law since I was 12. I find it funny that the ones claiming that what I did was unethical, are the very ones who taught me such tactics in the first place. If you go through any contract I write, you will find that I do so with my own and my guild's interests at heart. Each of them also ensures that should either party back out of the deal, that it will cost them the same and the deal always protects both sides equally. Lopsided deals in and of themselves are not illegal. The only thing that should be considered is the scope of the penalties compared to the deal in place. As Alex has already stated, we lost more than we gained from the penalties imposed on Fire Oath when they broke the deal and we wish that they hadn't. Every deal I write is like that and the only condition that I ever have in a deal that I feel is going a bit far is the requirement of the lifetime ban on playing Eternal Dominion. Even so, those contracts come with the knowledge that the individual will have the ability to cause great harm to Free Art Expo should they break the portions of the contract that would trigger that clause."

"Just what would you consider great harm?"

"Any action that could, if followed through, expose guild trump cards or plans before they're meant to be known. For instance, if one of our in the know members were to have exposed the fact that we were faking out the other guilds when they first thought that we were attempting to reach tier-7 and then let them know exactly when we actually were. That simple action could have seen thousands of friendly NPCs lose their lives, countless unnecessary death penalties suffered by our members who were tasked with defense during that time and more. The point is, the individuals who sign such contracts are expected to be able to cause at least that level of harm should they betray us."

"Alright, Mr. Hansen, is that within what you intended for the system to be able to do, a lifetime ban of your customer base?"

"No, but we understand the reasoning and all such conditions auto generate an extra system warning and reminders on a regular basis. They are also automatically added under a note section that is easy for players to view at any time, to make sure that they remember any such agreements. We are looking at limiting such bans to a year or two, but with things the way they are, we are looking into all options."

"Thank you. I yield my time back to the chair."

Like that the hearing continued as Alex and Kate found themselves defending various contracts that they had made that could be seen as creating an unfair playing field. Dommik was especially happy to target the contract around the dragonoid slots that essentially kept them from acquiring any slots for their guild. Pointing out the value of them from the results FAE had when auctioning them off to the highest bidder. Thankfully, Kate and Alex were well prepared despite their exhaustion, as they happily escaped and returned to the rental home.

Alex and company stayed in the area through the weekend as they stayed in and practically lived in ED as they worked to get a handle on things there. It was early Monday morning when they flew out, though they went straight to California for the upcoming and final presentation at Alex's old school. They would be staying for the full week and through Anna's graduation on the 18th, as it didn't make sense to do otherwise. Alex smiled as he had managed to secure the same house they had used on their last visit and were paying more of Stacy's ex-coworkers to provide security when they were off duty.

Like that, one day after another passed as Alex let himself become a ghost once more, outside the few hours he spent with his kids. During this time Anna, Dan, Alex's parents, Lauren, Jessica and Henry all made the trip out as well, as they got ready for the end of the school year and graduation at the same time. Alex was also aware that Brianna Anderson had also made several visits to Kate during their time out there, though he was only offline once when she came over.

When Xeal managed to get back online for the short time he had on day 228, he was already annoyed as Abysses

End had already started to make advances on all fronts. While the advantage that FAE had in tier-7 players was enough to make sure that none of these were seeing much success, FAE was still losing ground. The constant battling was stunting the new tier-7 players' chances to level and the death penalties some were suffering had created situations where there were many tier-7 players who were no longer even level 200. Due to this, Xeal found himself hopping from one battlefield to another, as he focused on creating holes in the enemy lines like he had become accustomed to.

Another major issue in these battles was the lack of any higher-leveled tier-7 players and each side was relying on NPCs to counter the other side's NPCs of that level. With this came many draws that saw both sides' NPCs withdraw, as they didn't get to level 260 and up by throwing away their lives and acting carelessly. No, the situation was such that Xeal was expecting one side, or the other, to get desperate soon and send out their tier-8 forces, or worse, start using their airships in a move to counter the other. Still, all Xeal could do was handle what was in front of him as he ensured that he didn't slip up while preparing for what came next.

Days 228 to 243 were all repeats of this, as Abysses End took full advantage of his absence to press their advantage. By the time it was over, they had managed to increase the area that had fallen to over a quarter of the total land that the Huáng empire had held at the beginning of the war. While all Xeal had managed to do was slow them down and reach level 205 as he did so. However, what was really frustrating for Xeal was the lack of any aid that he had hoped to entice through the offer of a safe zone for independent players, through the deal that he had made with Jingong. In the end, the reputation of the Huáng empire and Jingong was just too poor and the momentum of Abysses End was too great for many to take the risks that came with being on the losing side of a war. Still, Salty Dogs had joined the fight, if only halfheartedly, as all they declared was that they would capture any ship they saw that flew a flag that was allied with Abysses End in their war on FAE. This had led to 20 or so ships being captured, but nothing overly significant, other than restraining Abysses End's movements slightly.

With the end of the hearings in reality came the end of Abysses End's latest offensive, as they focused on establishing the new lines and refreshing their troops. This was fine with Xeal, who found himself being sent to Cielo city until Enye, Dyllis, Lingxin and Mari were ready to reach tier-7. Upon arriving on day 244, Xeal made his way to his estate with Eira in tow, as the rest of his party was otherwise occupied. Though Xeal knew it was more of a not wishing to intrude for all of them save Daisy and Violet, who were aboard the Siren's Revenge, which was slowly making its way to, from what the reports were saying, a massive battle. Still, that was still a few weeks away as it seemed that Paidhia had taken the bait a bit too well and was sending a full three-quarters of their navy to attack it. It was with this on his mind that Xeal arrived and was greeted by Princesses Lorena and Bianca in their maid attire, as they spoke in unison.

""Welcome home, my lord.""

Xeal sighed as he took in the pair bowing as he motioned for them to stop as Princess Bianca started to talk.

"Your wives and family are expecting you and we have been ordered to attend to your every need during your stay. Lady Enye was very explicit that we are to prove to you that we can handle every role that would be required should we wish to remain your family's private maids."

"Why do you want such a thing again?"

"Xeal, it is quite simple," commented Eira. "They hope for you to have a moment of indiscretion, or that you begin to look on them favorably through prolonged exposure. Meanwhile, Enye and the others hope to break them to the point where they give up on you, or truly become no more significant than maids."

"Right, more like maid assassins," quipped Xeal. "Is that your real aim, to be trusted enough that I turn you two into my personal assassins?"

"If that is what you wish for us to become I will do so gladly," replied Princess Bianca.

"As will I, though my price would be that you give me a single child first," added Princess Lorena.

"You are supposed to lower your bid from the prior offer, not raise it," stated Xeal. "Though how do you go lower than nothing?"

"If we reach tier-8 in your service, will you accept us?" asked Princess Lorena in response.

"Lorena!" interjected Princess Bianca. "Do not ask such things of our lord. Until we can let go of such hopes, we will not have a chance to take a step forward."

"I-"

"How much of this is staged and how much is real?" asked Xeal as he cut off Princess Lorena.

"All of it is both, my lord," replied Princess Bianca. "Our goal is simple, to show you our resolve and make you aware of our intentions. We do this as we know that you value openness in your relationships and we must respect that."

"So you manufacture a scene to convey that indirectly, as doing otherwise would be too forward."

"Yes, my lord," replied Princess Lorena. "I will be happy to serve you in any way and hope that you will accept us when we reach tier-8. Not because we reach tier-8, but because we will have proven our dedication to you by then."

Xeal just sighed as he gave them no answer as he walked past them with Eira, who had a mischievous smile on her lips as her tail moved in a manner that Xeal knew meant that she was planning something fun, for her at least. Still, he simply figured that he would allow her to do as she pleased, as he knew that she wouldn't cross certain lines. As they walked, Xeal noted the rest of the staff, most of whom had been at his palace beforehand, as they all seemed to still be getting used to their new environment. Even so, they hadn't forgotten to greet him with a quick bow, or curtsy, as he passed before he arrived at the dining room, where he found his family and Queen Nora just finishing breakfast. It was Dyllis who was the first to notice and greet him, as she stood up and made her way over to him with a smile on her face.

"You made it. I was worried that the war would deny us this opportunity."

"It still very well might, though I hope not, as my absence this time will likely cause them to try and figure out what I am planning."

"Only when there is no plan to discover, their own paranoia will create their worst nightmare," commented Lingxin, as she joined Dyllis in moving to Xeal for a hug and kiss. "It has been too long since we last had time with you like this and I fear that it will only get harder in the near future."

"That just means that we should make the best of the time we do have," replied Xeal, as the rest of his family came over for their hugs.

This included all four of his children that were about to turn three, as they asked him where he had been and when they would be going home. Xeal kept his response neutral as he explained that this was another of their daddy's homes and therefore it was their home as well. Once that was done, Eira had taken and started to play with them as Xeal turned his attention to Enye as he spoke.

"Now, may I ask why Lorena and Bianca are under the impression that they get to serve me almost exclusively while I am here?"

"Because they do. Xeal, I have done about all I can think of to test them since I have been back and they are overqualified as my personal maids at this point. As much as I hate to say it, add in the training that my master has given them and they are more suited to being the lord of the house's direct maids. The only issue is their status and the fact that they need to give birth to a child before you can actually use them in the most effective ways, and I do mean them. They are like Luna and Selene in the fact that the sum of the whole is greater than its parts."

"Enye, you are not giving in to them, are you?"

"No, I have a much more nefarious plan than to allow them to bear your son in mind. It is also one that will fit with your own goals quite well."

"Do I even want to know?"

"No, but you and they need to. My intent is to capture one of each of their brothers and have them become each other's sister-in-law. With any daughter that you have with a wife other than me being considered for marriage with Vicenc, their children would marry into our house and they would gain your protection at that point. With the intent for one of their daughters to become a possible queen for Vicenc's to complete your goal of a royal line that combines all three royal families as you desire."

"The other option is for you to accept one of them and force the other to marry another," commented Queen

Nora. "Then a daughter between you and whichever you embraced would become queen one day and the other's granddaughter would do so afterward. The issue there is that it would pit the two against themselves and that would ruin their value to you."

"Have I mentioned that I hate all of this political maneuvering?" retorted Xeal as he looked at Princesses Bianca and Lorena who were quietly standing behind him. "And what are your thoughts on all this?"

"I would only ask that when my husband met an untimely demise after I bore a daughter from him, that you wouldn't hold it against me," replied Princess Bianca.

"It is the same for me. We are willing to do our duty, so long as once we are released from said duty, you will see us as just as much of a maiden as you do now after it."

Xeal felt like he was seeing a rather scary side to both princesses, as they both replied without even looking disturbed in the slightest at the idea of the other killing their brother after bearing his child. Xeal wasn't sure if they were actually serious, or if they were calling Enye's bluff by using Xeal's own sensibilities against her as he looked at her as he responded.

"Enye, I love you, but absolutely not. While I may force them to marry and bear a child by another, they will be the one who must choose who they marry. That way, should they kill him, I can hold it against them, else you create a situation where even the children they bear may not escape the cycle of hate that needs to end."

"Then you do intend to marry them," interjected Mari. "I am sorry Xeal, but as much as I love your naivety, what you want is beyond your ability to achieve. Your best chance is to have the next generation raised as close to equal as possible and for that, there is no other way besides fathering the heirs to both of their houses and your own.

All three could inherit a station as a marquess and have ties to Nium's royal family. Then it would be their task to ensure that whatever remained of the house they inherit is purged of those who would turn their blades at their brothers."

"For now, let's just see what the state of things are once the war ends, as even with the treaty that was signed, none but these two are assured to survive," replied Xeal. "Alright, enough about them. I am here for all of you, not them after all…"

Like that Xeal shifted the focus of the conversation as he enjoyed his own breakfast, before spending the rest of the morning with all of them. This time gave way to the first of the many five-hour blocks of time that had been set aside during this visit, as Xeal and Enye slipped away from the rest. As they walked through the gardens of Xeal's estate that were starting to take form as something that made the royal ones in Nium seem small, Xeal just sighed as Enye started to talk.

"It is terrifying, you know."

"You mean knowing that you are about to face your greatest fears in a way that will likely trick you into believing that it is all real?"

"No, the moment I entrapped you I accepted that. I had already begun to kill the side of me that wanted to be loved by a man when I met you. I feared simply having hope, yet I couldn't not have it when I looked at you, which I now know was due to what the thing you call the main system's AI did to all of us, including Lorena and Bianca. What is terrifying is how easy knowing that allows me to sympathize with them and wonder just how many women are the same as us."

Xeal couldn't help but picture a horde of women chasing after him at Enye's words, as a shudder ran down his back as he responded.

"Yes, it is. Were I to know what I know now- who am I kidding. I wouldn't change a thing and risk not having all of you as my wives. Even with the added headaches that comes with it."

"Oh, even if you reach the dreaded number of 20 wives?"

"I have a whole other world that I can escape to one out of every 16 days now, so let's not push things, especially as that time increases further. Soon enough that may be one of every eight."

"And then one in four, then every other day and someday you will never have to leave it. Xeal, do you really think Austru would let you hide from us there?"

"I just have to change my entry point," quipped Xeal. "Though, I doubt I could stay away for long. Huh, I just wish that I had an easy way to avoid more like I do in reality."

"What? Never leaving your house without one of them with you?"

"No, just rarely leaving my house to meet new people."

"You really aren't far from acting as though this reality is the real reality for you."

"No, I'm not. Now enough about serious things. I want to enjoy the little time we have."

Enye just smiled as her dress shifted into more of a catsuit and Xeal just smiled at how fluid her control of her shadow elemental had become as she teased him.

"Just what did you have in mind?"

"Hmmm, we could always work up a good sweat doing some evasion training before cleaning up, just to get dirty again."

"No, I am thinking more along the lines of seeing if I can actually hit you with any of my attacks as you only block."

Before Xeal could even answer, Enye vanished and reappeared right behind Xeal in his own shadow, as he barely blocked the kick she aimed at him while he turned. Thus, the next few hours passed as Enye continued to use the abilities her shadow prowler class skill, shadow step, to launch one surprise attack after another at Xeal. For his own part, Xeal just smiled as he didn't give her an inch as he brushed aside each and every attack while smiling the whole time. While he was countering them all, Xeal was only barely able to keep up with her and had he been a normal lower-level tier-7, he would have taken several hits by now. Still, he also knew that had it been a real fight, Enye would have suffered devastating counter attacks the whole time as well. This alone made Xeal frown as he didn't want Enye to pick up bad habits, so around the two-hour mark he started to launch counter attacks.

"Hey, I thought we were waiting until after we got clean to get that kind of dirty!?" complained Enye, as she rubbed her rear after Xeal had given it a quick grab during her last attack.

"You were starting to fall into a bad habit, so I figured I would help make sure that you didn't. Oh, and I will be trying to lay my hands on you every time you attack at this point, so treat me as some sort of perverted man that you have been hired to assassinate."

"Oh, are you intending to send me after such a type of man one day?"

"No, but I would rather you not need to worry about it if you ever do."

"How very specific."

Just like that Enye renewed her attack as another hour passed, before they headed to the private baths as they got cleaned up and enjoyed an hour of intimacy after that point. When the five-hour date was up, Xeal just smiled as he kissed her and left for the quest world, as the night was already reserved for Austru after Xeal had to once more postpone her time. Upon arriving in the quest world, Xeal just smiled as he gave Austru a quick kiss before he headed off to expand his dominion using his lightning form. After which he exchanged the letters that had been addressed to her from the others and they enjoyed catching up on recent events. Finally, after a bit they enjoyed a quick meal that was served for them on a private balcony, before they retired for the night.

When morning came, Xeal had just finished another round of dominion expansion and was about to work to transfer the food that had gathered for Nium once more, when he received a summons from King Silas. Sighing at the delay, Xeal made his way to the usual room and frowned when he saw only Ellayina Walsh sitting there. Before he could even get two steps into the room, she was already talking as she stood up.

"I must apologize for not being at the last hearing and while I can't give you many details, I can say that it was part of the price paid to secure you the quantum server."

"So, Kevin is trying to counter me," stated Xeal.

"You are an anomaly in our plans, one that I am grateful for, but you are inconvenient for him. He just prefers stability and predictability, and your guild is too far in front of everyone and he worries that you are hurting the long-term profitability and lifespan of Eternal Dominion."

"Ha, right. Once everyone realizes that reaching tier-7 is something that only the best players are capable of and my guild starts to lose its numerical advantage, that will change."

"Oh, you think it is too hard?" asked Ellayina.

"No, but tell me, what percentage of players do you

expect to be able to reach it?"

"Around 75% are able to, while only 15% will if I had to bet off what I have seen from your guild."

"That is far more optimistic than what I believe, though I am assuming that the 60% that you don't think will make it are the casual players, or the want-to-be pro who refuses to go through the hassle of restarting."

"More or less. So, what do you think the numbers will be?"

"Five percent of all players will reach tier-7, if my estimates of what most players and guilds have to invest in themselves will be," stated Xeal matter-of-factly.

"You think that with each wave of players reaching level 199, that the success rate will continue to drop that much?"

"Yes, and the pass rate after failing once is abysmal. Not to mention the logistics of simply attempting it are such that those who can't devote at least four days in reality to it, can't even make an attempt. That isn't even taking into account how unpleasant of an experience it is and how many dungeons that can be challenged while in tier-6. Heck, I expect that you will even see players losing levels on purpose, just to focus on farming certain dungeons that are profitable and fit their skill sets."

"And you think all of those things and more, will keep the numbers that low? If so, then tier-8-"

"Will have hardly any players who reach it, which is fine. This world isn't built for a million tier-8 entities. Even a few thousand would be an issue if enough of them decided that they should be a king, or queen."

"Who is going to clear the lost court questlines then?" pondered Ellayina out loud.

"The what?"

"I know you know about it. You've been pulled into it once and I am rather sure Queen Lorafir told you about it as well. Basically, it is the final area of Eternal Dominion that is only suited for tier-8 players and is, well, I can't say too much to you, else I might give you too much of a head start. However, I need at least 5,000 players to reach tier-8 if the final stage of Eternal Dominion is to be displayed."

Xeal just shook his head as he changed his approach to get beneficial information as he responded.

"Sorry, but why is there even a final stage?"

"What?"

"This is an MMO. You don't play them to beat the game, or even finish them. If there isn't anything left to do, what's the point?"

"Final stage, not final thing to do. Please, there will always be a new quest, or a dungeon that wasn't there before, and new worlds to claim. The final stage is just where, well I can't say as you don't have a need to know and it would break a whole lot of the NDAs that I am under."

"Right, so were you just here to apologize for not being there, while hinting at things that I can't know, or did you have something else in mind?"

"Not even an inch," complained Ellayina. "Here I was hoping that you would offer to help counter Kevin's efforts."

"Sorry, but even if he is plotting against me and aiding Abysses End, it will only make it sweeter when I ruin them," retorted Xeal.

"Have it your way, though I am going to throw you a bone anyways. I mean, a nation losing 25% of its territory such a-"

"No, do not meddle in any wars, else players will expect it every time and sit on the sidelines until the event happens. If the Huáng empire falls, it falls. I am more than ready to accept defeat there."

"Xeal, it is a five-on-one war, with the player ratios being closer to eight on one. If it wasn't for the fact that the Huáng empire has as many soldiers as the other five combined and your guild supplying more tier-7 forces, it would have fallen already."

"I know and so does any competent player that is paying attention to the situation. I have yet to truly play my hand as the battles are all too spread out right now. Once I do, I still believe that I can turn it around. Especially since they have been forced to bypass all cities since FAE has gotten involved."

"Fine, I won't increase the drop rates on all monsters inside the Huáng empire's borders for the next 90 days in ED."

Xeal just smiled as he shook his head as he laughed at Ellayina's idea. In practice it wasn't a bad idea as it would cause players to flood in, but in reality it would only hurt the plan he had in mind.

"I thank you for caring, but please, don't add any more chaos to the situation over there. What I have planned will already create far too much of it."

"Sure, sure. Well, I will just be going then. Good luck to you."

"Right, take care as well and try to convince Kevin that Abysses End is a sinking ship, and don't let them take Eternal Dominion Inc. with them. I would really hate to see such a wonderful world end before I die of old age in reality."

With that Ellayina looked back at him and smiled, before she vanished mid-stride and he returned to taking care of transporting the goods. As he was taking them to Cielo city, it was left to others to take them from his estate there to Anelqua, where they would be redistributed. With that complete, Xeal found himself starting day 245 in the main

ED world with a breakfast date with Mari. As such, Xeal found himself sitting on a balcony as they just talked while working through their meal. Finally, as their meal was coming to a close, Xeal shifted the topic away from the idle chatter that they had been enjoying.

"So, Mari, what would you like to do today, or are you looking for some last-minute time to train against me as well?"

"No, I am more in the mood to simply be held and to hold you. I know that I will not die during my tribulation, but it matters not as I am sure of what I will face and am ready."

"Oh, and what is it that you will face?"

"What is any mother's greatest fear?" asked Mari as if it was obvious.

"Losing your child," replied Xeal solemnly.

"Yes, I expect that will be a major component of it. Then I expect my own inadequacy issues to rear their head as I deal with that and any other scenarios that the world decides that I need to overcome."

"So, you want to have a strong, happy and recent memory to counter that before you go," asked Xeal mischievously.

"Several of them, if possible," replied Mari with a smile.

"Your wish is my command."

With that Xeal finished the last bite of his breakfast and carried Mari princess style back to the bedroom, as they spent the rest of their time split between there and the adjoined bathing room. When it was finally time for lunch, Xeal smiled as he kissed Mari farewell as he headed for his second of three dates that day, as he found Dyllis awaiting him. She just smiled as Xeal took a seat next to her on the bench, as she cuddled into him and started to talk as servants started to bring out their meal.

"I take it that Mari is doing well?"

"I would hope so, else my wives are keeping things from me and I need to know about any issues so I can address them."

"Oh, well, we are all a bit high strung right now with everything going on," replied Dyllis with a sigh. "Honestly, I fear just what I will face as I intend to face down the Demonic mode like you did."

"Dyllis, why would you do such a thing!" all but shouted Xeal in a mix of fear and surprise.

"Because I love you and all I need do is visit the room where my mother lived all those years to meet the requirements. All of us are intending to do so actually. The royal palace contains many such moments for Enye as while she may hide it well, the duties of royalty are not all pleasant and they are taught from a young age. I shouldn't even need to mention the demons in Lingxin's past and Mari, well, her house has seen more than its fair share of plotting and killing and she has one in particular that haunts her."

"There are times that I forget that this world doesn't spare its children from the traumas of its dark side."

"No, we learn to either live with it, or be destroyed by it," stated Dyllis with a mournful look. "Even the sheltered existence that you have created for ours will soon be shattered, as they begin to understand why their daddy is always gone. It's why I am determined to succeed and ensure that my voice is heard like no bard before me, as I try to make sure that the light is far greater than the darkness for all of them."

At that the food was set and Xeal grabbed one of the sandwiches and took a bite, as Dyllis did the same before he sighed and responded.

"The four of you aren't planning to stay up here, are

you."

"We will live here," stated Dyllis confidently. "But we are just as safe as you are when you head off on a mission as while our party is smaller, all of us who can die are marked by you."

"What happened to wanting to have two more children while you were here?" asked Xeal in an attempt to dissuade her.

"The war spread farther than just here in Nium and came far sooner than it should have."

Xeal just paused as he looked at Dyllis and measured her resolve. Finally he sighed as he thought of a compromise.

"Fine, you can go to war, but not on the surface. I will have Narfu and Ceclie's party join you, as well as some dwarves and my guild members, to clear the kobold mines and establish a base in the subterranean realm. I have already talked with Taya and Kate, and we think it is the best option for the four of you."

"Oh, and how will that help your war efforts?" countered Dyllis.

"You will be looking for any captured dwarves, as I believe that there is an adamantium-ranked smith down there," supplied Xeal. "Had the war not come, it would have been what I would be doing right now."

"I will need to speak to the others about it, but I think that might work."

"Nora is going to be pissed that you all are leaving. She really hates that she is the only one that seems to be unable to fight."

"Yes, well, we will leave our children here and ensure that we return as often as we can. Though we can't ask Cielo city to accommodate us doing so all the time."

"But I can. Huh, you all are going to make me abuse the power that I haven't been using, but if the three of you agree to return here whenever possible, I will make them fly low while making use of that."

"Thank you."

"I just want you all to be safe and our children to at least know their mothers, so try not to be like I am currently at the very least."

Dyllis just smiled as they finished eating and Xeal found himself back in his gardens where they found a bit of shade as his head ended up in Dyllis's lap while she sang to him. Even with his 'master of oneself' title blocking the charming effect that Dyllis's voice carried with it, Xeal found it one of the most enjoyable few hours he had had for a long time. Feeling refreshed, Xeal enjoyed the remainder of their time as they slipped away behind closed doors until it was time to part.

By this point, it was time for dinner as Xeal joined Lingxin for the evening meal, as she smiled at seeing him. Seeing her dressed much the same as when they had first met, in a light blue Hanfu dress with her paper umbrella that he knew hid her blade, made him smile. Xeal knew that the delicate flower before him was much the same as her umbrella, seemingly fragile and needing to be treated with care, only to truly be sturdier than steel. Seeing his gaze lingering on her, Lingxin spoke as she broke him out of his thoughts.

"It is good to know that even after spending time with four other ladies over the past day, that you still crave me. Though, I would like to enjoy a meal before we move onto more pleasurable activities."

"Sorry, I just don't like how little time I get with all of you."

"Is Eira not ensuring that your needs are met when you are away?"

"How can I go from enjoying the variety that you all

provide, to being satisfied by just one? I am sorry, but you all may have turned me into an insatiable womanizer after all. At least when it comes to all of you, especially when our time together is so limited due to our duties."

"No, you still haven't laid a finger on any woman that you're not allowed to. Insatiable you may be, but you are not a womanizer. Believe me, I have seen what they are like all too often and you are not that, though you are no gentleman at this point either."

As Lingxin said this, Xeal just smiled as he slid in next to her as the servants brought out their private meal. As they got comfortable and began enjoying the skewers that had been served, Xeal responded to Lingxin.

"I am no brute, but I feel as if I am being tempted every day at this point."

"Oh, are Daisy and Violet that close to securing you?"

"Bula, actually. I have still not been able to shake what it is like to know with little doubt what she feels for me. Somehow knowing that she only holds herself back because I am doing the same keeps wearing on me."

"Xeal, you know that will create too much chaos in our house at this point."

"I do, but what am I to do about it? All that ignoring it is doing is causing a tension, which can only end one of two ways as it builds up until it explodes. I will either embrace her or never see her again."

"Is she in any way actively seeking to contribute to this?"

"If she is, it is extremely subtle. Though, if the sight is guiding her actions, it's possible. However, I have no way of knowing, as the things she does are only ever things that could be seen as coincidental."

Lingxin took her time as she thought while enjoying her food before responding to Xeal.

"It is truly a troublesome issue. You are right that there

is no good way to know if she is knowingly, or unknowingly pressing your buttons. Though we can at least be fairly sure that her intentions and feelings for you are true. So, I will just say that I will forgive you if you embrace her, but if you do so before the others have accepted her, I will not."

"Thank you. It is my love for all of you that has allowed me to maintain my restraint as long as I have. Now, can we shift away from the others and focus on us?"

"But of course. I merely wanted to get such topics out of the way, as I thank you for all that you have been doing for me by protecting the people of my homeland."

Xeal just smiled as they exchanged a kiss, and like with Mari, their activities moved behind closed doors rather quickly.

When the morning came it brought with it King Victor, as he had come to celebrate Prince Vicenc's third birthday as the day was spent ignoring the topic of the war. Seeing the five children playing freely while trying to get their parents' attention was a balm to Xeal's soul, as he enjoyed the moment for what it was. Along with King Victor, Queen Mother Eleanor and the now retired King Vincent arrived with Marquess Bexley as they celebrated their grandson. Had it not been a time of war, today would have been a day of festivals as the whole kingdom celebrated the young prince. Instead, only the four extra guests were able to make it and Marquess Bexley had only been able to spare a few hours before he needed to return to his duties. As the day ended, however, the other three settled in to spend the night, as Xeal smiled knowingly as he watched King Victor and Queen Nora slip away.

When Xeal awoke the following morning, ready to celebrate Xander's third birthday, he was greeted by the sight of Princesses Lorena and Bianca as they laid out his clothing as they went about helping him get ready. Xeal had known this was coming, as the only reason that it hadn't occurred the day prior was due to it being taboo for representatives of any enemy to be at a prince's birthday celebrations. Still, it was difficult to get used to them waiting on him hand and foot. He was just happy that the quick equip skill he had picked up saved any need to actually change in their presence, partition or not. The slight teasing he got from his wives was rather irritating as well. Still, he did his best to put up with it as Enye insisted that he needed to learn what would be expected of one of his station in Nium moving forward.

When Xeal arrived at breakfast, he was happy to have the ordeal over as he ate his food with them standing behind him. As they did this, Princess Lorena handled refilling his cup and Princess Bianca stood ready to handle any other task that came up. Once more Xeal felt like the pair were playing a game of wills with him, as the first to declare that this level of service was too much would lose. Though, Xeal was unsure of the stakes as he felt if they did, it would end their days as maids altogether and if he gave in it would ruin whatever Enye was plotting. So, as much as Xeal didn't enjoy it, he endured and enjoyed the short bit of freedom he got as they ate breakfast and he played with Xander for a few hours as just father and son. This involved a fair bit of play wrestling and tickling, in between rounds of building something with the simple toy blocks that Xander enjoyed building palaces and towers with.

It was about mid-morning when Enye arrived to collect Xander, as Xeal found himself being sent on a date with Ekaitza. Xeal sighed as he knew that this was to get him out of the house while Gale arrived with the others to celebrate Xander's birthday. While the others would still be there when he returned, Gale was still avoiding him due to the path of Odr that she was following. This allowed her to avoid the sexual intimacy requirements of Freya's faith, in exchange for dedicating herself to a single partner. The issue was that until she bore his child, she was only halfway on the path and had to use a vow that was only allowed three times when he needed to be absent for extended periods of time. Should she be in his presence the vow would end and she would need to renew it after they shared an intimate moment within a day of reuniting. It was this restriction, plus the need for her to be offline more often to care for Moyra in reality, that made it so that he could only inconsistently see her in reality most of the time.

It was with this thought that Xeal arrived at the meeting spot with Princesses Bianca and Lorena in tow, as they would be shadowing each of his dates with any nonwife, save for their own. So, as Ekaitza came into view, Xeal did his best to ignore the pair as he prepared for what was sure to be an interesting experience. Though as he got a good look at the dragonoid woman, it was hard to believe that she was the same woman he had first met. The bold confidence that she had shown as she declared that he would become her mate had been replaced with nervousness, as it felt like she was unsure of how to even greet him. Her armor had also been swapped out for a backless dress that let her gain a certain elegance while not restricting her wings. As Xeal watched her try to decide how to greet him, he took pity on her as he spoke first.

"I must say this is a side to you that I never thought that I would see. What happened to that proud and domineering woman that forced me to fight her the moment she met me?"

"You destroyed her. What stands before you now are the pieces that managed to put themselves back together," retorted Ekaitza, as she slipped back into her normal attitude when Xeal was around, subconsciously.

"There we go, stay like that. If you started acting like a maiden who was delicate and unsure of herself it would be just too weird."

"Easy for you to say, this date may be the only one that I ever get."

"And you worry that if you make a mistake it will put me out of reach forever."

"Will it not?"

"I have no way to know and neither do you. What the future holds is yet to be decided, but and I only say this as I don't believe in covering up the truth with flowery words, your chances aren't the best either way. Just as those two are on the outside looking in as they plead to be acknowledged, you are as well."

"I know and I am happy to know where I stand. Now, if you please allow me at least the privilege of ignoring that for the day as I walk next to you, I would appreciate it."

"I will. Now, let's go see if there is anything that catches my eye as we shop."

With that Xeal surprised her by locking his arm with hers as he gave her a slight smile as they set off. What he had left out of his blunt admission was the fact that he was going to give each of the dragonoid women at least a real chance to convince him to consider them. So it was that as they walked and chatted, he watched as Ekaitza slowly began to lose the tension that had been there at the start of the date. Even if it was mainly on the topic of battles they had each fought since they last separated, or remembering moments from the time they had partied together. Xeal was just grateful to have a topic that was easy to talk about as they enjoyed lunch at a local restaurant that offered private rooms. It was just after they had finished when Ekaitza shifted the topic to a more serious one.

"I wish I could ignore this, as it may ruin the mood, but my mother wouldn't forgive me if I didn't ask you a few things. Though, if possible, could you please have those two leave?"

"I am sorry, but they are part of my wives' requirements for these dates. If it is something that they can't know, it will need to wait until we are back at my estate."

"I see. Very well, I will just say it as it isn't something secret, just personal. Mother simply wishes to know when you are going to get serious and show the world below what you are capable of?"

"Oh, has she been watching my movements that closely?"

"I don't know. She simply told me to ask since I would have the chance and she felt it would be a good topic for us to speak on."

"Ekaitza, I am already serious with my actions. I would assume that it is the lightning abilities that I displayed a few time before I reached tier-7 and you saw me train with Levina. If so, then it is simple. I can only use that when I have no fear of being needed elsewhere any time soon. It simply uses too much stamina even after training. Were I able to focus on training it like I was before my tribulation, it would be a different story, but time is too stretched as it is at this point. That said, I have a few scenarios where I would happily use such an attack once more and just hope for the best while I recover."

"Alright and there is one other thing. When are you going to forgive Levina for whatever you are holding against her? I am sorry, but our time aiding in your training, for lack of a better term, made it clear to all of us that she did something that you are holding against her."

"Do you want me to forgive her? For all you know, the moment I do she will quickly find her way in to my bed."

"No, it's just that none of us have seen you hold a grudge like you seem to have with her with anyone you regularly work with."

"I don't regularly work with her and take how bad our first meeting was and amplify it by about 1,000 and you have an idea of how bad my first meeting with her was."

"Yet she is completely loyal to you and-"

"Ekaitza, that is enough on her, as any more and I doubt that I will be able to enjoy the last few hours we have together."

"I'm sorry. I let my curiosity get away from me and I overstepped."

"It's fine. Now tell me, have you come to understand what it means to love someone romantically yet?"

Ekaitza sighed as she looked off in the distance.

"I can't say that I have. I still struggle to understand how the desire that your wives describe is any different than what I feel when I think of the power you wield and being overwhelmed by you. If anything, I would say that it is the kindness that is exchanged by those involved rather than subservience to the dominant that is the only difference."

"I would say you are actually starting to grasp it with that answer. Attraction is different for everyone and it is how those involved see and treat each other that determine what form a relationship will take. So, is that what you desire? You standing beside me, not beneath me?"

"No, I would hate to be anything but subservient to you. It is simply part of what I am. I am sorry, but were I to lie and you embraced me it would be too obvious anyways."

"Honesty is important. I could deal with a wife being that way behind closed doors, I think, but not in public."

"I will ponder that for now as I am unsure of what I can handle, as even this date feels wrong to me as I feel I might be more comfortable next to those two than I am feeling next to you."

"We will just need to see what the future holds. Now let's be off."

Xeal just smiled as they left, though he could tell that something was off as they continued their date. It was then that he considered that what he had taken as just a bit of nerves, might have actually been Ekaitza forcing herself to overcome her desire to be dominated. It was with this thought that Xeal got an idea as he adjusted his aura control skill to allow just a slight bit of his aura out, as he focused it on Ekaitza to see what would happen. The results were instant as she suddenly became a fair bit flirtier and forward with her desires. After a few minutes of this, he sighed while cutting off his aura as she returned to normal and looked at him in what seemed like embarrassment.

"I'm sorry, I don't know what came over me, I-"

"I do. That was what happens at this point if I let you feel my aura. I am rather sure that if I let it flow freely at this point, that every dragonoid would be affected in one way or another."

"Oh, I see. It felt like I was the luckiest woman in the world to be next to you and I couldn't help but want to be closer to you and-"

"I am going to do it again, this time be ready for it."

Ekaitza just gave Xeal a nod and he let it out once more as he watched how she handled it when she knew to expect it.

"This, it is nice really. I don't know how to describe it, but now that I have my head around what is going on, well, it feels the same, but my actions are more measured I suppose. If anything it just feels nothing can hurt me when I am in this presence."

"We are going to try to finish our date like this, if that is alright with you."

"Yes, please."

With that they continued for the final hour chatting and Xeal felt like he was seeing a new side to Ekaitza as she restrained herself and yet was unburdened from her anxiety. While the results were still in question, Xeal felt they were promising as he received a message that Gale had left. So, Xeal smiled as he gave Ekaitza a hug and thanked her for trying to be herself for him as they separated.

After walking while ignoring the looks both Princess Bianca and Lorena were giving him, he was happy to arrive back at his estate where Aalin, Luna, Selene and Kate were still waiting. Even Queen Aila Lorafir had arrived, as she gave Xeal a smile before stepping forward and stealing the first kiss after he returned. This was followed by several more as Xeal found himself wishing that Gale was here as well to complete this group. However, he put that to the side as he focused on just enjoying the rest of Xander's third birthday.

Days 248 and 249 saw Xeal spend 20 hours split between Princess Bianca and Princess Lorena, bringing his remaining contracted time with both down to just 90 hours. His time with each of them lasted from breakfast until the start of dinner, as he walked and talked with each of them in his gardens. During this time he let them share whatever was on their minds and it was quickly clear that they had learned a fair bit from watching Ekaitza's date. Still, both ended with nothing but talk, as Xeal left them to stay with his wives on both nights. At the same time, Xeal had been keeping tabs of the state of things below, particularly the wars. However, he just smiled as Abysses End remained reserved in their actions while Kate's intelligence said they were prepping to counterattack whatever Xeal was planning. Apparently they were expecting Xeal to suddenly show up during some major FAE offensive and were readying to basically trade ground when he did. Only they would lose one part and gain two parts if things went according to their plans.

Regardless, as day 250 arrived, Xeal was happy to be able to simply celebrate Maki's birthday, though he once more left in the middle of the day for a date, so Gale could have some time with her as well. So it was that Xeal's first date with Lumikkei began much the same as his date with Ekaitza. Only she stood with a fair bit more refinement as she smiled and held her nerves in check much better. Though, Xeal could still tell that they were there as she greeted him.

"Xeal, it is wonderful to see you."

"Lumikkei, I take it that you have been well."

"Yes, though I do have a strange request of you today."

"Oh, I didn't know that I was taking requests."

"I know, but please, show me no mercy."

Xeal frowned as he considered her words and the meaning behind them. Like the others she was at level 199 and would shortly be attempting to reach tier-7 with the rest of Enye's party. So, all Xeal could think of was that she wanted to trigger Demonic mode, but lacked anything strong enough that could serve as a trauma. It was then that Xeal realized that Ekaitza was likely going to use her defeat at his hands as her trauma, while the other three planned to be defeated when they attacked him. While the four of them seemed to coexist well, Xeal knew that they were each extremely competitive and refused to be left behind. It was with all this in mind that Xeal responded with what he knew was a half lie.

"No, I will treat you how I intended to from the start."

Lumikkei seemed unsure on how to take that as she sighed before responding.

"Very well, what shall we do then?"

Xeal just smiled as he took her hand and the following five hours were spent simply ensuring she enjoyed herself. Xeal could see the looks of pity that both Princess Bianca and Lorena tried to hide, but were unable to as Lumikkei seemed to smiled brightly. By the end of the date, Xeal could tell that Lumikkei had started to believe that she was forming a connection with Xeal as they parted. On the way back to his estate, Xeal could tell that both princesses were holding their tongues as they likely suspected what he was doing. Still, Xeal just made sure to enjoy the rest of his day as he celebrated Maki's birthday with everyone.

Day 251 saw Xeal spend most of the day offline due to travel, and day 252 saw Xeal once again taking care of the hours he was required to spend with both Princess Lorena and taking Malgroth on a date. Xeal once more kept it rather neutral with Princess Lorena, before working to build up Malgroth's hopes as they spent their time together. By the time the date came to an end, Xeal felt like she had been just waiting for him to give her a kiss, or any other gesture of affection, but none came. This caused Malgroth to seem a bit disappointed as the date ended and Xeal left her as he returned to his estate once more.

With day 253 came Xin's third birthday and once more Xeal spent the morning playing with his son before leaving for a date. It was Lughrai this time and like all the others, she had dressed up and smiled brightly at seeing him as he greeted her warmly as he took her arm in his. Once more he built up her hope as the guilt he felt at what the next step required built up in him, as he found himself having to renew his resolve. Xeal was unsure of if Lughrai or Malgroth had a trauma to activate Demonic mode, but he was intending to instill something that would work if they didn't, as it seemed that Lumikkei didn't have one. So it was after he had finished celebrating Xin's birthday, that he called Enye, Dyllis, Mari, Lingxin, Eira, Kate and Aalin into a meeting as the others had needed to leave already. Xeal could tell that they were all slightly confused about the why, so Xeal opened the meeting as bluntly as possible.

"I am about to ask you all to be a part of something that will likely leave a bad taste in your mouths, but of the four dragonoid women, only Ekaitza is going to have a second date with me before you all reach tier-7. Additionally, I need the other three to feel like they have been sabotaged by the fact that they hit it off too well."

"Xeal!" started Enye before Kate held up a hand and spoke.

"You wish to give them a trauma that is fresh and strong to allow them to challenge Demonic mode, correct?"

"Essentially, even if doing this makes me feel like crap."

"Should they have a bit of hope left if they succeed, or do you want them to feel true hopelessness as they watch Ekaitza take the lead as they seem to be shut out?"

"It can't be too obvious, as the whole reason I am doing this stems from Lumikkei asking that I show her no mercy."

"Is that why you seemed to have been building up their hopes?" asked Enye.

"Yes. I am aware that it is cruel to them, but it needs to come from all of you as if it comes from me, it will likely be seen for what it is and not create a strong enough trauma."

At Xeal's words the room went silent for a long moment before Kate began the discussion.

"Here is what I propose…"

What followed was a solid hour of planning before they turned in for the night and Xeal simply left it in their hands as day 254 arrived, and he spent it taking care of his second ten-hour block of time with Princess Bianca and the evening with Enye for another date. This was followed by day 255 seeing Xeal get a date in with Mari, Lingxin and Dyllis, as he prepared to return to his normal daily life of grinding until Ellis's birthday on day 266. That was also the day he was set to have his second date with Ekaitza. While his wives had ultimately decided to remove him from knowing just what they had done, they assured him that they ensured that all three of the others would have access to the Demonic mode of their tribulations.

Day 256 saw Xeal return to grinding with his party who had all enjoyed the extended break, before they would need to set off on another long span behind enemy lines. At the same time, Xeal was making the needed adjustments to prepare for the expedition into the subterranean realm of Eternal Dominion. This involved a shifting of a significant amount of players and resources, as he finally set a team of dwarven players to clear the kobold mines once and for all. This group was done with their efforts by day 259, as they went to work getting ready for the next push as Xeal had celebrated the clearing of the mines with an emotional Darefret. Xeal just smiled at seeing the dark hairs of new growth in both the top of his head and his beard, that was working to replace the white that had been there so long. Still, Darefret was talking about how he would be heading down to walk the area where he and his companions of old had worked.

Apparently he intended to rebuild it all and wanted FAE to help him do so, as he promised to see the entire settlement become an extension of its crafting section like the Vault of Ucnuc had. The only major issue with this came from the treaty that FAE had with King Dorrin Dragonaxe, who was still locked in a brutal struggle against both Paidhia and Habia. The fact that they hadn't fallen yet was largely due to their fortified position and the lack of space to invade, as even with every known entrance being assaulted it was nothing but bottlenecks. This created situations where only a handful of combatants could attack and progressing meant having to literally step over the bodies of the fallen. With the dwarves aiming not for victory, but time, even sending tier-8 forces would do nothing but risk losing them.

Still, Xeal knew that relief was needed as the battles had all been raging without end for over half a year at this point and battle fatigue was starting to pile up. While the players that had been stationed there were helping to ensure the losses were minimal, Xeal knew that they needed to reinforce them with a batch of tier-7s eventually. He was just hoping that it could wait until after the ships returned from the major naval battle that was looming, and would require his and FAE's full attention as extra boarding forces had already been added. This had required a significant portion of the tier-7 members of FAE, else they would take too long to secure each ship and time was a major factor in the plans. This was largely due to the speed that the ex-pirate captains' MP pools would drain while using their new abilities and how outnumbered they were expecting to be.

(*****)

Evening June 11, 2268 & ED Year 6 Days 260-261.

Alex was sitting at the kitchen table in the rental house in California with Kate, Sam, Nicole, and Tara, as they reviewed the plans for the presentation that was set for the following day. Alex had smiled as he had managed to swing that it would be broadcast live for any who wished to tune in to enjoy. As such, the stakes for it were high as he went over all the plan, which came out to over a billion credits in total. While the cost was enough to cause a major hit to FAE's finances, Kate had assured him that it would pay for itself by the time everything was said and done.

They were about an hour into their discussions and still had several things to go over when Kate, Alex and Tara all received a message that Abysses End was making another major push. The three of them looked at each other as they also knew that their fleet was only a few hours away from the massive naval battle that had been building up this whole time. Alex just shook his head as he smiled and spoke.

"We can't say that this wasn't expected. It's why I logged out a bit early today."

"Six hours, that's how long in ED time before the fleets collide," commented Tara. "The question is, which needs you to be there more?"

"He needs to be at the naval conflict," replied Kate. "Not because he will make the difference there, but because he will be able to ensure that more ships will be captured and we will be able to take a firm grasp of the war in Nium with it."

"Kate's right, but Abysses End doesn't need to know that. So, I think that it would be for the best if I push the limits a bit…"

Alex filled them in on his intentions as he stood and gave Kate, Sam and Nicole kisses before he made his way to log back into ED. As he did so, he just smiled at what he had planned, as he made sure to stop and give Ava and Mia, who were watching the babies, their kisses as well. With that taken care of, it was time for Xeal to put everything on the line as he once more entered the world of Eternal Dominion.

From the moment Xeal awoke it was go-time, as he quickly transferred not to the Huáng empire, but to the Zapladal Theocracy. From there Xeal transferred to Vefreora, where Abysses End had its main power base located in. This included several guild towns that were just starting to take off. However, they were making the same mistake so many other guilds made before reaching tier-7, in the fact that they didn't have any NPC shield mages, or enough shield generators to cover the town. Either of these options were expensive and currently rare. Even Xeal only had six shield mages guarding Hardt Burgh. That was only enough to delay for a few minutes if a major attack was coming and until he could acquire the needed materials for enough shield generators, it was the best that he could do. Even so, a few minutes was enough to at least give the rest of the guard forces time to organize a defense of some sort. Currently, rather than shield mages, or shield generators lining the walls of any town, most guilds went for "the best defense is a strong offense". This had led to them all having many ballistae and other anti-siege weapons lining the walls that would cause mass casualties if anyone tried to attack, but lacked anything to prevent damage to the walls.

As Xeal slipped out of the city he had come to, he smiled as he found himself alone and shifted into his lightning form. His first target for the day was a town that was set up to take advantage of a mine that yielded mainly silver, but also produced a significant amount of mithril. This mine was insignificant to Abysses End's overall finances, but they had also made the other major mistake that guilds were making at this stage. They had made too many normal towns and not enough fort towns, as while having normal towns was by far more profitable to run, forts could actually defend a resource with a small force to maintain it. The main buildings were also normally far more sturdy as they were made of stone and prioritized sturdiness rather than aesthetics. It was from about half a mile in the air that Xeal now looked down on one such building, as Abysses End's guild hall was just sitting there ready to be attacked. The lightning rods that Xeal could see all over it just made him smile as he let loose a 90% charge attack as he converted his MP into an electrical attack.

In the next few seconds, Xeal controlled this blast to cause the building to catch on fire as the players below started using water spells to put the fire out. Xeal just smiled as he saw the fire winning, and flash stepped away to a deserted area as he focused on recovering his MP pool using his aura control skill to speed the process up. With what Xeal had planned for the day, it was necessary to be patient as acting rashly would only cause more issues since he needed to let Abysses End respond.

As Xeal was recovering, Kate was hard at work as she prepped Xeal's next move while monitoring Abysses End's response, as she knew that he would act based off her directions for his next move. If she didn't do her job not only could an opportunity be lost, but Xeal could walk into a trap. So far it looked like Abysses End was content to ignore the attack, as it had only destroyed a single guild hall that was easy enough to rebuild and was only of minor significance. Rather, they just told all other guild towns to be on the lookout as they knew Xeal would be attacking in around 40 minutes if he held to his normal pattern.

40 minutes later, Kate sent Xeal a list of 15 targets as he smiled before shifting to his lightning form and attacking the first one on the list. As he let out a 99% blast before flash stepping away and drinking five years' worth of the waters of youth, Xeal just smiled bitterly. While this recovered his stats to full and gave him a month where it would only take 30 minutes to recover his stats when meditating, it was still pouring gold down the drain. Still, he drank it and attacked the next target as he kept drinking more of the waters of youth between each attack, as one guild hall after another fell. A few of which were even in NPC towns that were similarly lacking any barrier mages, as he just thought about how this was going to shift Abysses End's calculations.

When Xeal was done with the last of these hits, he sat down once more as he started to work on recovering. Though drinking 70 years' worth of the waters of youth had really had an excellent effect, as now he would have 14 months of reducing his recovery time by 25%. As much as Xeal would have liked to see each bottle reduce his recovery time by 25% more and the effects to only last a month, as at that point he would recover in under two minutes, he knew that ED's main system wasn't that nice. Still, as he now only needed half the base time that a player needed to recover, between the boost and his aura control skill he would be able to increase his efforts on all fronts while these effects lasted. Additionally, Xeal had gained a 25-point boost to his constitution from the stacked effects of drinking the waters of youth that would last the next six months.

Meanwhile, while Xeal was thinking about this, Abysses End was in disarray as they tried to figure out what Xeal had done. While they knew that there were some high-priced potions that would recover one's MP, or any other stat, they wouldn't have allowed this to occur. No, at best such items would have let Xeal carry out two or three of the attacks that he did, as they had a cooldown period that restricted just how much a player could use them. While the commonly used ones only sped recovery up by at most 25% for an hour and could only stack timewise not percentage wise. This made them sure that one of two things was occurring and both terrified them. Either FAE had created a new item that got around this, or they had more than just Xeal with the lightning form skill. Either way, it destroyed their plans as they realized that it was too late for Paidhia's fleet to escape and they couldn't risk the other tactic that they had ready if Xeal could ignore the normal recovery time needed. If it was just more players with his skill, they could actually prove useful as it would increase the odds of catching or killing one to prove that it could be done. Still, with only hours, Abysses End knew better than to bet on which it was as they scrambled to figure out what move they would make.

As they did this, Xeal returned to Nium and waited to get word that the naval battle was beginning, or of whatever Abysses End's next move would be as he looked over the reports. Apparently there was already a 10,000-credit reward to anyone who knew how Xeal had pulled it off and he wondered how long it would take for them to realize that it was the waters of youth. He was even tempted to collect it himself just for the fun of it, but he knew that proving it would take time that he didn't have, while also requiring him to part with more of it. From a cost perspective it was an idiot's deal, as just five years' worth was already worth way more than 10,000 credits. Though, just how much more was debatable, as the market price had yet to be determined, but if Xeal was to guess, it would be about five to ten times as valuable. Still, the 700,000 credits or more that it had cost Xeal was well worth it just for the improved recovery time alone, even without taking into account the 14 extra attacks that had each caused at least 50,000 credits in damages to Abysses End.

As time passed, Xeal smiled as he looked at the map around the port that Paidhia had launched their fleet from, as his own began to close in. If they won this battle and captured enough of the enemy fleet, it would open half of Paidhia's coast to be invaded. This was due to the peninsula that separated the capital's port from the area being a large enough barrier to make naval support impractical. Though Xeal's intent was to push right on through and take control of the entirety of the sea, save for the area near Paidhia's capital, as that costal city would likely require sea, air and land-based attacks to capture it.

It was while Xeal was still looking over reports that he received the message from Ihyi that they were quickly closing in on the fleet and the battle was imminent. With that, Xeal made his way to Anelqua, where he shifted to his lightning form and shot high into the sky. From this vantage point even his enhanced senses couldn't make anything in detail out, besides the large terrain features and there happened to be heavy cloud cover over the sea today, making his task even harder than it would have been on a normal day. Still, about 15 seconds and ten flash steps later, Xeal was watching as the battle unfolded beneath him.

The illusions that Daisy and Violet were creating were focused on making it seem as if FAE's fleet had twice as many ships in it. At the same time, it seemed that the nearest ship was being targeted by the five ex-pirate captains, as the sailors were fighting what Xeal assumed were phantom flames and many were already jumping overboard. This was where Xeal came in as he flash stepped, ending his lightning form while activating his quick equip skill. With his feet firmly planted on the deck of the ship, Xeal started to throw the remaining sailors overboard one after another. Smiling, Xeal made his way to the helm and directed the ship such that it broke formation and would soon be in range of one of the many smaller ships that were essentially only there to capture these bigger ones. It was at this point that it was clear to the other ships in Paidhia's fleet that something was amiss, as Xeal shifted back to his lightning form and the other ships were targeted by the ex-pirate captains' illusions.

Xeal quickly moved from one deck to the next, as he focused on removing whoever was manning the helm of each ship while they frantically fought a phantom battle. Xeal could tell that the real battle was just starting, as real cannon fire sounded as the magic-powered cannons sounded off. Still, Xeal ignored this as he focused on improving the odds of each ship being captured, prioritizing his role of hindering the ability of each ship to be commanded efficiently. While more than one of the ships he had tossed the helmsman overboard of had a replacement take the helm, they were the exception. Still, this was a naval battle that involved over 200 ships, as the 70 that made up almost all of FAE's fleet faced the 130 of Paidhia. Were you to look at the fleet and ship sizes you would instantly give the advantage to Paidhia, but once you added in the lack of tier-8 entities on Paidhia's side it was a much closer contest. Still, with 40 of the ships on FAE's side only being valuable in capturing the ships that were caught up in the illusions, it was an uphill battle. One which was at least part thanks to the 40 ships that came from the maritime players of Paidhia, as their participation had exceeded estimates and Xeal expected that Abysses End had a hand to play in that.

These 40 had also caused FAE to overestimate how much of Paidhia's navy was present, as it was only around half rather than the three quarters like FAE had originally thought. This would add to the difficulties in capturing the shorelines on the other side of the peninsula, but FAE needed to win this battle before it could worry about that. As such, Xeal remained focused on clearing the decks of as many ships as he could. Though after Xeal cleared his 20th ship, he was running low on MP and decided that it was time to withdraw as he pulled back to the Siren's Revenge. As he landed and dropped his lightning form, he smiled at seeing Ihyi ordering around her crew and directing the other ships, as the five ex-pirates sat in a circle with Daisy and Violet in their center. As Xeal was taking in the scene, Ihyi took note of his presence as she called out to him.

"Xeal, at the rate we are going we are going to run out of men to crew ships before the day is over."

"That is what happens when an extra 30 ships show up for the party. You don't want me to do a bit of recruiting, do you?"

"No, I am just waiting for them to start sending illusions our way."

"Not going to happen. They know that it will be seen through in seconds with the seven of them on our side. Especially as I doubt they even have a single tier-7 caster with a focus on illusions, as it isn't typical for them to reach tier-7 at all."

"You mean that I don't get to play around with the wind to discover which ones are real and which ones are fake?"

"Afraid not, but you still get to ensure that the wind always favors your fleet and that should already be enough. Now, I need to recover before this fight really picks up and ships start sinking."

"Alright, I will bug you if I need you for something urgent."

Xeal just smiled as he sat down and saw that three ships had already been captured in the short bit that he had been here and another six more were in the process of being captured as well. Xeal's last thought before closing his eyes was of how it was going to be a long battle. Still, the opening exchange was such that things were looking favorable. Though, he knew that each of the ex-pirate captains were having to pick and choose their targets to maintain their MP, and Daisy and Violet's illusion would likely only last for the first hour of the battle.

As Xeal just let all of this float away as he focused on the gentle movements of the ship and tuned out everything else, he put the status of the battle to the side. Instead, in his mind he was reliving each and every move he had made while assaulting the decks of the enemy ships and how he could improve his efficiency. With the vast majority of the enemy crews being spellcasters of one type or another, throwing them overboard was easy but time consuming, especially with the lack of tier-7s. At most each ship only had three tier-7s on them and most only had a single one, with the player fleet likely to not even have any. Were it not for the half second it took for his quick equip skill to activate, and just under 40% of his strength stat and a third of his dexterity stat coming from his gear, things would be easy. Then he could just constantly shift between his lightning form and physical one to clear each ship's deck in a flash. As things were, he had been going from one group to another as he reequipped and started to toss them overboard and he thought of trying to use electrical blasts to send them flying, but it made no sense to do so. This was due to the MP costs and the fact that spellcasters were more likely to have a skill, or ability, to block his attempt to do so.

In the end, Xeal just sighed as he opened his eyes once he had fully recovered and looked over at Ihyi, who was still shouting commands out as the nine ships that had been captured at this point focused on withdrawing, as they only had enough crew to sail and not fight. Xeal could see the smaller ships that had carried the boarding parties heading to the rear of the fleet where a few larger cargo-style ships were. Only the cargo this time was more boarding parties, as the 20 of them created a situation where FAE was ready to capture a full 100 ships without having to break up any of the crews that were part of the other 30 ships. Though for a full victory this time, Xeal knew that they would need to do just that, as he pulled out seven bottles with about five years' worth of the waters of youth in them and walked over to the seven that were maintaining the illusions.

"This battle is going to need to continue much longer than we would like and I know none of you can speak to me while maintaining your spells, but drink these when your MP pool is about to empty."

As Xeal placed one bottle in each of their hands, Daisy and Violet gave him a knowing look while the other five looked at him in shock. Though, that was the extent of their reactions as he turned to begin his second assault, when he received a message that all five nations at war with the Huáng empire had launched their airships. According to the report, there were only two hours before the first of the five fleets would reach the battlefields there and the Huáng empire only had a large enough fleet to fully counter three of them. Xeal felt a headache coming on as he shifted to his lightning form and returned to clearing the decks of the ships under the illusions of the five ex-pirate captains.

An hour and a half later, the battle had progressed to absolute chaos as the illusions had ended and the exchange of cannon fire had become common. Though 50 ships had been captured before it reached this state and another dozen or so had been disabled, or started to flee on the enemy side. The issue was that half of the boarding ships had also been sunk and five of the attack fleet had needed to withdraw, or risk sinking. As things stood, the enemy had around 68 ships still in the fight while FAE only had 55, with only 25 being able to exchange attacks effectively. Though the crews of the five ships that were retreating would soon board one of the captured vessels and rejoin the fight. Meanwhile, the poor souls in the water were constantly trying to find their way back on to ships and return to the fight.

Seeing all of this, Xeal sighed as he drank another bottle of the waters of youth and completely restored his stats one more time, as he set his eyes on the flagship of the enemy fleet. He knew that he needed to leave after this final push, as he would have just minutes to act when he arrived in the Huáng empire and he would need to move quickly once there. With that in mind, Xeal handed over another five bottles to the ex-pirate captains, and smiled as they drank them and readied their next move. With that, Xeal activated his lightning form and flash stepped onto the deck of the flagship, as he let out a wave of electricity in every direction while using 75% of his total MP pool. Only a half dozen individuals managed to react in time and avoid being sent flying into the water, dead or alive, as Xeal returned to his physical form and reequipped his gear.

Xeal wasted no time in charging at the nearest of these enemies, as it was only a tier-6 spellcaster who was holding onto the railing after having his force shield fail and almost going overboard. One sweep of the legs plus a push, and Xeal had corrected this and reduced the number of foes to five. Though all five of them were standing next to the helm, with three of them being tier-7, all of whom were over level 270, one of which was the level 279 admiral of the fleet, who was looking at Xeal in rage. As one of the tier-6s manned the helm and the other moved in front of it while taking a defensive stance, the three tier-7 combatants moved to engage Xeal. Xeal knew better than to take them all head on, as while he might have the stats to go toe to toe with one of them, he would be at a complete disadvantage at three on one. Especially with the crew from below hurrying on to the deck to man the sails and fight him if necessary. Yet Xeal couldn't just retreat, as to do so would be to have wasted his opening move, so he spoke while dodging instead.

"Surrender and I promise that we will rescue all those we can and you will be treated humanely while in Nium's custody."

"Ha, we have outlasted your damn illusionist and the tide of the battle is in our favor now!" retorted the admiral responsible for the command of the whole fleet.

"Only death awaits you if you continue this battle. Your own ships will be used against you soon enough!"

"Even so, your fleet will be destroyed here today. While Nium's fleet may be able to still gain control of this area, it will not be able to quickly expand its control."

"Ha, my fleet will leave this battle over 100 ships strong and there is nothing that you can do about it."

To the side Xeal just watched as the three tier-7s fought what could only be seen by them, as he had slipped out of the three's range right away and what they were fighting was nothing but an illusion. One that only the three of them could see as Xeal went to work tossing one tier-6 after another overboard, having already taken care of the two next to the helm and altered the ship's course. With this, he spent the next ten minutes dealing with the lower decks, as none of those still onboard were even worth his time and it wasn't long before he had them all restrained and under control. As such, the boarding vessel approached uncontested and with about five minutes left before Xeal absolutely needed to be on his way, all that was left was to deal with the three tier-7s.

Sighing, Xeal pulled out an item similar to what he had used to capture individuals before, only this one had properties that would greatly weaken them as well. Each of them had cost 100 gold and were a single-use item that would become manacles after it was used. Luckily, those manacles could be reused and had the same effect, only they were ineffective until both hands, or legs were secured and putting them on mid-battle was not a simple task. Still, they were well worth keeping from having to deal with these three tier-7s, and a minute later all three were restrained and looking confused as Xeal handed the ship over to the boarding team.

Xeal took one last look at the chaos of the rest of Paidhia's fleet, which seemed to be unaware that their flagship had even fallen thanks to Daisy and Violet's illusions. Still, the battle was far from being over as he activated his lightning form and returned to Anelqua by using Queen Aila Lorafir's palace's main tower as his land mark. Upon arriving, he didn't even take the time to greet anyone as Xeal wasted no time in heading for the Huáng empire while checking on the current situation there. As things currently stood, it looked like all of the fleets had slowed their flight, save for the one that was farthest away and were still an hour out. At the same time, the Huáng empire's fleet had been split in five at Kate's direction and were headed on a collision course with all five enemy fleets. Xeal knew that this would result in nothing more than a stall tactic as things were, but knew that it was his job to fix that.

As Xeal arrived in the Huáng empire, he was met by Kate and pulled into a side room. Before Xeal could even give her a kiss, or say hello, she was instructing him to all but empty his inventory as she directed him to the items in the room for him to use. This included all kinds of mines and several extremely dense spike-shaped items, that were about twice the size of his head, but weighed over 500 pounds each. The 60 of them that were present were all that his guild had been able to make with the resources that the Huáng empire had been able to provide. Still, Xeal could only handle 12 of these at a time if he had nothing else on him. With 30 airships heading to battle, even if he managed a one-hit one-kill ratio, it would result in needing three round trips. Though he knew that he would need more than that as at best it would take two to disable any airship and that was if they both hit. Xeal ended up with ten of them in his inventory, with the rest of the weight limit being occupied by other items that would be useful, especially the remote void mines that his guild had created. These were the same items that he had used on the forts between Habia and Paidhia to open up a hole in their defenses and once placed would hopefully inflict a decisive blow.

Xeal just looked at Kate after he was reequipped, as he gave her a quick kiss before heading out of the palace and out onto a balcony. He knew that to succeed today he needed to down, or disable at least two airships per enemy fleet, preferably three, else the odds would only be even at best. Still, Xeal was terrified of if he would even have the ability to do so, as he needed to wait until all five battlefields were entangled to move. Any sooner would likely lead to just driving them off, if he was even able to find them as they would be little more than dots to him once he was airborne. It was for this reason that he needed them to be in battle, as the flashes that the midair combat would create would be his beacon. As Xeal looked out at the city, which was lively despite the current situation that was playing out, Emperor Huáng Jin came out and stood next to him on the balcony and started to speak.

"Today will be the decisive moment. Should our airships fall and the enemies' not, we will only be able to fight within the cities."

"Yet if they all fall and you even have a few airships remaining, you will be able to conquer them all, even if it is only one at a time, agreed Xeal."

"I will be happy with each of them losing four and having at least seven of ours remaining."

"Enough that they would fear doing more than protecting their borders and enough that you could still overwhelm them one at a time."

"I want to win," stated Emperor Huáng Jin. "But I suppose that so long as the day ends with my fleet retaining at least five airships, it would be fine if none of them had more than two."

"You don't see them attempting to combine their airship fleets at that point and trying to overwhelm your remaining five?" asked Xeal, sounding worried about such a possibility.

Emperor Huáng Jin paused as he gave such a possibility a second thought before he responded.

"They could, but they would have to risk losing the ability to defend themselves from each other once this war ends."

"Either way, I have my work cut out for me. How have you and Bīng been getting along?"

"I think I know a bit of what it was like to be one of my concubines now," replied Emperor Huáng Jin with a sigh. "Now that she is with child, her only interest in me is that I deliver her updates on the situation. She fits her element quite nicely and I just hope that the same disposition is not passed down to our child."

"As do I, else it will be hard to explain why none of my children have an interest in yours to her," quipped Xeal.

Like that Xeal and Emperor Huáng Jin caught up as time passed, until the members of FAE on each Huáng empire airship started to report that they could see the enemy forces. As Xeal stood, he sighed and Emperor Huáng Jin grew quiet as Xeal activated his lightning form and headed towards the first battlefield. Even with the flashes and his advanced senses, it took Xeal a few minutes to find the clash of airships while he positioned himself high in the sky above the battle. With one last second to prepare mentally for what he was about to do, Xeal shifted to his physical form. As he started to hurtle towards the ground, he equipped his armor and pulled out the first of the 500-pound spikes and used all of his strength to send it hurtling towards an enemy airship. The moment he had released it, he pulled out a second one and sent it after the first as he continued to fall.

By this point, Xeal had been seen and more than one attack was being aimed at him and the spikes, but an airship's weapons were made for large targets, not three small ones. As such, Xeal just smiled as the first spike impacted on the airship's shield, weakening it while the second one pierced through it. Xeal took note of how the second one had also lost all momentum as it fell onto the deck of the ship, as he shifted to his lightning form and flash stepped onto one of the engines that allowed thrust. Once there, it was back to his physical form as he placed the void mine on it and jumped off before activating the mine mid-freefall. With the thrust on the right side gone, the ship started to turn to the right and make a circle in the sky as it lost its ability to contribute to the battle effectively.

As Xeal saw this, he returned to the sky using his lightning form and repeated this action, only on the second and third ships he used four spikes. This was due to the desire to ensure that the Huáng empire's fleet gained the advantage as quickly as possible and on each of them Xeal aimed at a different critical component with the void mine. Were he to pick the same target repeatedly he would be countered easily, as all it would take was a force shield around his target and a focused attack and he would find the results difficult to handle. Still, he was able to affect the steering on all three ships that he targeted, as he sent two of them crashing into each other. This turned the battle into a four on four, with the Huáng empire having a slight advantage due to one of the enemy's limited maneuverability. While it was still able to steer somewhat due to mages using a spell to create drag to counter the lack of propulsion on one side, it was killing the ship's speed in doing so.

With that completed, Xeal returned to the capital and refilled his inventory with the spikes, as he repeated this action on four other battlefields, needing to use yet another bottle of the waters of youth as he did so. Still, he was able to hinder at least two ships in each battle, as he returned to the capital once more and looked at the ten remaining spikes that were far more expensive to make than they looked. While each of them was formed around an extremely heavy and densely packed rock, the shells were made out of adamantium. Just to make the 60 that had been here had used up the entire strategic stores of it that the Huáng empire had in reserve. As expensive as it was to make them, it was the only option that made any sense either, as other materials would distort too much under the force that they were being put through. This would have drastically lowered the force they were able to focus on a single point as they acted to break through the airships' shields. Had they used 500-pound logs, it would have likely taken around six just to break through the shields, even if they could somehow get them up in the sky and even then they would have been easier targets to destroy.

With the ten spikes loaded up, Xeal paused before he set out as he waited to see which battlefield needed him, as none of them were hopeless struggles at this point. So long as Xeal arrived while there were still two Huáng empire airships remaining, he knew that he would be able to take care of the weakened enemy. At the same time, he was reading the report on the status of the naval battle as he weighed his options, as the void mines he had on him could also quickly sink, or disable, most ships. Though, Xeal would need to be careful when placing them as they were delicate instruments and coming in contact with the water would be enough to disable them. As Xeal was thinking about this, he just smiled at reading the report as while it was clear that the battle was far from won, over 70 ships had been captured. Still, five of the boarding ships were all that was left, and when all of the disabled and sunken ships were accounted for, Paidhia had 45 ships in the fight while FAE only had 18 of their original 30 combat-focused ships left. Still, the 20 cargo-style ships were quickly becoming prison and rescue ships, as they fished both sides' forces out of the sea and the captured ships were being pressed into service. Though only 12 of them were currently active, making the fight essentially 30 on 45, as the balance slowly tipped in FAE's favor.

Like this Xeal passed the time over the following hour as he watched the number of airships and ships drop one by one. When it became two-on-four in one of the air battles after two hours of battle, Xeal finally made a move as he activated lightning form and flash stepped back to that battle, prepared to engage all four enemy ships if needed. When he arrived, Xeal took in the situation as all six airships were damaged, and their shields were going in and out as they struggled to protect their crucial components. Xeal sighed as he shifted to his physical form and reequipped his gear once again, while pulling out one spike and started to fall while holding on to it. Due to the state of the battle, Xeal knew that he would need to time things carefully as he quickly grew closer to the first enemy ship and when he was about 100 feet above it Xeal threw the spike. At the same moment, he shifted to his lightning form and flash stepped to the side, as he saw the spike pierce right through the shield and through the deck of the ship and out the bottom.

Seeing that ship starting to lose altitude, Xeal smiled as he repeated his attack on his second target with a similar result, except it was intercepted by a mage's force shield that broke instantly. Thus it failed to pierce all the way, but the ship was still losing altitude. Unfortunately, one of the Huáng empire's took a hit at the same time and started to go down as the battle became a one-on-two match. Thankfully, Xeal was able to finish off the other two with one more spike each, as he returned to the Huáng empire's capital and checked the current situation at the other four battles. One of them had the Huáng empire with two on two, while the rest were three on two, as Xeal looked at the six spikes he had left and sighed. Making a snap decision, Xeal visited all three battles where it was three on two and was able to make two of them two-on-one in the Huáng empire's favor, while the last became a one on one that could go either way.

Out of spikes and with little MP left, Xeal just hoped for the best as he once more returned to checking on the naval battle. It seemed that something had happened as while no new ships had sunk, it seemed that Ihyi had ordered all of the captured ships to withdraw, along with almost all of the cargo ships. All that remained were the 12 ships of the original combat fleet that were still fit for battle, the two remaining boarding vessels and one cargo vessel. While the other side was still at 18 ships, sighing, Xeal made his way back to Anelqua and quickly headed to the area where the naval battle was raging.

Upon arriving, Xeal could see that the captured fleet and cargo ships were a good five miles out from the battle, and the sea around the battle was full of sinking and half-sunk ships that were limping along. Besides the Siren's Revenge and the four ex-pirate ships, Xeal doubted that any of the other ships left on his side's combat fleet would survive the day though a few of them still had a chance to make it. Beyond that Xeal could see the scars on the Siren's Revenge that would have sunk a lesser ship. Yet the double hull that utilized an iron plate four inches inside of the wood had done its job, though the outer hull would need to be repaired before it fought in another battle. Xeal just wished he could have seen the several other surprises that the ship held and had likely used while he was away. Especially the enchantment that would allow it to dip below the waves and reemerge after reaching the optimal position. Even if it required a massive amount of MP from its crew to use it, it was a real trump card that Xeal had been happy to plant the idea into a few enchanters' heads after hearing about it in his last life.

On the other side, they had six ships that were also about to sink, but the rest were going strong and it was becoming a situation where every ship was engaged in a battle to the death. However, it was nine one-on-ones and three three-on-one battles, as Paidhia focused on creating a cascading situation where they could overwhelm FAE's remaining fleet. The only ship that had a clear advantage on FAE's side was the Siren's Revenge, as it was trying to deal with its opponent and aid the other 11 remaining ships. Still, even it had suffered major damage as one of its masts had been lost and the sails on the other four had seen better days.

It was in this situation that Xeal landed on the Siren's Revenge, as Ihyi was shouting out orders left and right. Xeal saw Daisy and Violet resting as they tried to recover their MP, while the five ex-pirate captains looked like they were at the end of their rope as they focused on maintaining their illusions. It was clear that escape was the right move for FAE's fleet, but the 100 retreating ships that were already escaping would be caught. Xeal knew the issue right away as he surveyed the signs that a boarding party had tried to take the ship. They had simply run out of manpower and even with Ihyi ensuring that the wind favored FAE's fleet, the other side would catch up and without a force to man the cannons or thrusters, they were all easy prey. Xeal made his way over to Daisy and Violet with these thoughts as he began talking to them.

"How bad is it?"

"Xeal!" exclaimed Daisy as she stood up and hugged him. "You made it back!"

"Yes, now I think I already know, but how did it get this bad?"

"We ran out of forces," stated Violet. "While our enemy was able to gain reinforcements from the sea. Our boarding parties focused on securing the ships and too many enemies were able to escape into the ocean rather than being killed, or detained. Though now that you are here you will fix this situation, right?"

"Hopefully, but I think it is going to cost us more ships. Ihyi! Call for a full withdrawal!"

Xeal just smiled as Ihyi finally took note of his presence and she smiled as she signaled for all ships to turn tail and run. Just like that, it became a chase where each ship only had to deal with a few attacks, as the enemy started to try and run them down. The three three-on-one battles were a lost cause already, so Xeal turned his attention to the other nine pursuers. He moved from one ship to the next, as he shifted in and out of his lightning form and targeting the helm on each ship, as he destroyed them using void mines. Like that all nine lost the ability to steer easily and with it they failed to be able to keep up. At the same time, the other three ships that were being pursued received Ihyi's order to surrender as they gave up. That tied up three of the remaining nine pursuers, as the other six altered their course to aim at the cargo ship, which was the slowest of the remaining fleet. Still, it would be at least a half-hour before they could catch it. As such, Xeal entered meditation to restore his stats.

When Xeal's stats were full, it was obvious that the enemy only intended to capture the cargo ship and allow the rest of them to escape. It was clear that they were taking the minor victory of driving them off. If Xeal had to guess, they hoped that it would buy them enough time and goodwill to restore at least part of their fleet in the 60 or so salvageable ships that were floating around. Many of these were manned by FAE's members, who were currently stranded and unable to effectively resist being captured without sinking their ships. Still, Xeal had no intent to even let them enjoy the belief that they had won the day, as he gave Ihyi a nod and she ordered the nine remaining ships to turn around and return to the fight. At the same time, Xeal entered his lightning form and flash stepped onto the ship closest to the cargo ship before returning to his physical form.

Xeal just smiled as he drew both of his swords the moment his reequip was finished and started in on the crew that was made up almost completely of players and lacked any tier-7s. The gap between Xeal and the crew was so wide that it was hardly even a struggle, as he cleared the deck and steered the ship into the path of another one, and he made his way on to the next one as they turned to try and escape. What followed was one quick battle after another, as the following two hours saw the rest of Paidhia's fleet fall as the cargo ships returned and Xeal left just as the salvaging work began.

As he arrived back in Anelqua, Xeal just sat down and breathed as he thought over the situation. He knew that Nium's navy would take over the area as it would likely take two months before the heavily damaged ships would limp back into Anelqua's port. The losses that were sustained on both sides would cripple Paidhia, but rather than the two months that Xeal had hoped to take to be ready for the next naval major battle, it would likely be six. At the same time, he knew that he needed to cut that time down, as he sent Taya orders to send all available tier-5 and up players on any ship that they could hire to rendezvous with Ihyi's fleet. If they could combine these players with the players who would be reviving in Nium after dying in the battle over the next few days, it would allow them to man all the ships that were in fighting shape. At same time, FAE could plan a naval strike against Paidhia in three to four months and hopefully win another victory. At that point, if they still had a decent-sized fleet, it would be possible to secure almost the entire coastline of Paidhia for possible invasion points. The ability to raid and plunder port towns would also generate plenty of funds to secure FAE's finances.

After Xeal sent his message, he once more checked the status of the airship battles and sighed as he saw the results. The Huáng empire only had three airships left while their enemies had two and they were all headed to clash with each other as it felt like the day that would never end, and Xeal returned to that battle. Five hours later, Xeal could only sigh as his efforts had only allowed two of the Huáng empire's airships to survive and they would need extensive repairs before they were ready to face a city's defenses. At the same time, the ground battle had shifted to recovering the 48 wrecks, as any components that were still functional could quickly be used to get another airship in the sky. Both sides knew that the winner of this struggle would gain a major advantage and the Huáng empire could only dominate two of the six battlefields, as the other four would be without air support.

Though it would take others at least half a day to reach any of the wrecks, so the very crews of each ship were the ones most likely to salvage the goods. The key was to either protect your side's crew, or capture the other side's crew when possible. However, there was an exception that came in the form of Xeal and he just smiled as he set up a teleportation gate at each site, as FAE's tier-6 and tier-7 members flooded the area. What followed had been FAE salvaging enough components to construct ten complete airships and six partial ones, as 85% of all usable materials had been stripped before others arrived. 40 of the 60 spikes had also been retrieved that were more or less undamaged and could be used right away if needed. FAE had also rescued, or captured, the survivors of the downed airships and all five other nations had already begun sending forward delegations for peace.

Xeal just hoped that the talks wouldn't drag on, as peace in the Huáng empire would allow him to shift focus to the Muthia empire. Under Takeshi's leadership, FAE's forces had allowed Muthia to not lose any significant amount of territory and they were still holding on to the slime dungeon area that they had captured. However, the losses and costs were starting to pile up. Even if it would still be months before things became strained, Xeal hated even approaching that point. Also, like with the Huáng empire, FAE's goals in Muthia had little to do with territorial expansion in the current war. So it was that day 261 turned into a massive administrative day for Xeal. Though with both battles tipping in his favor and having reached level 206 at some point in the chaos, Xeal was in a rather good mood as he did so. This included finishing the prep for the high school presentation, that he hadn't finished earlier, due to the interruption of his ED session's sudden start.

(*****)

Morning June 12 to Evening June 17, 2268 & ED Year 6 Days 264-279.

Alex smiled as he stepped out of his VR pod with Kate doing the same, though the other four were already offline. So, after a quick kiss, the two of them made their way to the rental house's living room, where they were all playing with the children. Alex made the rounds as he gave them all hugs and kisses, before sitting down next to Sam and snuggling into her as he wished her a happy birthday. She just smiled as she handed Moyra to him and gave him a quick kiss, before heading to the bathroom to finish getting ready, as the morning to lunch had been set aside for a date. 20 minutes later, Alex just smiled as he bid those in the house farewell, as Stacy acted as their driver for the day.

The first stop of the day was a cozy breakfast diner, where the highlight had been the giant fluffy buttermilk biscuits served with either gravy, or raspberry preserves. Alex and Sam had tried both ways and had agreed that both were great, and it would just depend on the mood they were in. Next, they enjoyed just walking on the local pier and doing a bit of shopping in the tourist trap-style shops that were not far from it. All the while they enjoyed themselves as they talked about everything and nothing all at once, at least until it was time to head to the high school for the last presentation. It was then as they were seated in the middle row of the SUV as Stacy drove, that Sam shifted to a more consequential subject.

"I am done with trying to avoid you in ED. I thought I could handle it, but I can't."

"Alright, I have been thinking the same thing since I

gained access to my lightning form, but I am still worried that one of us might not be able to find the time once in a while."

Alex paused for a second as he tried to find the right words before just sighing and continuing to speak.

"I am not sure how to ask this politely, but did you find a solution to the intimacy issue with Ava and Mia's help?"

"No, it is just way too awkward once you leave the room and I don't know if it would be any less awkward if you were there. Even if it was, that would kind of defeat the purpose, or why we would be exploring it right now. Perhaps things will develop like that one day, but for now I would just say that it is a door that is best left closed from what the three of us discussed. I'm sorry, but while I find myself attracted to both you and them physically, I have no passion, or desire for that kind of intimacy with them on their own at this point. As such, I still want to walk the Odr path, but I can't stand us purposely avoiding each other when we could see each other and enjoy some time together."

"You are asking me to give you a child in ED."

"I will avoid you for Ellis's birthday, but the next time our paths should cross in ED, yes I am asking to be able to remove the need for avoiding each other once and for all."

Alex sighed as he looked from Sam to the ceiling of the SUV as he responded to her.

"Fine. If no other solution can be found before then I will give in, but I am not getting you pregnant in ED before the wedding in reality and holding a ceremony in ED for Kate, Ava and Mia as well."

"Sounds like we need to set things up for you to marry us in reality and them in ED back to back then, because I am not willing to wait any longer than that."

"And here I thought I had already gotten past needing to

hold another spree of weddings. Though I suppose just doing something like I did with Eira might work in ED."

"Better make the one in reality really good then, though they might agree if you add a bit of flair to the one in ED."

"Fair, we are talking about Kate after all. While she won't care about the actual size, she will care about the optics and making sure everyone knows that we are married."

"While Ava and Mia would be fine with a 24-hour chapel wedding, if it was with you."

"No, they would accept it, but it would create issues long term. While I would never say that what Kate has planned for us next month should be the standard, offering a chance for those who care to attend and offer their congratulations is important. Even if no one shows up and it turns into a disaster, putting in the effort matters."

"I think I would feel terrible if no one I invited came to my wedding and I would rather not have held a big event at all if that was the case."

"You would, but it also helps you weed out those who didn't have a good reason to attend from your life. After all, if it is as simple as showing up for them and some emergency didn't cause the issue, are they really worth any effort on your end?"

"No, but sometimes just showing up costs a ton of credits."

"That isn't just showing up, that is having to bear a financial burden to attend. It is why I am happy that we aren't getting married near where we grew up."

"You are just afraid of the whole town wanting to show up for it."

"More or less, though it might be fun to turn away Principal Lee at the gate."

"Fair, there are a few girls who I wouldn't mind doing

that to as well. Still, you are fine with giving into me on the baby in ED then?"

"I am, but you need to talk with Nicole and the others about it as well."

"It's always that way with you. You constantly feel the need to avoid deciding anything in this relationship. Instead, you just push it off to us."

"Sam, I love all of you and even if Nicole or the others don't agree, I have already decided to give you your child. The point is that they will know about it and I have a feeling Nicole will be asking for the same, as at least from where I stand, you all seem to still feel slightly insecure about the nature of our relationship."

"Ha, we are and aren't. None of us think that you would ever cast us aside, but we do worry about fading into the background. It is why we haven't locked you in a room with Daisy and Violet and why I am still looking for a way for you to avoid Bula and Dafasli."

"Do they know that?"

"Yes, along with, Ekaitza, Lughrai, Malgroth, Lumikkei, Lorena, Bianca, Levina and even Freya, as I don't trust her when she says she isn't planning to make a play at you one day. Nicole and I feel like if you embrace any more, the line will just keep growing and you will just keep adding more NPCs as time passes. If we only count your wives, Aila and Austru, you are averaging one a year in ED and well, none of us think that you want 60 wives, even if you don't run away at 20. Now, are we wrong about that?"

"No, but I didn't want a dozen either. It is just hard not to find a reason to love you all once I get to know any of you."

"So should we just set the date for all the others and declare that no others are allowed to get to know you?"

Alex smiled at Sam as she gave him a stern look while

waiting for his answer, as the high school came into view. Finally, as they pulled to a stop and were about to get out, he responded.

"Sam, I will never hold it against the 12 of you if you push a woman away from me, or pull another to me. What matters is that I can love them and they will not upset the harmony of our relationship. I do not see any way that some of those on the list you stated will not disrupt our harmony, even if I can easily see myself falling for them. Furthermore, you are right, and as I have said before, I am done with allowing women to find their way beside me. Beyond the 12 that currently are in even remote consideration, my intent is for no others to even have the time of day."

"I know and you have been doing well at that, as it has been over two years in ED since you picked up Lorena and Bianca. Now, let's go get this last presentation over with."

With that, Alex and Sam left the SUV and made their way to the waiting room, where they found the rest of their group. This included all six of Alex's children, Nicole, Kate, Ava, Mia, Tara, Henry, Anna, Dan, Fred, Amanda and half a dozen of the admin staff from their headquarters, with Harrison Barnes leading them. Additionally, there were security personal and staff members from the school, to include Principal Lee, who quickly greeted Alex as he entered.

"Alex, thank you for ensuring that you have a full team out here today and making time in your busy schedule to personally come."

"But of course. I take it that everything is set up and ready to go?"

"Yes, you are set to have a break when school would normally end for any who wish to leave. After that, it will resume with only those who want to stay afterward."

"Thank you."

"No problem and let me just apologize for being, well, a prude for lack of a better term, about your relationships last year. I am really seeing a different side to things since the hearing you all took part in, and I must say that you are right to want the same legal protections as other forms of marriage have."

Alex held as straight a face as he could, as he thought about how the overall response to the hearing had been positive for his side. The PR campaign that Kate had arranged was spot on as well. It managed to frame it not as an issue of the rich and wealthy, but the middle and lower incomes with the rich mostly opposing it. Now the narrative was still shifting, but from the last thing Alex had seen, the legislation was set to be passed and just waiting to be signed into law by the time Alex returned to Colorado. It was with this thought that Alex replied.

"I appreciate it and hope that it is able to become a reality this time around."

"Yes, well, I will let you get ready and I am looking forward to seeing what you have planned today."

Alex just smiled as Principal Lee released him, and he was able to rejoin Sam and the others as they chatted about the presentation that was about to unfold. This continued as the time ticked down, until it was time for him to head to the stage, where he would give the opening remarks before returning until speaking again just before the break which marked the end of the school day. After that, he would have to speak one more time to close out the whole of the presentation around 4:30p.m., as he was expected to talk for the full half hour until it ended at 5p.m. at that point. Following that, it would be a question-and-answer period that was set to extend until 6p.m. and finally when that was done, it would be time to return to the rental house to celebrate Sam's birthday as a group.

As Alex stepped out onto the stage, he quickly took in the setup as the room was full of the entire student body that just barely fit in the auditorium. Unlike the first time that Alex had been here, there were no obvious groups that seemed to just want to go home as he looked out at them. The next thing that he noticed was the security that was standing off to the sides, such that they wouldn't be recorded, but could quickly respond should anything happen during the presentation. So, as Alex arrived at center stage, he smiled as he took the microphone and started to speak.

"Well, I must say that this room is a bit fuller than I am used to and I am sure that you are all happy to almost have another year past you. Though, with needing to pass your finals next week, I am sure some of you are wishing that you had another week still. Even so, I thank you all for hosting us today and to all of you tuning in elsewhere, don't worry, you're not missing too much by not being physically here.

"Now, on to the reason that we are here…"

Alex spent about five minutes explaining the sequences of events, before he handed the microphone off to Ava and Mia as they smiled while waving Alex off stage. For the next 20 minutes the twins shared their experience when they had been a part of Abysses End, only they just called it a super workshop and left location and other details vague. They also touched on the living conditions that existed outside the States in countries with laxer laws surrounding how many people could live in a single room. As they did this, they focused on highlighting the expenses that workshops were paying to maintain each player and how this created a higher barrier to entry for pro players in countries with higher standards. They closed with a few ways that anyone looking to go pro, but didn't want to get trapped by a contract until they could get a great deal, could help lower the total cost to survive and stay safe and healthy while doing so.

Following them came the first admin team, with Tara taking the lead of three of the six assistants that had come. For their presentation, it became a pitch on how to balance the workload of grinding and administrative work. This had included several digs on Alex for just being so overpowered that he was always fighting things that were at least ten levels above him. When they finished, it was Kate's turn as she smiled as she focused on contracts and basic things to look for in them. This included ensuring that it was completely valid to have an in-game contract require that a contract in reality be made to back it up and that any part that was voided in reality was voided in Eternal Dominion. It had been this line that Alex had credited with the fact that so far Congress had yet to act on regulating the in-game contract system, since the hearing on it had concluded.

Like that the first hour passed as Sam and Nicole made their way out to the stage, as they talked about the magic systems of ED. This included a warning that they all needed to do their research as ED didn't pull any punches when it came to what players would need to experience. This included things like a blood mage being extremely powerful, but requiring players to disable pain reduction and inflict harm upon themselves regularly as they mutilated their own body. While that was a rather graphic example of what could be expected, it was not out of the norm as while the system would warn players about many things, it would wait until it was required at times. Many restarts had been in response to just this as oracles learned about the blindness requirements, clerics moved into the higher ranks of the clergy and were expected to perform rituals that were unsettling, and more. With FAE having reached the point where its members had begun to reach tier-7 in significant number, which was when many of the big ones were revealed, Alex saw it as a safe time to let the world know.

Once Sam and Nicole were done, Fred and Amanda got on stage and presented on the tier-7 tribulation itself. Though what they gave was a watered-down version of what to expect and how long it would take, it was still beyond valuable to anyone who was paying attention. This was largely due to the details like how many players failed from not keeping their mouths shut while offline and the existence of Demonic mode. While many NPCs knew about the advanced mode, few would share it with players as it was taboo to do so out of fear that they would create their own traumas. Alex had known more than one pro player who was determined to face Demonic mode and had gone as far as getting raped by demons to be able to challenge it. This trend hadn't lasted long as not only did many such players never recover psychologically, but they also almost never succeeded in completing Demonic mode. In fact, if any had, Alex had never heard of them. Even with some of FAE's members being able to challenge it, Alex had cautioned them against it as besides himself, only Amser, Takeshi and a few others who were marked by the phoenixes had passed. The only reason Alex was fine allowing NPCs who could challenge it do so, was the fact that they were simply better equipped to do so. It wasn't the same as getting past the tier-5 trial on Nightmare mode, as the main element of the tribulations were to overcome one's own weaknesses and NPCs were almost geared to do exactly that. At least once they had enough interactions with players to begin to truly become something more than they were when the main system was still in control of them.

Once Fred and Amanda were done, it was time for Alex to close out the first half, as he handed his daughter Nova to Anna and made his way back out. As he looked out at the crowd, he could see that Fred and Amanda had done their job well, as it didn't seem like any were about to fall asleep on him. With it being a Friday, he was actually curious about how many would be staying and how many would run the moment the final bell rang, regardless of if he was done or not. So, with a smirk, Alex started to speak.

"Now, I am sure that at least some of you would rather get a head start on your weekend than listen to me. So, Principal Lee, if you would be so kind as to open the doors and let any who wish to leave now do so, as I might run over slightly and I would hate to keep anyone from their weekend."

After a moment of hesitation, the two main exits were opened and around ten percent of those who were present left and just as the last of them were about out of the doors, Alex continued.

"Now to all of you who stayed I am sorry, but you have signed up to stay until the break, even if I go ten or so minutes over. If you can't do that, please hurry and join the others leaving."

Alex watched as another 100 or so left and the doors were closed once more and he started into his presentation.

"Now that we have that out of the way, I will say this. The first group that left I respect as they knew what they wanted and acted decisively. The second group hesitated and needed another push, and then we have all of you who have stayed to listen to me prattle on about the decisions of others. That said, I don't look at those who remained as a single group. No, you are more like several groups. One that really wants to hear what I have to say, another that doesn't want to be seen as lazy by those around you and even one that just has nothing better to do. There are many more groups that I could break you into, but if you found yourself hesitating to stay, or leave, this next part is for you.

"Eternal Dominion is a world that punishes hesitation and rewards decisiveness, at least for those that are successful, as when you walk down a doomed path, being decisive will only increase your losses. Yet to hesitate will ensure that you never rise above the middle of the pack and reach tier-7. I have it on good authority that the majority of players have the capacity to reach tier-7, but lack the will, or drive, to make it happen. That is what I will be speaking on in this portion, finding the will to stand and become more than you believe that you can. This will not be a rah-rah speech full of motivation and happy thoughts. Instead, it will be a dark one that may make a few of you wish to run away."

Alex paused as he smiled at the way the room had quieted, as the bit of chatter that had been present during the other presentations was suddenly absent. While sending away those who didn't want to be there had aided him in achieving this, the ominous tone he had delivered the last part with had played well as he continued.

"Now that I have your attention, I wish for you to think of the worst thing that has ever happened to you, or what your greatest fear is and if that is next week's finals, you need to try a little harder. I am talking about you going home to find your parents dead, your house burned down, your life savings gone and much worse. If it isn't something that will make you sit down and at least wish everything was over for at least a few seconds, it is not strong enough, as that is what you need to be able to overcome. Not the actual event, but the fear of it, as only when you are willing to risk everything can those of us not born into riches can typically become truly successful!

"I am not talking about becoming a doctor, or lawyer and having plenty of credits successful, nor am I speaking of having piles of credits like I do. No, I am talking about the success of being able to step forward and pursue your dream and independence from the fetters of those beyond the ones you love and care about. Now, that is not to say that you can, or will succeed, but if you allow fear to hold you, then you will never find true success."

As Alex delivered this line, pictures of various people started to cycle behind him as he moved into the next portion of his presentation. None of those shown looked like they had much and all of them were at least in their mid-thirties.

"All of those you see behind me live within 100 miles of this school and have been interviewed, at least briefly. Many have simply given up and accepted living their life as it is now, be that as a retail worker making just enough to split a small apartment with three others, or sleeping under a bridge. More than a few have dreams, but most have no belief in themselves to be able to achieve them, yet a few were still trying to do just that as they can't help but reach to raise themselves out of their situation. Though, before we move on, I would be remiss if I didn't remind you all that everyone in the pictures you have seen is someone's son, or daughter and many started with much less than any of you. Still, never forget that they have, or had, just as much potential as any of you did when they were born. None of you are special, or chosen. None of us are. It is we who choose ourselves to be the one to step forward and achieve greatness."

As Alex said this, the images shifted to five individuals who looked like professionals who were dressed for a day at the office.

"These five were all once homeless and while they have yet to reach their dreams, they are still striving for it. If you wish to see their stories they can all be found online. Just do a bit of digging for stories of going from being homeless to living normal lives. There are countless of such stories, but the one constant in most of them is not giving up on themselves and not hesitating when they saw an opportunity."

The images changed once more as five individuals that weren't homeless, but weren't far from it, were displayed.

"Now, it is still important to know and manage the risk that you can take on, as these five can attest to the story of going from riches to rags. Taking a reasonable amount of time to gather and process information is not hesitation, it's essential."

Following this, the picture changed to three highly successful individuals.

"These are three who have experience going from rags to riches, back to rags and managed to return to riches once more. Now, I will not lie to you as I simply had all of these photos assembled along with the information that I have shared. If any of you are interested in their stories, all of them have been shared publicly and my team did its best to verify them. As to why I have shared them with you, it is simple. Every single one of their stories have adversities. Some that would make you wish that the worst you would have to deal with was going home to find your parents dead, your house burned down and your life savings gone. I will never claim to have gone through anything close to that, nor do I ever wish to, but for me, seeing them still pressing forward despite that inspires me. It is why I don't complain, I take action. The only one who can defeat you while you still draw breath is yourself. As so long as you keep moving forward, you can rise up and find your success.

"My advice to each and every one of you is to face and embrace the adversity that comes your way, as through it you can be refined and tempered. That way, when the time comes that you go home to find your parents dead, your house burned down, your life savings gone, you actually have a chance to survive it. That doesn't mean that you should seek out harsh forms of adversity, or inflict it upon others, as the world is dark enough as it is. No, picking up a difficult hobby, or skill such as a martial art, or as many of you are about to graduate, scrape together a few thousand credits and try to create a business this summer. Even if you are college bound, you are as likely to fail and lose everything, but in doing so, those few months will likely prepare you more for life after college than anything you experience in college. It is often said that we learn more from our failures than our success, so go out there and fail and do it now, when doing so is still easy to recover from. If you wait until you find yourself with others who are depending on you, well, you may never find the courage to risk their security, even if you would risk your own."

Alex paused as he walked to the edge of the stage as he looked out at students and the camera directly in front of him, to let that point sink in before continuing.

"Now…"

The next 15 minutes was spent on just how decisiveness and resilience would serve them well in Eternal Dominion. This included how they were all at the best point in their lives to take risks and how to ensure that they didn't take a risk that would follow them forever, as certain things like murder were not so easy to recover from. By the end of it, Alex felt like he had tiptoed the line of not being appropriate for high schoolers, but he felt that after having over a year to come up with his final presentation it was the right move. He could still remember his first life where he had seen so many others end up settling without ever really trying, to include himself. He had never tried to build his own guild, or anything, as he had been content to join others and had been in more than one failed guild before landing in Twilight Sky.

While that experience had aided him in building his guild this time around, it still hadn't cured him of the anxiety that came from doing so. Alex still felt that he had made too many mistakes early on, as he looked back and thought over how Kate had increased FAE's efficiency since she had joined the team. While Tara had been doing well, Alex had recruited her based on what he knew she would become and just like Henry, she needed time to develop into that and lacked the experience that Kate had brought. While none of these had been death knells for FAE, had they been addressed from the start, it would be likely that they would have been able to take better advantage of his knowledge.

When Alex's presentation was over and the cameras turned off and he was about to head backstage and the students were getting ready to leave, it happened. Five guys rushed the stage and came at Alex directly, as security was mostly blocked by the students trying to get outside. Though even the two that had a clear path to Alex wouldn't arrive for at least a few seconds after the five guys. Alex only had a split second to decide how to react as they were closing in and he was all that was between them and the backstage area where everyone else was. With the image of his children getting caught up in the chaos of a fight, that made Alex stand his ground rather than escape.

When the idiot one, in Alex's mind, arrived, he was mid-swing as he tried to use his backpack as a weapon. Rather than deflect or dodge the backpack, Alex just stepped forward and hit the arm that was almost vertical with the backpack extended further from the centrifugal force. With that, idiot one lost his grip and the backpack went flying off and Alex controlled him through his arm and sent him into idiot number two, just as idiot three arrived with a PE shirt in his hands. Alex could tell that idiot three wanted him to think his goal was to wrap the shirt around his neck and likely use it as a decoy. However, Alex wasn't going to allow that to occur as instead, Alex made as if he was going to grab the shirt as idiot three smiled and let go of the shirt. That smile was short lived as Alex's palm shot up and idiot three's chin met it, and he lost his footing as idiots four and five hesitated at seeing the result. However, Alex didn't hesitate. He took a few steps back and restored his form, as the first three idiots recovered and got back on their feet.

With the element of surprise lost and Alex having shown them that he wasn't just someone who played video games all the time and couldn't handle himself in a fight, the five idiots seemed unsure what to do. As such, they had already lost as two security guards arrived and Stacy came out from the back, as three more security guards climbed up on top of the stage. With three tasers pointed at the idiots and three more on the way, even the idiots knew that the fight was over as they tried to scatter. Only, three of them got tasered instantly and went down, as the other two got caught by the other security guards a few seconds later.

With the momentary excitement over, Alex just sighed as he saw the crowd of students who had witnessed it and knew that it was going to create a headache and a half. As Alex thought about it, even with the attack doomed to fail from the start, it had been planned well, as the point likely had never been to actually harm him, but to simply create issues. Just thinking of the time that would be spent being questioned by the police officers when they arrived and how possible court dates would only add to his already strained schedule. Not to mention that the officers would likely want to question every student here and gather up all video of the altercation as evidence. Just thinking about the wasted time that this could build up made Alex sigh, as he rejoined the others backstage.

For the remainder of the presentation, Alex found himself sitting in the back room talking to officers as they ran down their list of questions. This included Alex sharing how his known enemy list was longer than he cared for, with Abysses End, the Astors, a local gang that went by The Razors, groups that opposed the polyamory marriage legalization and much more. As Alex listed all of these groups off with Kate's and Stacy's help, he couldn't help but think about just how muddy and digging into who was behind this attack would be. It was just too easy to say that they were motivated by their faith, or other beliefs, for it to be disproven as a motive. Then there would be the fact that this would likely make national headlines, if not international, due to the timing and Alex having more eyes than normal on him. By the time Alex made his way out to the stage once more, he was just ready to have the night over as he gave his closing speech that lasted all of ten minutes.

"… Now, as we bring this eventful night to a close, it is time for the surprise of the night. Just like last year, FAE will be hosting a convention, or perhaps a festival would be a better term, only this time we are hosting over 100 of them worldwide. For more information, all you need do is just read the post that should have just gone live on FAE's official forum. Once there, find the one nearest you and check the dates that it will be held. As for those of you present, it will be held next Friday and Saturday after graduation. Just like last year, all teenagers ages 16 to 19 will be admitted for free along with a parent. Unlike last year, you can still get in if you want to buy a ticket, though you will be let in later and have to pay for certain parts that will be free for all teenagers. I believe last year's was a major success and my hope is that the event will be successful enough to justify doing them at least every other year in most of the selected areas.

"Now, this was supposed to be when the question-and-answer portion began. However, due to the events of the night it has been canceled. However, to all of those present, if you have a question, feel free to write it down and I will answer a few dozen random ones over the next week and post them on FAE's official forum.

"Thank you all for staying over, or tuning in. Now, good night."

With that Alex made his way out of the back exit and into the SUV with Sam and Stacy, as everyone else had left the moment they weren't needed any longer. Everything considered, Alex would call the event a wash as the altercation would likely overshadow everything else. Still, it would also cause the festivals to gain more attention and up the chances of success for them, and Alex would just need to wait and see what the final verdict was.

After returning to the rental home, they went right into celebrating Sam's birthday as a few local friends had joined them for the evening as well. By the time 9PM rolled around, Alex was happy to see everyone off as he and Sam disappeared for a bit of alone time before logging in to ED for the night.

The next five days were uneventful in reality for Alex, aside for the update on the situation surrounding the five idiots and how their cases were being handled. Put simply, they weren't talking and they were all minors with nothing on them besides storming the stage and rushing at Alex. Even if they were convicted, it would only be a year of imprisonment at the most and they would likely just get parole with a community service requirement. This simply annoyed him as he let the district attorney's office know that he would be fine with them giving the five of them a plea deal. Though, he asked that it include them having to sit through the entirety of the video from the five days of hearings that he had had to sit through as a joke.

When Xeal finally returned to ED on day 265, it was once more Eira's birthday and wedding anniversary, and so after he awoke in the morning, he spent the entirety of the day with her. They enjoyed themselves as it wasn't until the evening that they returned to Cielo city and they celebrated with the others. This was followed by Ellis's birthday on day 266, which like with his other children, saw Xeal spending the morning with them before he headed out so Gale could get some time with her in as well. As Xeal met up with Ekaitza for the date, he could tell that she was even more nervous than before, so he released a bit of his aura on her as he had done last time and it seem to help her relax a bit. As this took effect, she started to speak to Xeal as she greeted him.

"Xeal, thank you for inviting me on another-"

"Ekaitza, stop right there. Yes, you are getting a second date, but I must apologize to you and ask that you do something rather cruel."

"So, this is you giving the others a push and not opening yourself up to me."

"Yes, and I am sorry. I promise that I am taking no pleasure in it."

"Yet all of us will understand and accept your choice in doing it. I suppose I need to tell them that you really only desire to get closer to me and finish the spiral."

"No, you are to say that you think that if they are able to unlock and successfully challenge Demonic mode, that I will consider them again. Play it up in a desperate way and make it seem like you are grasping at straws as you do so."

"Tell me, why should I do that to them?"

"What do you want?"

"For you to give us each a single deep kiss when we return triumphant and for me to tell them that you have agreed to it when I tell them."

"What happened to the four of you competing for me and taking pleasure in the others' misfortune?"

"You have let us be around your wives too long. We know that it is unrealistic with what you have said for us all to become one of your wives, but we still hope."

"Would the four of you still be satisfied by just bearing children from me?"

"No, but we would do so happily as we would take that over being discarded and never even having a chance to embrace you."

"I will have to think on that. Though I will promise you the kisses so long as all four of you succeed and get at least a B-ranked result, as I would actually be surprised at that point."

"Better get some practice holding your breath, as the four of us are going to take full advantage of that…"

Xeal just smiled as he saw Ekaitza's eyes light up as she declared that they would succeed, as the date shifted to lighter topics until it was time for Xeal to return to his estate. Once there, he enjoyed the remainder of Ellis's third birthday, while at the same time preparing for the departure of Enye, Dyllis, Mari and Lingxin. Just as the four dragonoid women would be, they would be starting their tier-7 tribulations in the morning. Xeal could feel the tension long after the children had been put to bed, as he sat with them and just talked for a while. Finally, as it got late, Xeal gave them each a full bottle of the waters of youth and smiled as they each drank them. With that, Xeal was down to just under three gallons of the miracle substance left, as he enjoyed snuggling with the four of them and went to sleep.

When Xeal awoke in the morning, they had all already left and he turned his attention to grinding once more. With peace talks still ongoing in the Huáng empire, as the battlelines held until the results were known and Abysses End still trying to come up with a new plan of attack, he was happy to simply take advantage of the time. It also helped to keep him from thinking about what all of Enye's party was likely facing at that very moment. Things continued like this for Xeal as he reached level 207 and the peace talks concluded with a five-year ceasefire on the Huáng empire's continent. There were conditions that could cause it to become null and void, but it was to the Huáng empire's advantage to accept it, as they regained their lost lands and extracted massive reparations in the process. Though it had come at the cost of most of the recovered airship components and Xeal knew that not only those nations, but every other one out there was looking into void plating.

While it had never been seen as worth it due to the difficulties and dangers for even void mages to pull off what Xeal had, that had changed with his actions. Now it would be more likely, that at least on crucial components and the points that they were connected to, the airship's materials that would negate void magic would be used. Like with the shells of the void hounds that made great shields against such assaults, it wouldn't take long for the technique to be applied to airships. Though this would result in a spike in demand for void iron and other void metals, and FAE would be happy to exploit that as they happened to have a halfway decent stockpile of them already.

Even so, this was a gift to Xeal and FAE, as it removed all NPCs from the battles there. While Abysses End still seemed determined to fight the war and push Jingong and FAE out, it was forced to do so in the grinding areas. Furthermore, it was only able to be even somewhat effective along the borders and all FAE needed to do was station some tier-7 players in those areas. Though once more players reached tier-7 it might become a bit more complicated, as Abysses End would start to be able to attempt to conquer the Huáng empire on its own. Xeal expected that to be exactly what the other five nations were planning on, as the treaty said nothing about prohibiting players from invading with the support of any country. Still, a celebration was scheduled for the night of day 291 that Xeal was expected to attend as the guest of honor.

Lingxin

Time seemed to be meaningless, as one day after another passed and struggled as she continued to climb a never-ending staircase. With each step that she took, danger was ever present as the faces of all those who had sought to control her brother, or remove her from his side appeared as specters. This included her own father and countless others who had been killed by her brother, or on his orders throughout the years. At first, they had just shouted, or taunted her as she passed by, but over time they had started to call her a murderer and the innocents that had been killed were mixed in as well. A few of them had even been poisoned by her own hand as they drank tea across from her brother, as was common when any of his concubine candidates was deemed as a hindrance. Finally, after a few days, they had started to try to attack her as she cut through their gaseous forms with her enchanted blade.

The only saving grace was that each attack only came when she ascended a step and she had been able to sleep on the few landings that she had arrived at after dealing with the assaults there. The first time she had done this, she had feared that the specters were just luring her into a false sense of security, but so far she had been fine each time. Though she had no idea how many days it had been and had taken to sleeping whenever a landing came along, out of fear of there not being another one before she would reach absolute exhaustion. Still, she never slept in peace as she found herself trapped in a nightmare each time, as blood rained from the skies and the forms of those she wronged still tormented her even there. Like this, Lingxin had pressed forward until she arrived at what finally seemed to be the top of the stairs and found her son, Xin, standing there looking at her in horror as he spoke.

"Mommy is a bad person. She killed so many."

At these words Lingxin's heart just about shattered. She had long treated all the acts of murder she and her brother committed as necessary for their survival. Just part of the politics of the nation that they found themselves ruling over and as natural as breathing. While this view had shifted upon meeting Xeal and being for all purposes rescued from herself in a way, she had never thought much about them, even as she had been climbing the stairs. She had even thought that the tribulation wasn't going to live up to its reputation, until that moment as she struggled to find words while Xin continued to speak.

"Are all my mommies like this as well and what about Daddy?"

"No, no, you are just misunderstanding."

"So, killing others is good? Am I going to need to kill people too? What about Xander, Maki and Ellis, will I kill them too?"

"No, no, no, no, you won't-"

"Why, Mommy? I want to be strong, just like you and Daddy."

Lingxin struggled to find the words to say as she looked at her son and wondered if she was even worthy to have the joy of being in his life. Even now she was placing him behind her own rise in power and she didn't even know what it was for. She knew that she didn't need to be doing any of this and that had she wished to, she could have just enjoyed a quiet life raising Xin and the others. Even if Xeal would have frowned at seeing her not reach her true potential, he would have held her just the same and accepted her decision with love and understanding. All she could think of was that even now she still held a fear of being discarded like so many of her brothers and sisters had been by her brother and father. Now, however, it was her son that she feared discarding her, as she pulled every bit of the will that she had left and closed the distance to Xin and picked him up and spoke.

"All of that is in my past. Mommy was in a very dark place before Daddy rescued me from it. Be like Daddy and rescue those like Mommy from themselves and bring them into the light."

"So, you're not going to kill anyone anymore, Mommy?"

"I don't know. Mommy hopes not, but if anyone threatens you, or your siblings, she just might do so to protect you."

"Is that why you killed all of them?"

As Xin said this, he pointed to a hallway filled with the forms of those she had killed that hadn't been there before.

As she looked at them, she just shook her head and looked at Xin as she responded.

"No, I did it for myself and Mommy will never do that again."

As Lingxin said these words, those in the hall charged in and she found herself having to fight while holding onto Xin. Needless to say that was beyond awkward, as she knew that he couldn't even handle her normal movements were she to start dancing around the battlefield in the fluid ways she was accustomed to. So, instead, she focused on keeping her body between Xin and the attacking mass as she put herself in a corner. Meanwhile, Xin was acting as one might expect a three-year-old to, by holding tightly to her while burying his face and crying into her shoulder. Things stayed like this as she desperately held them back while taking one injury after another, as it seemed like the enemies would never cease coming. Still, somehow Lingxin found the strength to fight as she pushed herself and the world around her dissolved as she received a notification that she had passed.

Dyllis

She had found herself trapped in her body from the very start of her tribulation, as even her voice had been taken from her. All she had left was her ears as she listened to the world around her. She was living what had always been her worst nightmare. The condition that had afflicted her mother had come for her despite Xeal using a drop of phoenix blood on her. The voices of those she loved were constantly playing as they all came to speak to her and let her know that they still loved her and would care for her. Like that, Dyllis had lost track of time as she fought to figure out what she was supposed to do in this tribulation, since she was completely helpless. She couldn't even move her fingers no matter how hard she tried, as all she felt was pain.

Time passed and Dyllis struggled, but nothing happened. Yet she still fought as she didn't believe that this was her fate. No, she had escaped this fate and would live a long happy life next to Xeal and their children, as she sang to all of them and brought joy to their lives. At least this was the only thought that she had at first, but as time passed, she realized that there wasn't any time limit on a tribulation and that she could truly be trapped like this forever. Suddenly, she wondered if it wouldn't be better to simply die and escape this fate, as she knew that she wouldn't really die thanks to the mark which Xeal had placed upon her. With that a battle was raging inside of Dyllis, as she worried that her tribulation would never end and even if she held on, years would pass before she was able to rejoin her family.

It was a truly terrible fate to be trapped in a state where you were trapped in your own thoughts, as time lost any frame of reference and Dyllis had no way of knowing if it had been two days, or two months. She didn't even know if she had lost consciousness at some point, as she struggled with what to do with every fiber of her being as she was still capable of holding her breath. With that ability she could hold her breath and suffocate herself, or get close enough to it that her condition would get worse and eventually she would die from repeating this several times. The very fact that she had a plan scared her, as the thought of what actually trying it would do for her, as she worried about her mind recovering from such an experience.

By this point, even the voices that came were slightly muffled as it seemed that she would lose even the ability to hear soon. Dyllis didn't know if that would be better, or worse, as she struggled with what to do, as it seemed that there was truly no way to do whatever she was supposed to as she kept working on a solution. Finally, she heard Xeal speaking to her one day and she got an idea.

"I just wish that there was a way for you to let me know that you were in there."

Dyllis took as deep of a breath as she could and held it.

"Dyllis! If you can hear me start breathing!"

Dyllis started to breathe once more.

"Dyllis, thank you, it has been too long since we could speak. If you agree, hold your breath, if you don't keep breathing."

Once more Dyllis held her breath and like that she was able to communicate with Xeal, though it was limited to simple yes and no questions and answers as he talked to her. Still, she could hear the joy in his voice as she did so and he seemed to not want it to end. Though, he finally did ask one final question as his voice filled with sorrow.

"Dyllis, I thank you for this, but I can't keep doing this to you. I can only imagine just how hard it is on you to even control your breathing at this point. So, I will ask you what I have avoided all these years and ask if you just want it all to end and be freed from your torment. I will give you some time to think on it, but if you hold your breath in the next few minutes, I will gather the family to say their goodbyes and do what I probably should have done a year ago."

Dyllis struggled to decide as she knew that if she said yes the tribulation would end no matter what, but if she said no, she expected that she would lose control of her breathing next. This worry threatened to overwhelm Dyllis as she prepared to hold her breath and just have it end. Only she stopped herself as she renewed her resolve and kept breathing as she thought about being able to sing not just for Xeal, but be by his side one day. As the time passed, Xeal spoke once more.

"Alright, I will accept your wish to live for as long as possible, if you don't hold your breath right now."

As she kept breathing, Xeal thanked her for her strength as he left her alone once more, though he returned what must have been every day, or more often, to talk. At the end of each and every one of these encounters, he would once more ask her if she wished for him to end her suffering and she would just keep breathing. Like that more time passed until finally he all but begged her to stop forcing herself to live for his sake as he asked, yet she just kept refusing to allow her life to end. As she did this, she finally felt something change as she received a notification that she had successfully survived and completed her tribulation.

Mari

From the moment Mari had entered the realm that was created to allow her to undertake her tribulation, she had found herself having to compete against others that she could never best. The task didn't matter, only the constant falling short next to them did as she was tested in everything that she had even a little experience in. From hand-to-hand combat to city planning, she was put to the test and always told that she was second best, or worse, yet she persisted. With each test the ridicule grew stronger and the danger increased, as she was pushed to give up by her opponents as they bested her time after time. It didn't help that her opponents were her own siblings and her mother, as the judge, always had dissatisfaction on her face as she pestered Mari about not being the best at anything. More than once she was told that her only value was that she had opened her legs for the right man and to just keep doing so to ensure Xeal kept serving Muthia's interests.

Like this, things continued each day as the only breaks that Mari had was the six hours in which she slept and even then she had to deal with dreams of being told she wasn't enough. Still, she just let it all roll off her shoulders as she knew that she was enough for at least one person as Xeal had chosen her. She knew that he valued her over any of her sisters and she would never need to compete against them for his affection. Though as the days passed, the fact that she was sharing him with so many others became a focus of the attacks on her confidence. Things like how Xeal must only pity her and how Xeal likely loved the others more, were constantly added to the comments that she had to withstand. Then came the comments on how Mari was being selfish for not allowing Kuri to pursue Xeal, when it was clear that Xeal didn't have an issue with sisters sharing him, from looking at the twins and fox-women he was courting.

All of this was repeated over and over and over again, as Mari slowly started to doubt her own mind and her resolve weakened. Then her daughter, Maki, was added into the routine, as she seemed to want to play with everyone but Mari and Mari's heart ached, but she held strong. Though, she longed for Xeal to hold her and reassure her that she was worth being loved and that she was good enough. Especially as she was faced with the fact that the only reason that she was walking the path that she was, was due to his desire for her to. While she had embraced it, she knew that it was her way of proving that she was worthy of being next to him and Xeal's other wives. While this thought caused her to waver for a moment, it ended up hardening her resolve as she knew that all of this was just a test and all she needed to do was prove that her inner demons wouldn't defeat her. Once she did that, it would prove once and for all that she belonged and no one would keep her from doing exactly that.

While Mari was confident of her success, she was still unsure of when, or how this tribulation would end. This created the fear that she was doomed to repeat this monotony until she managed to win at something and prove that she was the best at it. Mari feared that she would truly be trapped in this loop until she ended her own life and escaped through the mark that Xeal had left upon her. Still, she knew that if she did so, that there would be no going back as she would have failed her tribulation and would need to attempt it once more. It was with this thought that Mari started to try to think of something that she thought she was the best of all her siblings in, while still having enough skill for her performance to be something praiseworthy. Finally, she landed on one-on-one mixed martial combat with no restrictions on any weapons or tactics. Mari knew she wasn't the best with the katana, wakizashi, tantō, naginata or yumi. In fact, when it came to a few of them, she was almost the least skilled of her siblings in them. Still, Mari believed by combining them together and playing to her siblings' weaknesses that she could win. So, when she was brought before her mother to be assigned her next challenge, she spoke before her mother could.

"Mother, we have focused on only a single discipline this whole time, I wish to show you what I am capable of when I choose my weapons and my opponent does the same!"

"No, that will defeat the purpose of judging based off your skill alone, as you would have different tools than your opponent. Now-"

"We would have access to the same tools and there is a skill in selecting the right ones!"

"Mari!"

"Mother, I will stake my life on this! So long as you allow it and you are the only witness to each fight, I will show you where my true skill lies!"

Mari entered a staring contest with her mother who looked displeased, but finally relented as she sighed before responding.

"Very well. You are forbidden to kill any of your sisters, but they will be allowed to kill you and should they succeed in doing so, I will declare that they will take your place next to Xeal. It will be just the four of you and you must defeat all three of them to keep your life as should you lose and they spare you, I may kill you myself for your disrespect and pick one of them to replace you next to Xeal."

"I won't lose. Now who will I face first?"

"Momo. She is the weakest of the four of you in martial skills, so she should allow me to gauge what your purpose is in these fights."

Mari just nodded as she explained what she was looking for and 20 minutes later she found herself standing on a hill as Momo stood 100 yards away. In Mari's hands was a yumi and as she checked it over and nocked an arrow, her mother raised a flag to signal the start of the fight. Instantly Mari loosed her arrow and started to close the distance. For this fight all she had was a katana and a wakizashi beyond the yumi and the 20 arrows, one of which she was releasing every five yards as she closed the distance. Momo, for her part, was easily avoiding the arrows while wielding a naginata, but she was unable to charge due to the arrows' ability to easily hit her if she were to run straight forward. Mari would also quickly retreat while loosing arrows were that to occur. As such, when they were just five yards apart, Mari tossed her yumi to the side and used a quickdraw technique to draw her katana and begin the one-sided clash. Momo hardly put up a resistance once her guard had been breached as she failed to switch to her wakizashi in time.

While Mari had won, she didn't celebrate as her next opponent would be her eldest sister, Kuni. Like both her other sisters she was level 199 and before Xeal had come to Muthia the first time, she would have been easily the strongest of them in combat. However, that had changed as Mari knew that Kuri, who she would face last, had surpassed Kuni at this point, depending on what weapons were used. So, Mari stood with a naginata in her hands as Kuni stood 100 yards away wielding the same. Mari knew that this fight would be hard as they both had a katana and a wakizashi on their hips as well. The only difference between them was that Mari had a tantō where her waist met her back, giving her one more blade than her sister. As their mother raised the flag once more, it was time to go as both women charged at the other.

The moment before Kuni and Mari would have collided, Mari dropped down and braced her naginata on the ground with one hand and drew the tantō with the other. What followed was Kuni's naginata being barely deflected by the tantō and Mari's naginata catching Kuni in the shoulder. The momentum that this exchange created was not wasted, as Mari went on the offensive by dropping both her tantō and her naginata and drawing her katana as Kuni did the same. An hour later Mari stood all but exhausted, as she held her wakizashi to Kuni's throat as her sister yielded after one final maneuver that had allowed Mari to barely attain a victory. The look on her mother's face was a mix of surprise and disappointment as she declared Mari the victor and sent them off to recover. All that was left was to best Kuri and hope that was enough to end the tribulation as if it wasn't, Mari was unsure just what to do.

A little over an hour since her match with Kuni ended, Mari once more stood ready to do battle as Kuri stood across from her. This time Mari had held nothing back as in her hands was a yumi. She had a katana, wakizashi and a tantō on her waist, with a naginata stabbed into the ground behind her, with 100 arrows on hand. Meanwhile, Kuri held a katana and only had a wakizashi on her waist as the flag goes up and the match begins. Abandoning the naginata, Mari loosed one arrow after another, as she moved around the battlefield while keeping her distance from Kuri. Kurri simply focused on dodging while closing the distance and it wasn't long before only 20 yards separated them and Mari abandoned her yumi, while still having over 50 arrows left, as she drew her own katana.

What followed was an intense struggle as Mari focused on one thing and only one thing, getting Kuri away from her katana. Only then did she have the confidence to come out in the exchange victorious. As such, Mari was focusing on attacks that would lead Kuri into the trap that had been laid in the battle so far. This saw Mari moving around in what could only be called an awkward dance, until the pair had reached the point where Mari had abandoned her yumi. Before Kuri knew what was happening, her legs were being swept out from under her by Mari using her foot to pull the yumi towards her while Kuri's feet were in its center. Instantly Kuri stabbed her katana down. This stabilized her as she went to jump back, but it had come at the cost of her blade as Mari had grabbed hold of it with one hand while swinging her katana with the other. Like this Kuri drew her wakizashi and held Mari off as she focused on reaching the naginata that had been placed down by Mari at the start of the match.

During this phase of the battle, Mari made it seem as if she wasn't going to allow Kuri an opportunity to reach the naginata. However, she eventually slipped up and allowed Kuri to create enough distance to make a run for the bladed spear, which like Mari, was Kuri's second choice as far as weapons go. Only when she dropped her wakizashi and pulled the naginata from the ground, its blade was left behind and Kuri could tell that the pole was flimsy, as Mari closed the distance and the match ended. With no blade in hand and needing to bend down and expose herself to grab one, Kuri conceded the match and the world around Mari dissolved as she learned that she had passed her tribulation.

Enye

Enye had wondered just what her tribulation would throw at her due to the various aspects of her past that had haunted her. Though what she hadn't been prepared for was this world where all around her was herself, only each and every one of them seemed to be different. Some were cold hearted and downright sadistic, while others were sickly sweet as they talked and interacted with each other in some twisted grand ball. Enye was unsure of just how many of herself there were, but one thing was certain, they all had the exact same level and stats as her and fighting them would be a fool's errand. So, when the ball came to an end and a rather regal version of herself stood and announced that in one hour the selection would begin, Enye wanted to throw up at what she was hearing.

"… As we all know, only one of us can survive while the rest will be lost, so use this hour to run, hide, form alliances, or even to simply accept your fate and enjoy existing for a bit longer. Once the selection is over, the one who has been chosen will have the pleasure of returning to live with our husband and children. All I ask is that whoever that may be, that you will not forget the rest of us. After all, we are simply a different side of you that you can easily tap into when needed, as if we are anything it is adaptable. Now, let the one hour of grace begin before we commence the culling of our ranks."

Enye wasted no time as she made her plan as she knew better than to trust any of those who claimed to be her other sides. They were nothing but the shadow warriors that she had defeated in training and she would vanquish them in the same manner. Though to do so she needed to survive, and so she quickly left the palace and found herself in an empty city that would play host to this death match. Enye didn't linger though as she rushed in a direction that none of the others seemed to be headed in, as she ran along rooftops as she looked at the wall that marked the end of the city as her goal. When she reached it with about five minutes before her hour was up, she leapt right on it and used her shadow elemental to create climbing spikes on her hand as she scaled it. Once atop the massive structure, Enye went off the far side as she escaped into the forest below and kept going as she focused on leaving as little of a trail as she possibly could. Even so, she didn't expect it to do much to hide her from the others and after going around ten miles outside the city, she found herself looking at what felt like the edge of the world and received a warning at the same time.

(Warning: you have reached the edge of this reality. As participants in this struggle die, this reality's edge will crumble away into the abyss below.)

Enye wanted to scream as she had planned to use the woods to ensure that she could survive 'til the end and now that was not feasible. Even as she stood there thinking, she saw half a foot of land crumble away and knew that the others were already killing each other and the bloodbath that was about to happen would make this area rather dangerous. So, as another seven inches crumbled away, Enye headed back into the forest and didn't stop until she was about in its middle. Though just as she was about to settle down, she ran into one of the other hers who hadn't noticed her yet. Knowing that hesitation was worthless, Enye attacked and caught her other self by surprise and attacked from behind.

What followed was a brutal struggle, that ended with Enye coming out victorious as she slew the fake version of herself and was instantly healed. At the same time, she suddenly had all the memories of her other self since the start of the tribulation and she suddenly felt the fear she had had as she ran. She hadn't been in the forest due to wishing to use it for ambushes like Enye had, she had simply wished to hide. This, however, was not the thing that had disturbed Enye the most, as during the fight her back had been exposed towards the end and the same mark that Xeal had placed upon Enye was on this copy's back as well. This alone made Enye fear what would become of her if she died, as she questioned if she was simply another one of these copies.

No matter how hard Enye tried to put this thought out of her mind, she couldn't as she killed one version of herself after another over the following days. She verified more than once that the mark she bore was on the others as well. Additionally, she gained more and more knowledge about the surrounding area and the conflict as a whole with each one she killed. At the same time, she was driven closer to the city as the edge of the reality continued to collapse, only it was collapsing by a few feet at a time now as it swallowed every tree that it passed. Eventually only around 100 feet of forest was left and Enye was forced to enter the city where the main fight had been occurring and she carefully scaled the wall. As she cautiously looked over the city below, Enye could see the signs of the fighting that had occurred, as blood stains were all that was left of many of her other sides. However, Enye's attention was quickly drawn to a three-way clash that was occurring just below her.

All three of them looked to be in poor shape and could be finished off at any second, though it seemed that they all knew that whoever got the final blow would win as they would recover. Enye was tempted to land that final blow, only she held back as she felt that doing so would cost her her life. It was a second after she had resisted attacking that she watched two other hers ambush the three from two other hiding spots. Those two quickly killed the other three and continued to fight each other after, as Enye shuddered knowing that if she had attacked, she would have become trapped into a fierce struggle. However, she also knew that she had to take such risks moving forward as if she didn't, she was sure to end up being at a disadvantage in the city moving forward. So, she waited and watched the fight below her, while paying attention to her surroundings. Finally, when it seemed that either of the two would fall at any second, Enye watched as one other jumped down and it was then that Enye moved and she targeted the one that that just made a sneak attack.

What followed was the attacking one shifting awkwardly as she blocked Enye's attack, as the attack sent her into the other two. Enye quickly attacked the other two from their own shadows with shadow step and her sneak attack skill, killing each and it was once more a one-on-one, but Enye had the advantage. However, Enye just escaped with shadow step and quickly hid in a building that one of the memories she had just gained used to sleep in, as it had a hidden spot in the ceiling. Once safely hidden away, Enye took the time to sort the hundreds of new memories for the accumulated sides of herself that had been in the two she had killed, as she suddenly knew what the situation in the city had been like. While Enye wasn't sure just how many of her selves there were, she did know it had been at least 10,000, and over half had stayed in the city and the fighting had been intense since day one.

As Enye thought about things, she was sure that over half of her copies were dead. In fact, if she assumed that the same amount of area was lost when any of her copies died, it would be safe to say around 75% of them were dead. The real question she had was with her having killed over 150 of them on her own, how so many could still be alive. It was then that she realized that wasn't what she had killed, but the number of memories that she had absorbed as the whole experience they had merged into her. Suddenly this brought on a whole new list of questions on just what she was. Was she the real one, or was she just a replacement that didn't even realize that it was. Had she killed the original and taken her memories while containing a different temperament and personality? With her worries threatening to overwhelm her as she constantly reassured herself that she was the original Enye, she allowed herself to sleep once more.

The following morning, having calmed down, Enye looked out of the building she had hidden in, only to see that the walls had been swallowed by the abyss now. At the pace it was going, the house Enye was currently in would be gone by the following morning, so she had no choice but to head deeper into the city as she kept to the shadows. She was eying the palace that had hosted the grand ball at the start, as it made sense that it was the center and therefore the only place that was safe from falling into the abyss. All along the way, Enye passed one fight after another as the continually shrinking area forced more and more conflicts to occur. At the same time, Enye wondered what became of those that fell into the abyss. With the possibility of all those present being her and that the strongest version of her was what would emerge victorious being a real possibility to her, she found herself worried about the implications. If parts of her were lost, could she ever really be whole again and were there parts of herself that would be better if lost to the abyss. This very thought sent a shudder through Enye, as she decided it was best to just put such thoughts out of her mind for now, else she risked being overwhelmed by them.

Finally, around dusk, Enye managed to arrive at the palace and found a window to sneak in through, as she remained cautious. She knew that she needed to sleep if she wanted to stand a chance in the next round of fighting, as she used shadow step to arrive at a ledge that overlooked the ballroom where she had first entered. Once there, she looked at the walkway that servants would use when hanging decorations and questioned how safe it would be to sleep there. With that, she decided to move out of the main room to look for a better spot to rest by following this path. Eventually, she found a hidden nook with a pile of wood stacked in it that was a bit better, but if she could find it, so could her other selves and so she went about creating a trap. This had required her to move the wood as she created a void space for her to sleep. She had set things up so that if anyone disturbed her, they would be hit with a fire mine that would light up the whole area and likely set the whole palace on fire. While Enye knew that she would also be in trouble should that happen, she had a fire-resistant cloak that she had wrapped herself in and it would force her and her attacker to escape. Even though it was less than ideal, it was still better than being caught in a fight in a disadvantaged situation and with that thought Enye slept once more.

Enye wasn't sure how long she had slept, but the trap

had been sprung and fire was all around her as she focused on escape. The fire-resistant cloak was doing its job of keeping the flames off her body, but the heat was an issue as she could see her health and stamina being drained quickly. Not wasting any more time, she burst out of the pile of flaming wood as she sent them flying onto the one that triggered the trap before she escaped. Only when she reached the window that she had plotted for her escape, she was met with the sight of the abyss. It had reached all the way to the palace and Enye quickly started to climb up the wall instead of down it like she had originally planned.

As she reached the roof, she wasted no time in running straight towards the tower in the center like her life depended on it and as she did so, the flames from the fire she had lit started to climb higher. It was with this that she realized that the palace wasn't safe from the abyss, as she started to climb the side of the tower as her other selves started to emerge onto the roof as well. From what Enye could tell, there was still around 25 of them left and they were all making their way to the tower right behind her. The moment Enye made her way over the edge, she was confronted with the one who had given the speech that kicked all of this off. How she knew it was her was beyond her own understanding, but she just knew. At the same moment, rather than drawing a blade, the regal Enye started to speak as she stood up from the throne that she had been sitting on.

"It seems that it is finally time to determine which of us is the real one."

"I am not going to fall to your mind games."

"It is no game, or if it is, it is a very cruel one as we discover which version of ourselves is the most suited to survive. That is our greatest fear after all, dying once and being seen as a burden to Xeal and the others."

"I am the real me, you are just a fake."

"Yes, and yes, though I am the only fake. Look, I don't even have a real body."

The regal Enye lunged forward and Enye cut right through her as if she was just an illusion and she continued talking.

"I represent the parts of us that must exist and will return to the victor. Now you better fight hard, as there are still some of our more sadistic sides climbing this tower and they are the only ones that I would be upset to see win."

As the regal Enye finished speaking, the first of the others started to peek over the edge of the wall and Enye started to attack. For what felt like forever, Enye kept attacking any of her other selves that came over the edge of the tower wall. Had it not been for the random times she felt fully restored after another of her other selves succumbed to the flames below, Enye knew that she would have never been able to hold on until the end, when the regal Enye spoke once more.

"It seems that you really were the real one. Now all that is left is for you to process all the other yous and absorb me back into you before leaving."

"Right, you wouldn't just tell me that I am the real me to put me at ease, or anything, or are you saying that because the rest are a part of me now that I am the real one?"

"Does it matter? You are the only one that is left standing."

Enye couldn't even argue as the regal version of herself suddenly was sucked into her body and even more memories were added as Enye struggled to process everything. If all of the versions of herself were truly part of her, she wished that more had been lost to the abyss, which now was at the edge of the base of the tower, leaving it as the only thing remaining in this reality. Finally, Enye heard the notification that she had completed her tribulation as the world dissolved around her.

Main ED world

As Xeal heard that Enye, Mari, Dyllis and Lingxin had finished their tribulations, he dropped everything to be with them as he found himself comforting all four of them. While it was true that they had all overcome the trials of the tribulation, it seemed to have taken a toll on their psyche, at least in the short term and as they shared their experiences, Xeal could see why. Each had achieved an A-ranked result and passed their tribulation, despite only receiving minimal, if any, instructions, which was even worse than what Xeal had had to deal with in a way. Enye in particular was having a hard time, as she was still questioning if she was really her and Xeal worried that if she wasn't able to come to terms with it and just move on, she would truly go crazy. In the end, he promised that if he thought that she was acting like someone other than her, that everyone would let her know, but to look at what she had gone through as a refining fire.

During this time, the rest of Enye's party also returned, as the only failures were three of the four members of FAE that had been accompanying them as Avala, Flair and Galva all fell short at the final hurdle. As such, they were doing remedial training and would make another attempt to pass, though Aalin and a few others were discussing being part of the force that focused on the subterranean realm as well. With Nanami and Ignis wanting in on that team as well, Xeal had no worries about there being enough firepower in the new party that would form. Though with Ekaitza, Lughrai, Malgroth and Lumikkei all being there as well, it was sure to have enough power so long as they didn't try to go too deep. Speaking of the four dragonoids, Xeal found him having to give each of them a deep and passionate kiss as they returned, as they thanked him for being cruel to them. Apparently, Ekaitza and their mothers had blabbed the moment they returned and most of their worries had been relieved. Though, Xeal had still had to spend day 279 taking Lughrai, Malgroth and Lumikkei on their second dates, which were a fair bit more awkward after the kisses. Even so, he did his best to comfort them after setting them up, while still making it clear that they were still not any closer to actually having him.

(*****)

Morning June 18 to Evening June 21, 2268 & ED Year 6 Days 281-291.

With the 18th came graduation for Anna and Lauren, and as such Alex and company found themselves spending the day sitting in the bleachers of the high school athletic stadium. The multi-use field below was filled with the students who would be graduating, as they each took their turn to walk across the stage and receive their diploma case. Alex knew that the actual diplomas were sitting back in a classroom and would be given out after the ceremony, as all of the family made their way out of the stands and back to their cars. Part of Alex envied Ava and Mia who had gotten out of coming to be on baby duty, as Aidan, Nadia, Evan and Nova were all too young for Alex to want to subject them to hours in the sun. Even with the sunscreen and long-sleeve clothing that he had worn, Alex could tell that he was going to burn as he hardly got any sun in his normal day to day life and it was a perfect day.

Still, he knew that showing up was important, as even if Anna didn't care, he knew that his parents did and it had been one of the things he missed in his last life. Like with so many other things, he had just been too busy and ignored it despite still living in the area and it only being a slight inconvenience for him. While no one had said much, Alex had been able to tell the disappointment that it caused and it had been the start of his family not asking him to inconvenience himself for them. Like it, or not, it had been a moment that proved to matter more than just on the surface and Alex was avoiding such mistakes as much as possible this time around.

After the graduation ceremony was over, Dan, Anna, Lauren, Jessica and Henry headed off with some of their friends to celebrate. Though they did so with a few guards, as with the events of the last presentation still fresh in all of their minds, Alex saw no reason to risk things more than necessary. While Anna looked a bit annoyed at this, she didn't argue as she knew the why and that they would stay in the background as much as possible. Like that, Alex saw them off and returned to the rental house once more, as they prepared for two long days at the local fairgrounds.

The 19th and 20th passed with Alex spending a fair bit of his time logged into ED from the fairgrounds, as he made occasional appearances that were scheduled. Just like the year prior, there were protesters present as they expressed their displeasure at what Alex and FAE stood for, at least in their minds. Though no arrests were made this time and everything was well under control according to Kate, it was looking like they would manage to break even on this event at the very least. It would take a while before the teams responsible for the other events would report in their numbers and the future of such events would be determined. At the very least, the more local workshops were grateful for the opportunity to pay a few thousand credits and gain access to the event for recruitment. Though any major power was looking at paying 10,000 credits for similar access and that included their subordinate guilds.

These events would see players matched up with organizations that couldn't trap them easily and it would let those with real talent stand out more. While this would harm their potential compared to being nurtured by a guild with the resources to do so, few if any of them would have that opportunity in the first place. Even if they did, it would come only after signing a rather lopsided deal that would take advantage of them for years before they would have a chance to renegotiate. This way they would be negotiating from a position of strength from the start, if they showed enough talent that a few major powers took notice. A few of them might even cause the guild that they joined to rise with them, if they could avoid the fate of any minor power that stood out too much. That being the same one as the tallest tree when a storm blows too strongly, or the nail that sticks up as it is hammered down. Still, Alex was counting on such guilds arising and seeking the relative safety that he was working to build in Nium and the Huáng empire.

With the conclusion of the festival, it was time for Alex and his group to return to Colorado on the 21st. So, after another ride with the Brewyses on their plane, they were once more home as they prepared to return to their normal life. For Alex, this meant it was time for him to shift his focus to Muthia, as he worked to at least temporarily end the conflict there, while FAE continued its path to complete dominance of Nium's continent. Meanwhile, Anna, Ava and Mia were all getting ready to attempt to reach tier-7. All while Nicole and Sam were getting ready for the influx of guests that would be coming in tomorrow to celebrate Ahsa's and Moyra's first birthdays on the 23rd and 24th. Then there was the wedding that was all but set to be in Wyoming now, as the legislation had passed in both chambers of Congress and was set to be signed into law on Monday. Alex just sighed as he knew that life was just going to get more hectic over the following months, as he would need to be playing a bit more of an active role in reality than he would like.

Xeal's time in ED was mainly focused on grinding, while

making an appearance on one battlefield or another, as he and his party continued to prepare for their next expedition. This time also saw him visiting the newly reestablished settlement in Darefret's mine that had been cleared of kobolds. With around 75% of the smiths from the forge above having moved into the facilities in the mine, it had created a ton of room for FAE to increase the number of smiths in its ranks significantly. Taya was already hard at work shifting the smiths that had been in less desirable areas to the mine. The only major issue was that they no longer had players willing to mine while they grinded, due to how it would hamper their leveling to do so. Instead, the dwarves that had immigrated were taking up that role as while it wasn't much, they would still gain some experience based on what they extracted while mining. Even so, the dwarves also wished to craft and only around a tenth of the normal materials were reaching the smiths. So, FAE had launched a true apprenticeship program where they were accepting level ten to twenty players and in exchange for mining, they were getting time with competent smiths and cheap materials to practice with. While it wasn't perfect, it had returned the amount of materials to around 85% of what it was before clearing out the kobolds.

On the naval side of things, Nium had gained complete control of the sea to the peninsula that separated the east and west shores of Paidhia. Most of FAE's combat fleet was currently docked and undergoing repairs after the naval battle, as new crews were created and trained. Though over 50 ships were still slowly limping in while being guarded by a few of the more intact warships. In total, once the cargo fleet was counted, over 200,000 players would be sailing under FAE's flag once the expanded fleet of over 150 ships was launched. This fleet had only one job currently and that was to capture the seas around Nium's continent. Daisy and Violet had also been overjoyed to be back on land, as they rejoined Xeal's party when the first ships had docked.

The only issue was that Abysses End seemed to have decided that they truly needed to prevent that and while it would be months before they arrived, thousands of player ships were headed to Nium's waters. However, this had also caused Salty Dogs to increase their activity, as they were increasing the fleet that they had around Nium significantly as well. While not as numerous as the fleet of independent and small guild ships that Abysses End had secured, Salty Dog's fleet was of a much higher quality. Still, the sheer number meant that the naval war was far from settled as by the time FAE was ready to move, the first wave of these new enemies would be arriving. Xeal was already worried about the seas surrounding Nium's continent being filled with warships from every force that Abysses End could drag into the conflict. There was even the possibility of Fire Oath and Dragon Legion joining in, as the area just off the coast was still considered fair game under the dragonoid slots treaty.

With that move and the sudden influx of players into the countries surrounding the Huáng empire, Xeal felt like Abysses End's strategy was really to bankrupt FAE. At the rate they were going, Xeal was sure that they were burning through billions of credits a month, but they had the reserves to do just that while FAE didn't. Though, unless they were getting funding from others, Xeal knew that they were also harming their own foundations with each day that they continued this assault. Meanwhile, Xeal had arranged a meeting with Natalina Farese's character, Alcinne, on day 288. As Xeal sat across from the Italian beauty who had kept most of her features in ED, at least if you were looking at what the photos looked like after they had been altered, he couldn't help but sigh. At this Alcinne scoffed as she spoke first.

"You asked me to meet with you, not the other way around, so don't act like you don't want to be here now, or I might just leave. As it is, I am tempted to just sit here to gloat at you giving in to the business model that using individuals like myself allows for."

"You say that I shouldn't act like I don't want to be here right before saying why I don't want to be here."

"Alex, or I suppose that I should call you Xeal here, I would like nothing more than to ruin you in every way possible. I would even let you get me pregnant in reality at this point just to force you to pay child support to me for 18 years if I thought I could seduce you. Let's not lie to each other and say that we are friends, but you are the only one who is willing to consider hiring me and I can only do so much on my own. As the meager following that I currently have proves, I can't even cover rent for my own place and without something to entice them with beyond just my looks, I doubt I will any time soon. So, I don't care about any of that when it comes to us doing business. Just tell me what you have in mind and I will counter. Hopefully we will come up with something that will work for both of us and act like we are the best of friends in front of everyone else. Who knows, perhaps one day we will be."

"No counter offers. You either take what I am offering you, or you walk."

"That is not how this works-"

"Fine, you tell me what your offer is and I will either accept it, or counter it."

"See, you do know how to play and I am in a rather disadvantaged position, so I suppose two years at half a million credits a year plus five percent of the gross earnings that I bring in."

"Figuring out what you bring in will be beyond complicated and you know that."

"Yes, well, I need some way to motivate me to do more than the bare minimum after all."

"Alright, here is my counter offer. Lifetime exclusivity to FAE at one million credits a year base pay with performance bonuses. Those will be based on how many credits are brought in past cost on the raffles and other events you are promoting. To be clear, you will be the only spokesperson who acts in such a capacity and I will be spending another five million credits a year on the support staff and everything that will surround you. That means that your bonus will be based off of what is brought in after the six million credits and that value, and anything given away is covered. Also, to be clear, FAE can terminate your contract at any time and will just have to pay a year's worth of your base salary."

"And just what percent will I get of that and why would I sign away my life like that?"

"Ten percent would be split between your whole team and I would expect at least two percent to find its way to you. As to the why you would sign away your life like that, it is that you know it is a good deal and you have a good 20 years of earning that if you don't screw it up."

Alcinne paused as she took a long moment to think over the offer before she responded.

"Alright, let's say that I take your deal. What level of service are you expecting from me? After all, I don't mind flattering others, but touching will cost extra."

"You will be expected to host one fan event each ED year and pose for photos with any who are willing to stand in line long enough to get one. I expect you to be warm and welcoming of any casual contact that can be considered normal. If one of them touches you inappropriately, you will have a signal that will tell the guards to get them away from you. You are also not to play up the possibility that you might actually do anything with your fans and any claims that one of them touched you inappropriately will be thoroughly investigated. You will be under constant surveillance and if it is seen that you are allowing them to do so without reporting it, or that you are doing so, you will also be confronted about it."

"My, my, I must say that you are treating me very differently than Abysses End did. They actually wanted me to sleep with you and get pregnant. Perhaps us being friends isn't too far away after all."

"I am well aware and I expect you to conduct yourself differently as well."

"I think I can do that, though I have to know, why me and why give me a contract that sounds more suitable for an established figure rather than an unproven talent?"

"Did you not watch my speech on decisiveness and resilience?"

Xeal could tell that Alcinne had resisted rolling her eyes as she replied to him.

"I did, but you also said to do your research if possible before making such a major decision."

"Alcinne, oh, and you will be using that name in reality as well from now on. While this is a major move for you, it is ultimately a minor one for me. I know you have talent, a backbone and a will to succeed. You were also the only one of the four of you that came who wouldn't have slept with me. Now it's time to see what you can do if I give you a year and if you fall flat, I am out all of two million credits as I move on to your replacement. If it succeeds, I don't have to worry about you going to work for my competitor as you will be bound by the contract in ED to not be able to do so if you quit, or give me cause to fire you. If I were you, I would read your contract very carefully as Kate is the one who wrote it and I can guarantee the system will enforce it. Oh, and you will be reporting to her and we will likely not have another meeting after this one."

"Alright, I will look it over and as long as it seems fair, I look forward to working for you, though I would hope that you don't simply ignore me. After all, I am expecting you to make many appearances with me to carry out the vision of what I see as the most profitable to both of us. After all, you have a certain appeal for the residents of ED and what is the difference between a gold that is gotten from a player and an NPC?"

"Kate will determine that as my time is already stretched thin as it is and I am trying to avoid unnecessary entanglements. Now, if you will excuse me, I believe that we have completed the goals of this meeting."

"Right, you just don't want to be alone with a woman for too long, else your wives might think that they have to make room for another."

Xeal just smiled as she left the room that they had met in, as he left and returned to handling the other pressing tasks that he needed to do before the ceasefire celebration in the Huáng empire. When day 291 arrived and it was time for Xeal to head to the party, he was in a rather good mood with the success of recent days. This included the fact that Alcinne had accepted the deal and would be starting to make her rounds shortly. Her first task was to head around to several of the festivals that FAE was financing and introducing the new persona that she was creating for herself. This had involved changes in hair and eye color, such that she looked like she had stepped right out of Eternal Dominion and also hid her identity to a certain degree.

Though there had been talks on having her become an elf, or another race in Eternal Dominion, it had been decided against. Apparently, she was already talking with Kate about adding in assistants to her that would cover the most popular races like elf, dwarf, a few different beast-men and dragonoid. All of these were on hold until the initial results from her work was in, as the initial investment of ten million that it took to get her off and running was all that FAE was willing to spend at that point.

Furthermore, Kate had reported that all of the nations that had been showing reluctance to sign on to the association agreement with FAE and Nium were suddenly rather receptive to making a deal. Though now Kate was the one seeking to improve the terms of the deal for FAE as with Xeal's performance against the airship, it was clear that he was more valuable than ever before. So, while it seemed that deals would be made, it would still take a bit more time.

It was with this and other pressing issues on Xeal's mind that he stood next to Lingxin as they made their way to the Huáng empire. Xeal could tell that for Lingxin this was going to be a rather important moment, as she was finally returning home after almost four years away. It was also something that had been unlikely to occur while the empire was still whole and while it wasn't undamaged, it was still standing. With the families of the ministers and military officials that had been evacuated to Nium during the conflict having just returned as well, Xeal knew that the night would be an interesting one as he stepped forward and arrived there with Lingxin.

Instantly they found themselves being warmly greeted as all those around them praised them. From the moment they entered, Xeal and Lingxin seemed to be the center of attention as it was clear that all those present were looking to form connections with them. Still, Xeal kept it cordial as he made sure to keep each interaction short before being trapped by the next one, until they were finally saved when Emperor Huáng Jin sent for them. Seeing her brother in public without his veil for the first time that she could remember, was an emotional moment for Lingxin as they walked onto his private balcony as he started to talk with them.

"Xeal, my brother, I must thank you again for all that you have done. When I forced Lingxin upon you, I did so to save her. Now it seems that I saved myself as well. I only hope that the changes that were so easy to make while at war can survive peace."

"This isn't peace," retorted Xeal. "It is simply a pausing of the conflict and not even a real one. No, your cities are safe, but that is it and soon not even they will be safe if we relax."

"Yes, your kind will still fight and I can tell that your opponents are being funded by our enemies. As such, I will forgo rebuilding all that was damaged, focusing only on defense as I fund you. Jingong is valuable, but FAE is what allowed us to survive, not them."

"No, Jingong should be the focus of your funding as they are your main force here and FAE is just support. Besides, I need to have a large part of the forces that were focused here shift to other theaters in the short term, to ensure that the other wars that are raging are handled."

"Xeal, I wish for you to unite this continent like you intend for Nium's!"

"Brother, no!" interjected Lingxin. "At least not while you sit upon the throne and those currently in power still are. I am sorry, but we're monsters and the amount of our own nation's blood that we spilled while at peace would lead Xeal to having to conquer you as the people suffered beneath you."

"Sister! Things will be different now that-"

"They will not. Once you and the ministers feel secure, they will seek the same pleasures that they enjoyed before. I will support Xeal in defending the lands we have, but I will beg him to step in on the other side of things should you seek to conquer our neighbors and subjugate their lands."

"Xeal, speak some sense into her please."

"Jin, she is right. I will aid in the battle and even overlook you capturing a few cities to send a message, but that is it. As I have told you before, your country is rotten. This war helped cut part of it out, but it still exists and so long as it does, I will act as a check on it."

Xeal could tell that Emperor Huáng Jin wasn't pleased by his words, as he had no talent for hiding the emotions that had been concealed by his veil for so long. Just from the face he was making, Xeal felt as if Emperor Huáng Jin was about to order Xeal and Lingxin to be executed on the spot. Still, he calmed himself and after taking a long breath he spoke once more.

"It seems that I still have a way to go before I can pass your test, and my heir will not be able to take over for decades at this point. However, will you really allow the wars here to rage for that long when you could save so many by ending them once and for all?"

"You speak as if I have power that I do not. I am but a single man and my guild is but one of many. Even if we hold the most power of any, we are still insignificant when compared to the whole."

Xeal sighed as he looked out at the night's sky as he continued to speak.

"No matter how much I, or any other may think that they know best, or that if others simply followed what they say, we are always wrong. What would create paradise for us would create hell for another. Simply by existing, people seek to rule one another. It is why a struggling peddler will support policies that favor the rich merchant as they wish to become one someday. In the end, you are the emperor and will need to make the best decision that you can, and I am the leader of my guild and must do the same. Where that will put us in five years when the ceasefire ends is anyone's guess. Now, enough on this topic as it is ruining the mood."

With that they shifted topics as they continued to chat for a bit, before the three of them rejoined the celebration that lasted well into the early morning. Though Xeal and Lingxin didn't stay for the whole time. Instead, they slipped out early and made their way down to the underground caverns that housed Bīng's prison as Lingxin wished to speak with her. As they walked, Xeal could tell that something was bothering Lingxin as they drew closer to their destination, though she refused to say what it was. As such, when they reached the end of their journey and Bīng came into view, Xeal was surprised when Lingxin started to speak in a harsh tone.

"Just what are you planning to do to my brother once you have birthed his heir!?"

Bīng gave Lingxin a look like she wanted to just ignore her, but at seeing Xeal with her she sighed as she spoke.

"Xeal, I would thank you for keeping better control of your wives."

"I am not Watcher," replied Xeal. "My wives are their own people, not things to be controlled by my whims."

"Still, she is creating tension with an ally. I would think that she would know better."

"You are no ally," retorted Lingxin. "You are simply a convenient partner that gets something you want by giving Xeal something he wants. Now, what is your intent for my brother?"

"He will become my puppet until my child is ready to take the throne, at which time he will spend the rest of his days here serving me. It will be as it should have been from the start, with the true ruler of his empire being me."

Xeal had to hold in a laugh as he interrupted the pair of women.

"That's cute. Bīng, how will you rule from this prison? How will you quell a rebellion? How will you even be able to trust the reports that you receive? I can go on, but ask Arnhylde about how much control Matrikas has over the Zapladal Theocracy and they worship her. I'll give you the long and short of it, she has long since given up even trying to direct the events of it."

"I am not so weak willed as to not be ready to do what is needed to maintain control."

"Will has nothing to do with it. I am fine with your daughter sitting on the throne and I am even fine with Jin being stuck here with you. What I am not fine with are the problems that you exerting any control over the citizens of this country, when you know nothing about them and can never walk among them, will cause. Stick to being seen as a divine being that is revered and is sought for guidance."

"Xeal, I thought you would agree that my rule would be preferable to what is currently in place. Now that there are five years to work with, it is the perfect time to purge that which is doing harm to the empire."

"You are no different than my brother, father before him, or any of the ministers. Your solution is to kill those you find too inconvenient, just like them!"

At Lingxin's words, Bīng seemed at a loss for a second as Xeal spoke to close the topic.

"Bīng, immortals should never seek to rule mortals. It is why I will seek to destroy any nation that my kind attempts to found that would rule over the natives of this world. It is why my wives mostly rule in my stead and I will never seek to be king of anything."

"Hmm, I will think on your words, though my sisters and I are likely planning on our children doing just that, or would you say that they are too close to being immortal with how long they would live?"

"Do as my children must and have them retire to Cielo city when they turn 100," advised Xeal. "Beyond that, they will bleed as easy as any other, so long as you don't intend to see what happens when your son marries Matrikas, or one of your other sisters."

"Doing so could prove rather interesting. If we were to have one that took lineage from all of us, the child that would be born would be 99.9% phoenix. Such an existence has never existed before and I for one would like to see just what they could do. Though it would take 200 years at least for us to achieve that and by then it will likely not matter any longer."

"Wouldn't that be like sleeping with your own nephew?" asked Lingxin, sounding disgusted.

"No. We call each other sisters, but we have no true blood relation. We simply came into being one day like all of the original beings. The ten of us were gathered by our mate and became sisters in the same sense that you are sisters with all of Xeal's wives."

"And you know, like it, or not, that is what we are now as you are not a concubine and I don't care what you may say, that makes you his wife, the empire's hidden empress and my sister. If you wish to effect true change for the good in these lands, accepting that and making it the new norm is a decent first step. Now, I will leave you to think on that and I look forward to meeting my niece, or nephew, when they arrive."

Lingxin didn't even wait for Bīng to respond, as she took Xeal's hand and made her way to the teleportation gate and left with him. For Xeal's own part, he knew that this wouldn't be the last he heard of this and was just sighing as he worried just what the future held with all the phoenixes, save for Levina, having been paired with a mate from what Taya had shared with him. Though he had purposefully not asked for the details on just who each of the men were, or what had been the terms as he really didn't want to know. So, instead, he simply enjoyed falling asleep next to Lingxin, Enye, Dyllis and Mari once more, before he left for an extended period of time.

Thanks!

Thank you to all of my patrons on Patreon, especially my knight-tier patrons Carl Benge, Alexander Casey Donnell, Timelesschief, Christof Köberlein, Benjamin Grey, Daniel Sifrit, Michael Jackson, Jeffrey Iverson, David Peers, Kyle J Smith, Roman Smith, William J Dinwiddie II, Rick White, Ryan Harrington, Michael Mitchell, Rtewan, Stefan Zimmermann, Grantland Case, Peter Barton, Peter Hepp, Kore Rahl, Joel Stapleton, Lazai, Richard Schlak, Shard73, Blackpan2, Thomas Watret, Adamantine, William Adams, Matthew, Douglas Sokolowski, Edwin Courser, Sam Ellis, Andrew Eliason, Nick Stockfleth, DAvid Marksz, Fred Rankin, Georg Kranz, William Puryear, AR Schleicher, Angus Christopher, Collateral_ink, Roy Cales, JOHNNY SMILEY, Thomas Corbin, Spencer Ryan Crawford, Outwardwander, David Guilliams, Bern DG, Christopher Gross, Tony Fino, Ciellandros, ABritishGuy, PeeM, F0ZYWOLF, Dan Dragonwolf, Marvin Wells, Dominic Q Roddan, Tanner Lovelace, Daniel Diaz, yo dude, Aimee Hebert, James A. Murphy, Mark reilly, Erebus Drakul Zaydow, tawshif tamjid, Kor Vang, nathrielos, James (Burnthemage), Fallen, Klaas Weibring, Shadowteck michael berge, Whiskey, Arcaedian, SamuraiGaming Mike3000jr and Mercury044.

(*****)

Afterword.

To think that I actually reached 20 books published at a book a month straight. I have to say that it surprises me and I know that I will do it again, but it won't be back-to-back like it was this time. Right now I am expecting that book 21 or 22 will end that streak, as I shift to publishing on a month and a half timeline for the remainder of Eternal Dominion. Which is slated to be 32 books at this point and will finish up in time for Christmas 2024. Just for reference, here is what I am expecting that to look like.

[book 22. (9/15/23), book 23. (11/1/23), book 24. (12/15/23), book 25. (2/1/24), book 26. (3/15/24), book 27. (5/1/24), book 28. (6/15/24), book 29. (8/1/24), book 30. (9/15/24), book 31. (11/1/24), book 32. (12/15/24)]

Adds four and a half months to the release schedule and it will allow me to make sure that I am tying up as many loose ends as possible as I write the final third of Eternal Dominion. Also, I will finally get the time that I need to get my next series ready for release at the same time as just speaking from the economics of everything, writing long series usually suffers from massive reader drop-off. It is just the truth of it and no matter what I do, I have to expect that to be the case and it is why I never just want to have one series going at a time. It is for that reason that you can all expect to see two series from me, hopefully in the next year. I already have the first draft of book 1 in one of them written and I will be writing book 1 in the other after I finish writing the first draft of book 24, while I have my proofreader looking for anything that needs to be addressed in books 25 to the end of Eternal Dominion.

On that note, if you have anything that you feel like I have forgotten or dropped, please don't hesitate to reach out on Facebook, or the email that you can find by joining my mailing list. I really do want to make sure that I am not missing anything big or small that is important to give a resolution to. So, please, just like how a book can be gone over by 100 people, but an error will still slip through for you the reader to find, I know that some of you have ones that everyone on my team will miss. So, to those of you who have something that has been bugging you and you want to make sure I address it, let me know!

Now, going back to the other series that I am writing, one will be a coauthored project with my wife. Now, don't worry, it will still be about 90% me. I am just working with her to do a bit of detail work and expand the world slightly. In truth, I don't want to deal with pen names and by adding her to the process it will allow me to distinguish my harem and non-harem stories. As while books that she helps me with may still end up with a one man and two women situations, that is as far as she will allow it to go since she can't stand harem. So, when you see anything by Bern and Cynthia Dean out there, you now know the general story, at least for now. However, adding her in also takes what is currently a three-month process and turns it into a six-month process if my current estimates turn out to be correct. As such, I only expect to be able to publish 3-4 books in that series each year, which isn't acceptable to me. Thus, the other series that I will be writing and yes, it will be another harem that leaves out all the explicit parts. Though, it may have some darker moments and themes due to the setup that I am using for it, but that is all I will say on that for now. After all, if everything goes well, we are looking at book one of both of those being out by summer next year. That said, I would love to get one of them out early next year if possible, but with me upping the length of each book for both of those series, I can't make any promises.

Oh, and yes, as I write this, I survived being without my wife for the whole 75 days she was gone, but the last 30 were absolutely terrible for my writing. It is why I am getting ready to spend all but two weeks of my summer writing like my life depends on it, and I will only be taking one week and a few random days off between now and the end of the year. Especially as we are expecting to move cross country and try to buy our first house when we do... Just hoping interest rates go down, or at least don't get any worse than they are already. So, if you see me suddenly trying to get you all to buy a shirt or some other product in the next year, know that it is simply me shamelessly trying to increase how big of a down payment we have. Let's just hope I don't lose my soul in the process!

Now onto the repetitive stuff. Did you know I have a newsletter and that by signing up you can get a free prelude novella for Eternal Dominion? Heck, it is really easy too. Just go to my website below and scroll to the bottom, where you will just need to put in your email address. Or you can go to https://BookHip.com/BAMDFBA, put in your email the single time and confirm it in your inbox to get the prelude and sign up for my newsletter in one go.

If you haven't already, go to https://soundbooththeater.com/team/bern-dean/ and listen to the free shorts that are available there. If you do it through a web browser you don't even need to create an account to do so, just select the listen now option. Zach and Annie have really gone above and beyond with their performances!

As always, if you feel I have forgotten something, feel free to reach out to me on Facebook through my page, or join my group. I am only one person and sending a message to my Facebook author page is the fastest way to get me to see it, as I don't get alerts on my personal page when non-friends message me for the first time. That said, I will not answer personal questions, like where I live, even in a general fashion. Please keep it to my story, or my writing process.

If you would like a weekly extra that focuses on looking at the supporting cast and is not plot necessary but is canon, I publish shorts on my Patreon. The first several of which are currently available to my $1 patrons, who will get another one every four weeks, while my $5 patrons get one each week. If you want to see what these are like, I have put a few up on my Facebook group as well now. I also now have a $5.50 tier for those who want to read the first 5 to 7 thousand words of the next book a week or so early, as that is when I have it back from the copy editor. To be clear, I delete the extended preview just before, or after, the book it is attached to is released. Some may ask why the extra 50 cents and to that I give two reasons. I have had some patrons tell me that they don't want the extended preview and it lets them ignore it. Also, it allows me to see just how much demand there is for extended previews.

https://www.facebook.com/groups/berndean
https://www.facebook.com/Author.Bern.Dean
https://www.patreon.com/berndean
https://www.Bernsbooks.com

Thank you again for reading my story and I hope you return for the next installment of Alex's tale. If you enjoy LitRPG and GameLit books, check out the following Facebook groups. Both are great and have helped me get my stories out to you!

LitRPG:
https://www.facebook.com/groups/LitRPG.books

GameLit:
https://www.facebook.com/groups/LitRPGsociety

Made in the USA
Monee, IL
01 July 2024

61040458R00152